THE KING'S TRIAL

M. L. FARB

For the Gibson Family

ML Farb

Editing by Bookaholics Press LLC, Provo Utah

Front cover design by Rachael Wilkinson, RaeLaRey@gmail.com

Published by M. L. Farb

Contact the author at mlfarb.author@gmail.com

CONTENTS

For Erin and Rachael. You've been there from the first "once upon a time."

1

THE SHADOW DOES NOT CRY OUT WHEN TRODDEN UPON

YOSYPH

I discovered I was a prince the day they sentenced my best friend to die. Not the prince of this land. No one would mistake me for him. Prince Halavant is the meat of every woman's gossip—muscular, fair-skinned, golden-haired, and an intolerable spoiled brat. He'll be appointed our king next year when he reaches the divinely appointed age of eighteen. If his mother, the 'glorious and beloved Queen' of Lansimetsa, allows him to take her throne. I doubt he'd cross her in anything.

No, I'm not that prince. I'm not handsome or popular. I'm opposite of Prince Halavant in every appearance, and most don't even notice me. That's why I hear the gossip. No hushed titters when I walk by. I don't mind being invisible, except when it gets the hangman's noose around Jack's neck.

It was hot that day. I hefted a sack of barley from the wagon onto my back, then onto the growing stack in the White Goose's courtyard. A breeze cooled my sticky, sweaty clothes and brought the scent of baking bread, horse, human waste, and the gallows.

Three days, I signed, *and still they leave the fellow to rot.*

"May he rot there forever," Father's mellow voice belied his words, "if it means they never hang another."

Unlikely. But I nodded.

"Did you bring the herbs from Devron's farm?" Father asked.

I wiped the sweat from my forehead and dried my hand on the hem of my tunic. It wouldn't be good to mix fine spices with salt water. I opened a small barrel. Ginger and coriander tickled my nose and pushed out the other scents. In the middle of the nest of spices sat a purchase list—apples, barley, grapes—it continued with more items and prices. Curling doodles flowed around the words.

He didn't have— I started, then stilled my hands at the sound of bare feet slapping the cobble. Timothy, my towheaded brother, burst into the courtyard.

"They've taken Uncle Jack!" he gasped, his feet already turned back the way he'd come.

Not Jack, too! I launched after Timothy.

"Yosyph, wait!" Father's heavy boots thumped behind me in an unsteady rhythm.

Timothy skirted the crowded square and the gallows, then ducked into an alley. He darted like a mouse around barrels, under hanging clothes, and over a dead dog before disappearing around a corner.

I pushed through the wet linens. A yellowed sheet clung to

my arm and pulled from the line. I flung it to the side and rounded the corner.

Ten paces ahead, the alley opened. Five men in the Queen's red surrounded Jack. His chestnut hair tumbled over his down-turned face. Rope bound his legs and arms. Two other soldiers dumped arm-loads of arrows onto a pile of bows next to him.

One soldier shook Jack by his shoulders. "Why does a cobbler need fifty bows and hundreds of arrows? Traitor!" Then he spat. A tobacco-yellowed glob hit Jack on the forehead and rolled down his nose.

"It was for—" Jack began.

"I don't need to hear more of your lies." The soldier kicked him behind the knees and sent him tumbling to the ground.

My hand flicked to my side for my sword. It wasn't there. I never wore it in the daylight. Even if I had it, they'd kill him if I rushed in.

I slackened my jaw, uncurled my hands, and slumped my shoulders—sliding into the role of a dumb, harmless, half-wit.

Timothy jumped from foot to foot in a doorway a short distance from the men. Father panted up beside me. I felt his hand on my shoulder, and I let out a slow breath. *Ready,* I signed. Timothy looked at us, Father nodded, and Timothy darted toward the guards.

I hated when he did that. Even though he was a scrawny kid, the Queen's men could be unpredictable. I forced my shoulders to slouch again.

"Get out of here, you brat!" The soldier snatched Timothy's ear.

Father strode forward, and I shuffled after him.

"Timothy!" Father said. "What are you doing?" Then he turned to the grizzled soldier. "Please forgive my son's interruption. I know it's not much, but to pay for his bothering you, may I offer a tankard of ale?"

The soldier shoved Timothy away. "One for each of us."

"Of course. What flavor would you have?"

"Make mine spiced cider."

"Anise beer," shouted another soldier.

Thank you, Father. Now my part. I scuffed a boot on the cobble twice. Jack turned his head.

His face was puffed with purple bruising, one eye half closed, and his front teeth were missing.

I stepped back. Stop being a ninny, I told myself. You've seen worse. But never on the face of a friend.

I flicked my fingers. Small movements disguised as mere fidgeting. Please Jack, remember the code. Even after eight years, he still struggled with it, though he was six years older than me.

I'm getting you out, I signed. *One hour.*

His eyes widened. He signed, his movements hampered by the ropes. *No. Wife, children. Out—city.*

I'll get them out.

His shoulders relaxed.

But I'm getting you next, I signed, flicking my pinky against my thigh in the sign of my most solemn oath.

A soldier hauled Jack to his feet and shoved him forward. He stumbled against the ropes that held his feet, then settled into a shuffle. Wait, wait, wait—my blood thumped in my neck. The last soldier turned the corner. I turned in the opposite direction and sprinted the two blocks to Jack's home.

Anna opened the door to my pounding.

"Yosyph?" She wiped her flour-covered hands on her apron. "What brings you here?"

She knew my signing even less than Jack. I opened my little-used voice. "They've taken Jack. Get the children. We have to go now."

Anna blanched. "Samuel, Susan." Her voice trembled under the soft words. "Get Charlie."

The dew of the pre-dawn hours made the stones of Fairhaven's outer wall slick. I bit my tongue as my hand slipped and my chin hit the top of the wall. It'd been years since I'd slipped going over this wall. Nervous? Ridiculous! I'd gotten Anna and the children out of Fairhaven, and they'd be sailing to safety instead of sold into slavery. Soon, I'd get Jack out, too.

I crouched on top of the wall and looked over the crumbling adobe buildings and rambling alleys pocked with the still forms of homeless and drunks, their hopeless ranks growing daily. My efforts did little to stem that tide, at least for now.

Beyond the brick homes and the sleeping market square stood the inner wall, twenty feet of masonry wide enough for two men to walk abreast. The prison nestled against the inner wall, a squat windowless building stretching hundreds of feet along the curving wall, hidden from the delicate eyes of the nobles, but not from their noses.

Mansions sprawled behind the inner wall with their domed roofs, gardens and broad avenues. Beyond them rose the fortress wall and the palace—a granite castle matching the wall, ghostly gray in the last of the moonlight. Limestone cliffs backed the city to the east, stretching far to the south and gradually falling level with the ground to the north. Each of Fairhaven's three walls curved around to meet the face of a two-hundred-foot cliff, forming bands of a gray rainbow with the palace as its dark heart. I clenched my fists.

Stop it. Jack needs me.

I flicked my eyes back to the prison. Guards, wall, more

guards, locked doors, and shackles to pass by and unlock unseen. I pulled my mottled cloak closer. Father told me that when I stood still at night, my dark hair and skin blended with the shadows, and with my cloak I became a shadow. After years of practice, I'd learned to slip around the edge of a lighted door without notice.

I could get into the prison. But leaving with a non-shadow proved more difficult. I'd only succeeded thrice. With so many condemned to death, I had to calculate how many lives could be spared and how much of a coward I could stand to be.

I leaped down the eight feet from the outer city wall and rolled to absorb the impact. The moon followed me through the rambled streets past Jack's home. I touched the wall where I'd played wall-en-ball with him and his children. The paint was worn thin from the repeated thumps.

Torchlight flickered in the market square. I raced forward, my leather shoes shushing against the ground.

"For the last time," a nasal voice whined, "who else is plotting against our kingdom?"

I clung to the wall and glanced around the corner. Jack stood on the gallows with a noose encircling his neck. The judge, with his powdered wig askew and his black robes rumpled, stared at Jack. The flickering light played across the judge's long nose and sneering mouth. Ten guards surrounded them, and a full-bearded guard gripped the trapdoor lever.

A guard raised a whip. "I'll make him talk."

I dashed from barrel to crate.

"No, no." The judge yawned. "I've had enough of him. You tortured him all night long, and he's still as closed-mouthed as a turtle. It's enough he's admitted to being the Yorel. The others will fade without him."

I darted forward in the scudding shadow of a cloud.

"The morning won't come soon enough." The full-bearded

guard rubbed the trapdoor lever. "We'll string the Yorel up where everyone can see what color their 'hero' truly is. Nothing but a yellow, broken coward."

Fifteen feet away. I wanted to race across the open square, but if they saw me, they'd pull the trapdoor lever, and his neck could snap. I dashed along the edge in the shadows of the market awnings.

The judge straitened his askew wig. "He hangs now. I'll not risk him escaping. He's a slippery one."

The guard reached for the lever.

Stop!

"Wait!" The judge's voice jumped an octave. "Wait until I get off the platform."

The men chuckled as the judge scurried off the platform. I lunged forward. It didn't matter if they saw me now. I leaped onto the platform and barreled into the man holding the lever. His weight worked against him as I pivoted him over my shoulder and tossed him.

"It's a shadow demon," the judge screamed.

The guards drew their swords, but several stepped back.

Thank you, judge, you are actually helpful tonight.

I darted between the guards to where Jack sagged, half hanging himself in weariness. Swords slashed. One nicked my cheek, another ripped my cloak. I wrenched the wrist of one of the guards. As his wrist snapped, he bellowed and dropped his sword. I grasped the back of his quilted vest with my other hand and flung him into the soldiers behind me. Grunts and thuds let me know several fell from the platform.

I caught the rope above the noose and hacked it. Jack crumpled with the frayed noose still around his neck. I slung him over my shoulders as the ground dropped from beneath us. One soldier stood on the platform, his hand on the trapdoor lever.

My knees protested falling six feet and landing with Jack's

added weight. You'll survive, I told them as I sprinted across the market square. The judge squealed and scuttled away from me. I disappeared into the darkness, angry shouts of men fading behind me, and Jack's breath wet against my neck.

2

DUSTY MEMORIES LIE BENEATH THE LONELIEST NIGHTMARES

YOSYPH

I don't know how I got Jack over the wall and to Gaven's. The moon slipped behind the trees as I stumbled through a tangle of herbs to a vine-covered door, set deep in a hillside. A raven croaked, and Gaven ushered us in, putting me to work setting Jack's bones and bandaging wounds.

Nightmares usually end with the coming of day, but this one bled into the morning hours. Sunlight filtered through a vine-smothered window. It danced across Jack's foreshortened fingers wrapped in bandages and broken arms set in splints. Yet he lived.

At dawn, Gaven went to bed, and I sat to watch over Jack. The mid-morning sun shifted to fall across his face.

"Anna," Jack moaned, turning his head away from the light.

"She's safe and so are the children." I touched a cloth to his feverish brow.

He opened one eye; the other had swollen shut. "You saved me."

"I wish I'd gotten to you before they did this." I vaguely motioned to his fingers.

Jack's hands flinched. "Queen's Wrath! I can't feel my hands!"

I touched the back of one of his hands but he didn't react. "It should be temporary." I hoped. "Gaven rubbed a clove ointment over your injuries and forced drugged ale down your throat to help you sleep and take the edge off your pain. I'm glad you don't hurt."

"Oh, I hurt," Jack laughed and then coughed.

I forced a smile. "You should sleep."

"I can't. My body is prickles and itches and numbness. My mind is racing in a hundred directions at once, like the time we got into your father's coffee supply and brewed up a triple-strength cup with enough sugar to turn it to sludge."

Stimulated by a sedative? That was Jack, always in motion. "Slow down. I'll listen as long as you want to talk."

"I didn't tell them anything." Jack closed his eye. Deep lines creased his forehead. "I screamed and swore. But I didn't tell a single thing."

"I know." I shuddered and bathed his brow again with lavender water.

"I even led them astray." He grimaced. "I told them I was the Yorel. Thought they'd stop removing parts of fingers and just kill me. It worked. Don't know why they believed me. I'm nothing like you."

"You're a far better man." I'd have cracked under the same torture.

"No, I'm not," Jack raced on, his speech slurring even more.

"I've never saved anyone's life. I haven't given up a kingdom to be a servant to foreigners. I've—"

"What kingdom?" I cut in, my voice rough in surprise. The drugged ale addled him.

"Your kingdom." He opened his eye again. "The one your mother came from. The desert people, you know, from her letter."

"What letter?" I had no idea what he was talking about.

Gaven poked his head through the doorway. A rumpled nightshirt hung on his slight form. His gray eyebrows formed a storm cloud over his eyes. "Why are you agitating the patient? You're always playing a mute, except when I ask you to be quiet. Now let him rest!" He grabbed a pestle and bowl and crushed herbs while glowering at me.

I nodded and turned back to Jack, flickering my fingers in apology.

"You don't know about the letter?" Jack asked in a quieter voice. "The one hidden in the cellar wall?"

I shook my head. I would find it as soon as I got back.

"I was sure you hid it there. It's two stones down from the one where we hide the logistics. I found it by mistake one day. I'm sorry I didn't tell you." He shrugged and then winced. "I didn't want you to know I'd read something so personal."

Gaven poured the herbs into a mug and mixed it with water. He held it to Jack's lips. "Drink this. It should help you sleep." He touched Jack's brow, creased his own, and turned a stern eye on me. "I'm awake now, and you have work to do. So get going."

The crush of the market-goers filing through the city gate almost matched the stampede of questions pounding through my head. I ducked into the White Goose taproom. The fumes of alcohol enveloped me. Father stood behind the counter and glanced at me with question-filled eyes.

A drunk voice rose above the hum of voices. "A devil, he was." A soldier, the one I'd tossed from the hangman's platform, hunched over his tankard. "Took that yellow slinking coward straight down to where he belongs."

"I heard," said another soldier, "the Yorel called up the shadow demon to free him."

I coughed to cover my laugh and nodded to Father to follow me.

The door slammed against the wall. General Jonstone strode into the tap room, followed by two others, each in richly ribboned uniforms. "Ho, Hadron! Prepare my room and bring forth the Shiraz, the one from the year the king died." He turned to the others, and chuckled, "What a joke it will be."

Why did the general come now? Any other time would be welcome, but why now?

Father hurried over to him, bowing. "I am pleased you grace my humble tavern again." He then turned to me. "Yosyph! Go prepare the General's room!" He pointed upstairs, his eyes full of questions. I'd not even told him Jack was alive, though I supposed he guessed it from the tavern talk.

I snatched a dust rag and climbed the stairs to the second-floor drinking room. It had been months since the general had visited the White Goose.

"Hurry," General Jonstone thundered from the door, "I have a mighty thirst to slake." Then to the younger officer I'd not seen before, the general confided, "You'll see, best wine in the kingdom."

"But is it wise?" The boy-faced officer's gaze darted around.

"Tush. Look at these walls. Thick." Jonstone pulled the young officer in and shut the door with a resounding thump. "Listen. Can't hear the ruckus below. And," he pointed to me, "a mute, half-wit serving boy. Been serving me for years. Never a safer place, nor better drink."

"But he's a desert savage!"

"Come now. Half-breed, half-wit, it amounts to the same thing." He held up his cup. "Here boy, my Shiraz!"

I poured the Shiraz, then stood off by a corner, my face blank.

"See, like a dog. He'll wait until I call him to get us something else."

I smiled inwardly. *If you only knew.*

Jonstone downed his goblet of wine in a few swallows, then turned to an older officer with a thin goatee. "Evans, having much trouble with the census?"

The census? The last months had been full of soldiers knocking on doors, counting children, asking their ages, and moving on. It was a bother, an invasion of privacy, but something done by many rulers before and innocuous enough. The worst of it had been an increase in taxes and imprisonment for those who resisted. The census was one of the lesser evils in this land.

Why was Jonstone interested in this menial number taking? He oversaw a cancerous network of spies who kept tabs on the people of Lansimetsa, making some disappear, and bringing others to an unjust trial—those I didn't get to first. None of the census info would be new to him, would it?

Evans stroked his goatee. "The people don't like it. Most ask what business is it if their ancestors come from east, west, north, or across the sea. And they look even further askance at the religion question. It's a touchy thing, and some have gotten violent."

They asked about ancestry and religion? Father answered for me when the soldiers asked at our door. Witless mutes can't answer questions. *Father, you are supposed to tell me those things.*

"Of course they do," Jonstone said. "Who wants their gods

questioned? But you've given them a good cell to say their prayers in, I hope."

"Always. Thankfully, we only have to wait for the soldiers to return from the villages at the edges of Lansimetsa. Then I can leave this headache behind." He rubbed his temples, then glanced at Jonstone. "May I ask, why does Her Highness desire this information?"

"It isn't my place to guess at her inner workings."

"You know, but you won't tell us." Evans held up his goblet for more wine.

Jonstone thumped the table. "You're right! I've kept this under my belt for long enough. It's time for you to enjoy it, too."

My stomach knotted.

"The census is but the boring beginning to a desperately needed cleansing. It will show, by the people's own words, who are truly Lansimetsian and who are but foreign leeches, draining our land, taking our riches, and spoiling our bloodlines. Do you know how many admit to impure bloodlines?" His voice rose, "A full third of the people! Another generation, and they will outnumber us."

The younger officer's eyes grew wide. "But what will you do to them?"

"What should've been done long ago. Clean the land of them. At the end of the last harvest, we will harvest *them*, chain them together and send them as the animals they are to slave in the mines."

The knots in my stomach grew until acid burned my throat. How could they expect to succeed? The people wouldn't stand by and watch their neighbors taken as slaves.

They might, a thought hissed. Hadn't the last royal play showcased the superiority of the full-blooded Lansimetsian farmer and made the Northern minister a fool? The Queen funded its performance in every major city. The people loved it. And in the play before, a half-blooded prince of the desert murdered his wife. And before that? How long had this been going on—a year, two? All my life, I'd become so accustomed to the ridicule and ignorance, I'd been blind to the growing plague of prejudice. Fool!

"But," the younger officer continued, oblivious to Evans' quick shake of the head, "aren't most of them farmers and laborers already? Who will feed the kingdom? Who will serve us?"

Jonstone focused his watery gaze on him, "Farnsworth, do you always question so much? You'd do well to guard your tongue. This once, I'll answer your question and forgive your impudence."

Farnsworth shrank back as Jonstone leaned toward him. "Others, pure-blooded people of our land, will take over the farming. There won't be any more poor because everyone will have enough land to support them and us. Oh, we'll keep a few special ones around, like personal slaves and that idiot in the corner." He waved over his shoulder at me.

I stood with my head slumped forward.

"See he doesn't even comprehend what we are talking about —a slouched-shouldered, empty-headed specimen. That's what happens when you mix blood. Besides, the gems the foreign scum dig from the mines will enrich our nation far beyond what the paltry farms do. Have you not heard of fireside tales of the Roc's nest in the desert? We've found it. We'll need thousands to excavate it."

Fools and criminals, the lot of them. A third of the people! I couldn't fake the deaths and hide away the victims. I flickered my fingers in a silent prayer: *May the plague fall upon these men and bless the Queen to choke on a bone. May the people be freed from her cursed shadow before autumn harvest*. If only it was that easy. So far, all my prayers required earthly intervention.

Jonstone held his goblet out for more wine. "I've answered your insolent question, Farnsworth. You owe me a favor, a trifle to prove your loyalty." I almost splashed him as my hands shook, but he kept his gaze on the shrinking officer. "You know the young lady who visits the palace each year, the one with the bright red hair?"

"The one betrothed to the prince?"

"Yes. The Queen doesn't approve. Your errand is to make sure she finds herself in a new and more heavenly world before the sun sets tomorrow."

"I—I—" Farnsworth sputtered, and Evans kicked him. "Yes. I'll do it tomorrow, when she goes out for her afternoon ride."

"Good, because if you can't do this small favor, you'll lose my trust, and that would be a pity."

Farnsworth blanched as white as the towel over my shoulder.

I almost felt sorry for him, because I wouldn't let him kill her.

A lone candle flickered in the closed drinking room. Dawn would come in a few hours, and the last customer had left minutes before. I unrolled the yellowed, cracking vellum and weighted it with stones. My eyes blurred as I read the delicate script. My mother's script. The curling curves of my mother's tongue, like water dancing across the page. It must be from the emotions with Jack and the planned enslavement. I didn't cry. Ever. I blinked hard and blew out a quick breath, then read.

My son, I fear I will leave you soon. Lest you forget, I will tell you again what you must know. I am Tanyeshna, of the Kishkarish tribe. If you desire to return to my people, you must walk the King's Trial.

The way is difficult, but if you succeed, they will welcome you as the prince you are.

A prince? A memory formed, shrouded and indistinct. I tried to catch it, understand it, but it shimmered and slipped away. I shuddered and followed the flowing words to a map. A vague path marked the *King's Trial* leading to a grassland hidden in the desert, to my mother's people. Each landmark was a fountain of words, warnings, and advice. One said, *Stone Forest*. I startled as I heard her rich voice in my mind. *The trees shimmer in glass and marble, a mage's sorrow, the starvation of a people.* I read on, pulling dusty memories from beneath my loneliest nightmares. Some slipped away like a canyon echo. Others burst in color. Her voice in my mind grew stronger with each word, even as the writing grew weaker. Words trembled and letters slid sideways. Below the map was a slurred scrawl. *I love you, my son.*

I rubbed the taut muscles in the back of my neck. Two more sheets lay beneath this one. But those words seemed so final. I wasn't ready for final words, not from her, not even though she'd been gone for almost as long as I could remember. I breathed through my nose and moved the top vellum aside.

I am stronger today. Her writing cramped together as if afraid there would not be enough paper.

I brushed away a tear from the vellum.

Your father is dead. I never told you about him. It hurt too much. But now I must. He was everything I hope you will grow to be—honorable, kind, gentle, brave. He was also an Ura-ubiya, a man of this wetland. I gave up everything to marry him—my people, my land—and I would again. Do not blame him for what we have suffered.

We hoped for a child for many years. But when my husband developed the bane of his fathers, I knew I must seek the sage of the Truven Island to lift this curse on my womb before he died. I did not know I carried you when I set sail. By the time I reached the isle, I could feel you fluttering within me. The sage gave me his blessing, promising you would bring peace to a torn land, but only after you had walked through deep shadow. Thus far, his prophecy is too true. He also warned me—

The sentence ended in an ink splatter. Long finger marks smeared the ink off the paper's edge. The next page contained a different writing, Father's writing, not my real father but the only one I'd ever known. The Lansi missed pieces of letters as if he was in a hurry, and couldn't dip the pen often enough.

Child, your mother asks me to write for her.

On the return voyage, pirates attacked. I pled with them to not kill me, for the sake of my unborn child, and I would be a servant to them. The captain agreed and marked me his slave.

I stopped reading and massaged my forehead, my palms covering my eyes. It did not block the images. I saw again the skull marks burned into her hand and cheek, her beautiful earth-colored skin puckering around the scars. Hot, salty days, she scrubbed, spliced, tarred, and cooked, until her fingers bled. I search for memories before this, but the earliest were working beside her, and then later as a cabin boy. When the captain was in a good mood it meant sweets, and when he wasn't, it meant a flogging. I flinched my shoulders, feeling the muscles roll under the lines of old scars.

But not at nighttime. Nighttime was ours. The pirates drank until we ceased to exist to them. Midnight brought lessons of history, writing, signing with my hands—taught in the rocking of the ship, lit by a stolen candle, curled up in a nest of ropes, hiding, hoping not to be noticed. Learning to not be noticed. I smiled, remembering. Mother whispered the most comic things about the pirates, such that when I saw them the next day, I'd shake with silent laughter.

Seven years I served them, until I overheard the captain say he was selling you the next day at port. That night, I threw us over-

board. We made it to shore, and we were back in this land. But all has changed. Your father is dead. And soon I will be, too. I love you. I will always watch over you. Never forget you are a prince. Live true to your heritage.

I closed my eyes and imagined her arms around me again, her breath playing through my hair as she whispered stories. Strange it should hurt so much, remembering. Sharp pain caught in my chest like the barbs of an arrow being slowly pulled out. I turned over the page. Again, Father's script.

Yosyph, you are my son now. I do not know when I will give you your mother's words, but not yet. You are still too little and too solemn. You must learn to forget and be a child again before I will burden you with them. I promised your mother to care for you. I promise you I will love you as a son.

I had forgotten, or at least pushed seven years of my life into the cellar of my mind and locked the door. Now with that door open, the memories staggered piecemeal into the light.

The drinking room door creaked open. Father stood with his hand on the latch, as if uncertain whether or not to enter. "I see you found her letter. I never knew when to give it to you. Besides, you'd probably have tried to leave for wherever that map leads. You were too young."

"Where did you find her?"

"In an alley, in the middle of winter. She had wrapped you in her shawl and shielded you from the snow with her body."

"I remember now." I shuddered as the words brought the sharp cold back to my skin. Her hands were ice as she clutched me to her bosom. "She gave her life to save mine. As I must give mine to save others."

"You never did grow out of your seriousness."

"There's not much to laugh about. Especially not now."

"I find it amusing General Jonstone comes to share his greatest secrets in the safety of this room. Can you imagine his face if he knew the Yorel served him wine while planning a revolution here?"

I snorted.

"What are our numbers now?" Father's brow knit as he looked at the spread of papers I'd brought into the room. Stained and creased receipts from all parts of the land for grapes, grains, apples, mushrooms, and other supplies to create the White Goose's drinks. Swirls of my mother's language, written in my hand, edged each one.

I chuckled then sighed. Why did I remember the writing when I'd forgotten the teacher?

I set aside the last receipt and rubbed my forehead. "Each town now has a captain with at least twenty men willing to fight. Some even have fifty."

"The Queen has thrice that stationed near each town. We are still too weak." Father's brow knit tighter, and his jaw worked in and out. "We need more men."

"The people will rise against the Queen when they hear her plan. A full third of the people enslaved. There are many who would defend their neighbors. We'll have enough." *But it will be a massacre if we are not organized*, I added silently. My mind sputtered. How could we organize so many without the Queen knowing? I had a hard enough time keeping our little, disjointed groups from the knowledge of Jonstone. We'd been more than lucky, so far. Three years! We couldn't remain secret much longer.

I stood and placed my hand on my father's shoulder. "You're right. We need more men, trained soldiers, organized, ready to fight. That is why I will gather an army of my mother's people, my people. I am their prince."

3

THE WOLF PUP STILL BITES

YOSYPH

I stopped the wagon inside the porter's gate. The backside of the castle loomed beyond the craftsmen huts, stables, and barracks—the invisible bones that kept the palace running.

I'd visited Jack earlier that morning. My conversation with him rolled through my head. He had some color in his cheeks. He'd make it through, if infection didn't set in. His parting words were hopeful for one so recently brushed by death.

"Yosyph, don't worry about me. Get the army. Overthrow the tyrant. And, if you meet a pretty maiden—a redhead by chance—don't get fumble-mouthed with her."

I shouldn't have mentioned going to rescue Katrin. Jack never lost an opportunity to tease me about her, not since I'd commented how pretty she was. I was only twelve back then. Another reason to speak less.

"Ah-hem." The steward stood tapping his foot.

I jumped to unload several casks of fine mead and boxes of bottled wine.

"What's this?" he asked, as I pulled out a smaller box with one bottle.

I motioned to the label. *Compliments to the prince's bride.*

"Wooing future clients? I'll get it to her." He glanced over my shoulder. "Or better yet, you give it to the prince."

I turned around to see the prince stomping down a garden path, whacking at bushes with a stick. Sun reflected off his white ringlets. Was he bleaching his hair now, or wearing a wig? He used to have wheat-yellow hair. His skin showed he spent hours outside each day, somehow turning it gold instead of ruddy or brown. His face had the round softness of luxury. It was little wonder the women compared him to a god.

"Prince Halavant," the steward called out, "Hadron, the vintner, has sent a special gift of wine for your bride."

He turned toward us, his brows furrowed and lips tight. "It won't do any good. It would have been perfect for our picnic, but she'd rather go riding without me. I imagine she's climbing *our* oak or skipping stones on *our* pond, without me!"

He was an angry, spoiled godling, not yet full grown. But at least he told me where to find her.

I turned to leave as he continued his rant.

"I'd like to thrash someone. But everyone even the least bit capable is on duty. Not one can spar. Nothing is going right today." He turned. "You, what is your name and service?"

Why did he, of all people, notice me? I motioned to my throat.

"He is mute, sire," the steward explained. "The son of the vintner."

The prince studied me closer, then nodded, "You stand with the ease of a swordsman."

I dropped to a slouch.

"Though too tall and lean to be much of a match. Still, I see no better options. You may have the privilege of sparing with your prince and future king."

I slouched to the sparring yard. Perhaps he would rethink fighting me if I looked incapable.

The prince grumbled, "Pointless, worthless day. Left to spar with a mute commoner. Could it get any worse?"

I could think of a hundred ways.

He grabbed one of the dull metal practice swords and tossed another toward me. I leaped to the side, letting it clatter to the ground. I fumbled as I picked it up.

"He has no more skill than a practice dummy. I could take off his head."

I rethought my strategy. He stood shorter than me, but heavier built and held himself with the balance of a dancer. I shifted my weight to my toes and gripped the sword, point down. Defend myself or not? Run? Wait. Watch. Two long breaths.

He sneered, then lunged, driving his sword toward my chest.

I threw myself to the side, barely keeping to my feet. The prince's sword slid by my arm as he stumbled past.

I turned to face him. He roared and swung his sword downward. Metal screamed as I tried to deflect the blow. It was like trying to stop a falling cask with a metal rod. I pushed myself off the weight of the swords and spun aside with a slight stumble. It was getting harder to pretend clumsiness while avoiding blows.

He was like a bear. If I wasn't careful, he'd break my arm or crack my skull. I ducked to avoid the latter.

"Stop dodging and fight, coward!" He whirled around with another crushing swing.

I didn't like taking orders from him, but fighting instead of dodging seemed sound advice if I didn't want to be crippled. So much for my half-wit mask. I leaned away from his swing while flicking my sword under his blow, striking him lightly across the ribs.

His Royal Rageness drew back and blinked. Had I injured his pride? I could end up in prison for scratching his pampered flesh. I tensed my legs, ready to dash through the open porter's gate.

"Unexpected." He adjusted his sword grip from a fist to a fencer's hold. He rose to his toes. A hint of a smile creased his green eyes. No longer a bear, but a panther.

I blew out a held breath. No prison sentence yet, but broken bones still probable. I raised my sword to full preparedness.

He attacked with a rain of thrusts and forehand, backhand, and overhead cuts. I parried and blocked and counter-attacked, grateful he no longer put all his weight behind the thrusts. My ears ached with the clash of steel, and my hands grew slick with sweat.

"Ah! You are skilled for a commoner."

I flicked my blade up, deflecting a blow thrust at my midsection.

"Are all desert people this good?" He panted. "Or only the half-bloods?"

I replied with another blow to his ribs, this one a solid thump. I tired of him, and he could see I wasn't a half-wit, so why hold back?

He grunted but held his ground. "Yes." He attacked with greater force. "You are definitely a misfit of a man, too tall, and with those green eyes staring out of that dark face. How can you stand to look in the mirror?"

Enough! I twisted my sword around the prince's and wrested it away.

He looked at the fallen sword for a moment. His eyebrows rose to his hair and then dropped tight against his eyes. Foolish!

I knelt and handed the sword to him. I was a subservient nobody soon to be forgotten.

His hand touched my chin, lifting it. Silent laughter escaped into shuddering gasps. "You really are a novelty. I look forward to our next match. You must teach me how you did that last part."

I rose and bowed in acknowledgment. Foolish boy, but perhaps not fully spoiled—yet.

The steward closed the gate behind me. I'm sure he was shaking his head. The story would travel. I could no longer pretend to be the mute, half-wit serving boy. Mute perhaps, but no half-wit. I needed to be a desert prince and gather an army. So why did I feel so forlorn losing that bothersome identity?

Father would be implicated. Ten minutes later I entered the White Goose and motioned for him to follow me to the courtyard.

He nodded as I finished reporting. "I'll be gone before noon. But you must be on your way."

I glanced at Timothy playing at the back of the courtyard and swallowed bile. Time for all of us to disappear. An easy thing for me; I was never noticed, well almost never. I rolled my shoulders to work out a knot of concern. Why had the prince noticed me? Maybe he wasn't as dimwitted as people thought. I rode out of the city.

My yellow-gray horse shivered his skin beneath the saddle.

"Sorry Flax." I patted his neck. "I'd let you roll off the harness itch, but we must hurry."

Flax shook his head and snorted as we turned from the main road. Twin oaks arched over the path, marking the start of the royal forest to the north of the city. Only nobles were permitted to enter, and first-time trespassers risked a broken leg. There was no way I'd pass for nobility, but I had explored the forest before, and both my legs were still intact despite my foolish escapades.

Half a mile into the royal forest, an oak sprawled across the forest floor. The lower branches bowed to the ground like so many slides and stairways. A turreted house perched in the mid branches—the prince's castle. Over the years, I'd watched him play there with the red-haired girl, Katrin. They were sweet as children. She might still be. It'd been six years since I'd last trespassed. I climbed into the tree. No one.

I turned from the tree and rode toward the pond. *Please let her be there.*

A woman's voice pierced the quiet.

I dismounted and slipped forward. A lily-covered pond nestled in white pebbled banks. Hydrangea and roses grew half-wild in a garden once planned and then forgotten. The scents stabbed my forehead and reminded me why I disliked gathering the petals for Father's rose drinks.

At the water's edge, a young woman stood beside a white horse. She flipped a stone into the pond and it skipped twelve times. If the prince liked novelty, she fit it. Hair the color of an autumn maple trailed down her back in tight curls. Paprika freckles dusted her cream skin. She burned brightly in a land of brown and flaxen tresses.

"She says I'm not fit to be a queen." Katrin flung another stone. It skipped once, hit a lily pad, and sank. "Too ungainly, too brash, too forward. She's nothing of grace herself, all dominance and force."

I stepped from the trees.

She continued to rant. "I shall not be frightened away by her threats. I shall not! She tells me she shall make my life miserable if I don't refuse to marry her son! Oh, how could she be Mother's best friend and such a beast to me?"

I stepped closer. Still, she didn't see me. Sometimes, not being noticed was bothersome. I cleared my throat. She whirled, a thin dagger appearing in her hand. Good, so she wasn't oblivious to the danger.

"Who are you? What are you doing here?"

I held out my weaponless hands. "I've come to warn you. The Queen has sent her assassins after you. I am sure they are looking for you as we speak. Come. You will be safe." I stepped closer.

"Get away from me," she warned.

"Please listen." I took another step.

She flicked the dagger like she had the stone. I should have been prepared for that. I flung myself sideways as it grazed my shoulder. She leaped to her horse, kicking it into a gallop. I heard the twang of an arrow being released from a taut bowstring. The white horse reared high, an arrow protruding from its left flank. Katrin screamed as she fell backward over the withers. The horse dashed away into the forest with the arrow still bobbing in its flank.

The cutthroats were here already? I rolled to my feet, my shoulder stinging under the torn cloth. I sprinted toward Katrin, whistling a screech owl call. Flax whinnied. Why did I leave my sword on my saddle? So I could watch her die instead of scaring her?

Two men entered the clearing. One was the boy-faced officer from the Jonstone meeting, his eyes blinking rapidly as he held a bow half-taut. The other was a short and muscular man, muttering with disgust while stringing another arrow.

I dove toward Katrin, and something ruffled my hair as I hit the ground. An arrow bit into the ground an arm's length from her.

"Fool of a shot," the man yelled at the officer, pulling his own bow taut. I lunged forward and caught Katrin's foot, yanking her to the ground. Her dress billowed. An arrow ripped through the silk.

Flax burst into the clearing, knocking over the shorter archer. The officer turned at the noise. I leaped to my feet, grabbed Flax's saddle, and swung upward as my horse twisted around.

The officer nocked an arrow and raised his bow toward us. Too late for him. I kicked the bow from his hands as Flax struck with his front hooves. The officer fell with a grunt. A knife flew by where his chest had been moments before. Katrin, now standing, had a third knife in her hand.

Flax spun about with the pressure of my knees. "My lady!"

She glanced at me, then behind me, then dashed toward the trees. Another arrow ripped through her dress, causing her to stumble.

Drat that short archer.

I galloped level with her and grabbed her under her arms. She struggled, making me almost lose hold.

"Don't you want me to save you?"

Flax kept galloping as I pulled her up into the saddle in front of me. Another arrow sang past and buried itself in a tree by my head. More arrows flew, but none found their mark as I charged through the trees and left the bowmen far behind.

4

FIRE BURNS THIEVING FINGERS

YOSYPH

Flax's sides heaved beneath us, and white foam lathered around his mouth. He'd galloped until we left the royal forest behind. We'd finally entered the unkept forest north-west of Fairhaven. A stretch of barren land sat ahead of us, one of the old king's protections against surprise attack.

"We are safe for now." I lowered Katrin from the horse.

She pulled away from me as soon as her feet touched the ground and stood swaying for a moment before her knees collapsed beneath her. She landed on her backside with a small *oof.* Blood crusted across her cheek where either a branch or arrow had scored it. White petticoat showed through gashes in her green linen riding gown. Her hair covered her face and back like a skein of tangled yarn, with a hundred knitting needles of twigs.

I reached out to help her ups.

She batted my hand away, pushed her hair from her face, and glared at me.

What? I signed, fingers flickering. *I saved you. Why do you look at me as if I were an ill-behaved servant who interrupted your morning walk? You'd have died.*

I only said, "You're hurt."

"The palace physicians will tend to them. Take me back." She stood, wincing as she placed weight on her left foot.

"But—"

"You shall be rewarded for saving me."

"No." *Does she think I did this for a reward?* My fingers signed my thoughts.

She took a limping step. "No, you don't want a reward? You're a noble-minded hero out to save a damsel? Or no, you won't take me back? And why do you twitch so much?"

I stilled my hands. "You'll die."

"Halavant will protect me."

"No." I turned away from her. She wouldn't let me help her, but I wouldn't take her back.

"Can't you give more than a monosyllable? You don't think Halavant can protect me? Even if he couldn't—though he certainly can—I can protect myself."

"She'll find some other way: poison, strangle you in your sleep, false accusation and death sentence, or—" I trailed off. Why was I still talking to her?

"Oh, you do speak in sentences. And who is this 'she'?"

"You know as well as I do."

"Go already." She turned her back on me. "I don't need you."

My throat tightened around words I shouldn't say. My fingers tensed to sign words not fit for her ears. But what good would either do? I rubbed the foam from Flax's mouth and flicked it to the ground, then mounted him.

"Wait! You're leaving me here?"

I half-smiled. She thought she could force my hand with pouty defiance. "Yes."

Her shoulders slumped forward. "Take me to Conborner."

Not that I wanted to help her anymore. "I have a friend who can help you get there." I reached out to help swing her onto Flax.

She glanced heavenward, sighed, and took my hand. "Don't get so close." She settled sidesaddle in front of me.

"If you don't want to touch me, you'll have to sit in front of the saddle."

The moment stretched as neither of us moved. She felt like a statue, her stiff side against my front, and her legs rigid over my left leg. Flax whinnied a question, I flicked the reins, and we moved on.

All afternoon, she complained as we trotted down the road, when we stopped to let Flax rest, and even while we ate good bread and cheese. She continued the ungrateful monologue clear until we'd reached the edge of a town.

"Finally," Katrin muttered, "a proper place to eat and rest."

We rode past the first thatched homes. "My friend is but a two-hour ride from here."

"I'll not spend the evening in the saddle. Do you forget I'm injured?"

Not that she'd let me do anything to tend to her injuries. I'd offered several times. But she always looked at me like I carried the measles. So I watched as she pulled twigs from her hair, washed her scratches in a stream, and bound up the worst of the scrapes with strips of her underskirt. She limped about, her ankle probably twisted if not sprained. I carried several helpful herbs. But no, I didn't know why I even tried.

"There's the inn," she said. "I'll stop here."

A two-story building with wooden shingles stood off the road to the East. The low sunlight glinted off dirty glass windows—a luxury that advertised expensive rooms with lice from previous occupants. The hay in the stable would be cleaner. I tightened my knees to bring Flax to a trot, but Katrin slipped from the horse in the short pause before he responded.

Flax coughed. I touched his legs. They shook with exhaustion. A drop of rain hit the back of my neck and slid under my cloak. The sun slipped behind the fast-moving clouds.

Fine, we'll stop here, but not because Lady Pout wants to.

I led Flax to the stables before entering the Thirsty Stallion, an appropriate name for the inn. It smelled as strong as any stable, though of human sweat and old ale instead of manure. It hummed with the voices of farmers discussing crops and merchants bemoaning brigands.

In the middle of it all, a roundish, white-haired man stood next to Katrin. She said something, and the man raised his eyebrows, motioning to the floor above them.

His deep voice carried across the commons, "Our rooms are the cleanest you'll find outside the palace itself. Only ten coppers."

She shook her head and pulled a coin from a fold in her skirt. Gold glinted.

"Yes, my lady," the man boomed. "A bath and our finest room, and I'll get our herbalist to—"

Katrin muttered something.

"Yes, I can keep my voice down," he said, only slightly softer. He motioned a serving wench over, and Katrin followed her from the room.

I half smiled. The innkeeper held his own, in his own simple way, against her pride. I gave him four coppers for a meal and a place in the stables.

At dawn, I'd head off. Lady Pout carried enough riches to get wherever she wanted. No need to take her any farther. I fell asleep to that pleasant notion and the sound of horses munching hay.

I jerked awake, staring into the night. What had awakened me? I strained to catch any sound beyond the continuous patter of rain on cobbles outside. Nothing. I pulled my cloak tighter around my shoulders and nestled back into the hay. Then I heard it again—a muffled cry.

I peered out the loft window. Two men carried a large cloth-wrapped bundle through the driving rain. The smaller man mounted a horse. The other, a tall man with massive arms, lifted the bundle when a foot shot out of the folds of fabric, striking him in the chest. He grunted and hit the bundle with a meaty fist. The bundle flopped, red hair spilling out as the cloth slipped sideways to the ground.

No! I didn't save her just so brigands could take her.

In the moments it took to buckle on my sword and saddle Flax, both men had mounted. Katrin lay limply over the neck of one horse. The smaller man gripped the back of her white slip, his hand much too close to her rump. Filthy rat!

Flax whinnied in the darkness of the stable.

"Still." But the command came too late. I froze in the stable doorway as the larger man turned in his saddle to look back.

His eyes passed over me. He turned back, muttered something and drew his sword, laying it across his lap.

I followed them a hundred yards back, keeping them in sight

but out of earshot. The two bandits were black splotches in a gray night. Driving rain stung my face.

The men veered into the forest. I nudged Flax to follow. The path split in two directions and twisted. I couldn't see more than ten feet either way. Drat! A crack of branches sounded to the left. I followed, stopping every minute to listen over Flax's own clopping. After about ten minutes, the sounds stopped. I continued my course, and moments later, found myself at the edge of a clearing.

An old cottage squatted among the tall grass, its decaying roof almost collapsed from moss and ferns. Light streamed from the window, and the two horses from the inn munched at grass outside.

I hid Flax behind a cluster of trees and stole across the dark meadow.

Deep voices carried from the cottage. I ran to the shuttered window and peered through a knot-hole. A candle lit the room with wavering light. Two men, one thin with a goatee and a cap flopped over one ear, and the other tall and muscular, faced each other with Katrin sprawled on the floor between them. She glared at them over a dirty gag. Her bare arms twitched as she strained against the ropes. Mud and dirt stained the front of her once-white slip.

The thin man finished knotting a rope. "She's a mite more than pretty. She'll fetch a good bit of gold as a slave, especially if General Jonstone is looking again. He's always in need of fresh flesh. She's exotic enough for his tastes. And since the rest of the band ain't here, we can split the coin fifty-fifty."

It seemed the fates were determined to kill her. Assassins one day, and by night, brigands ready to sell her to the man who would kill her without a second thought—once he was done using her. I'd heard him boast before that no pretty woman lasted long in his household. No one deserved Jonstone, not even Katrin in all her condescending, ungrateful pride.

I wanted to burst through the door before they could speak another word, but the big one had his sword, and the thin one's belt held three daggers. If I burst in, they might kill her. I breathed deeply and relaxed my tensed muscles. I had to draw them out.

The thin man reached down to stroke her leg.

Katrin rolled sideways and swung her bound legs against him, knocking him backward to the floor.

"Cat's claws!" He pushed himself back to his feet and kicked her in the side.

Katrin groaned and curled up.

The big man chuckled. "She'll be plenty of fun for whoever buys her, but don't damage her too much."

Enough! I ran to the men's horses and untied their hobbles, then slapped them with a leather strap and howled the long mournful note of a timber wolf. The horses screamed and bolted away from me. I howled again as the cottage door burst open, and both men piled out.

"Bloodsucking bats!" The large man lunged after the departing horses. "What's a wolf doing so close to town?"

The thin man stood in the open doorway, light spilling around him. He glanced back in, but another yell from his companion drew him to chase after the horses. The sound of the men crashing through the brush faded into the driving rain.

I dashed into the cottage. Katrin lay curled on the floor, moaning through the gag, her eyes closed. I knelt by her and touched her shoulder. She exploded like a spring-loaded toy, arching her back and swinging her legs around. I jumped back in time to avoid her bare feet in my face. Then she froze, her eyes fixed on me, full of fear, anger, and surprise.

"I'm here to help," I whispered. Anyone else would be broken and sobbing by now, but she still fought.

I sawed at the ropes with my dagger. First, her hand bonds. She snapped them apart before I had even cut through. Her hands scrabbled at the gag and tried to yank it from her mouth, but it was too tight. I slid the dagger under the gag, into the tangle of her hair, and cut it next to the knot. She spat out the dirty cloth and gulped in air. I braced myself for a scream, but instead she said with a shaking voice, "My feet."

I cut the ropes on her feet while she rubbed her arms where the bindings had cut into her flesh. Her slim ankles bore red marks. Her slip had risen above her knees. Heat rose in my cheeks, and I forced my eyes back to the rope I was cutting.

I jerked my head up at the scream of rusty hinges, followed by a bellow.

"Toad's venom!" The large man drew his sword, mud pasted to him like he'd fallen several times in his attempts to catch the horses.

I dropped the dagger and leaped to my feet, drawing my sword. I stepped in front of Katrin.

"Move over, fool," she hissed. Her own dagger flew by, embedding itself in the man's gut.

If he'd bellowed before, he now roared. He charged at her like a wounded bull, swinging his sword in a wild arch. I stepped toward him. Our swords met and locked, metal screaming. His red face drained of color as we strained against each other. He wavered and fell over.

Deep gasping came from the doorway. The thin man stood bent over with one hand on the door frame. His eyes were closed for a moment, but when he finally saw the grisly scene, he squealed like a pig and dashed into the night.

"Coward." Katrin pulled the dagger from the fat man's gut and wiped it against his leggings. Blood flowed freely. He would die if we didn't stop it, but he deserved it. He'd surely killed others.

I grabbed the gag and shoved it against the wound. "Hold this."

Katrin raised her eyebrows. "You'll help him?"

"Just hold it."

"You're crazy." She knelt down, pressing the gag none too gently against the wound.

I whistled for Flax. When he trotted up to the door, I pulled herbs and bandages from my saddlebag. It took a few minutes to pack the wound with yarrow and stem the blood. After binding the wound, I pulled a blanket from a bed in the corner and laid it over the man.

I buckled the saddlebag. "Let's go."

"Why did you help him?" It wasn't a condescending tone, but a real question.

"I'll leave a note at the inn with directions to this cottage. The villagers can come to get this brigand. He has to be alive to meet justice." What I didn't tell her was that I'd seen enough death, and I couldn't let someone die without doing something about it.

Katrin shook her head. "You could have left him to God's justice." She shivered, and I realized she still stood in the thin slip, her arms bare to the shoulder, and her mid-calves showing.

"Here." I pulled off my mottled cloak and draped it across her shoulders. The hem dragged on the floor.

She pulled it tight about her, glanced at the man on the floor, and looked up at me, her eyes full of questions. "Why do you keep helping me?"

"Let's go." I guided her out the door with my hand on her shoulder and helped her onto Flax. She huddled in my lap, her body shuddering against me as we rode in silence through the twisting wood back toward the inn. I wanted to hold her tight, help her feel safe, but my arms stayed awkwardly to either side of her.

"I'm sorry." Her whispered words slipped through the falling rain. "If I'd been you, I would have abandoned my quarrelsome self."

My thoughts blustered. "I'm only doing what any man of honor would do."

As we came to the inn, Katrin slid from the horse. "I've caused you more trouble than my life is worth. I'm nothing to you, no more than that bleeding bandit. I don't want you to trouble yourself any more for me. Please go."

"Your life is worth a thousand times more than his." I bit my lip as the words slipped out. Now she'd think I was being forward. "I'm sorry. I didn't mean that. I don't think of you that way."

"If your friend is two hours from here, you'll be rid of me soon enough. I'll get my dress so you can have your cloak back." She slipped into the inn.

Curse my foolish tongue! How should I speak to her? I was much better as a mute. Sealing my mouth against further hurtful words, I finished the note detailing how to get to the brigands' nest and pasted it to the inn door. At least that bit of filth would be cleared up.

Katrin slipped out the door moments later. She glanced at the note, froze a second, and then allowed me to help her mount Flax. Within minutes she fell asleep, leaning into me with the unresisting trust of a child. I put one arm around her and rode into the night.

5

ANCHORED BETWEEN DUTY AND HONOR

YOSYPH

The rain eased as we approached Devron's farm. I shook my head, scattering droplets from my hair, and yawned as gray dawn crept over the horizon. Flax had lumbered along at a steady walk through the downpour.

Katrin slept curled up sideways on the saddle, her head bent forward against my arm. My mottled cloak wrapped around her like a blanket. I stifled a shiver. I didn't want to wake her. If I did, she'd pull away from me, and I'd lose her small measure of warmth.

She must have heard my thoughts. She stirred and pulled the cloak tighter. "So, you are the Yorel." The cloak muffled her voice.

She must have seen my raven stamp on the note. I did it to ensure the villages believed the note, but didn't think of her seeing it. Foolish. I shook my head, hoping she would believe me.

She pulled the cloak from her head. "It would be easier to talk to you if you spoke in words instead of head shakes and twitching fingers."

"I'm not the Yorel. He's a myth made up by the people to give them hope, like a shadow demon is made up to scare children into going to bed."

She shifted and studied my face. I tried to ignore her and watched the road ahead.

"Are you?" she asked after a minute's scrutiny.

"Am I what?"

"A shadow demon?"

"No!" I laughed.

"That's better. Your laugh is more pleasant than your serious voice." She touched my cheek, turning my head toward her. Heat spread from my cheeks to my entire face before creeping down to my shoulders. "I think you are both. My eyes keep sliding sideways when I try to study you, like anything else should be more important. You feel shifty. But when you get angry or laugh, you're easier to focus on. Is that why you're so serious?"

I shook my head, puzzlement muting the blush. "I don't understand what you are talking about."

"You don't, do you?" She tapped a finger to her lips, her brow crinkled up in concentration. "Maybe you are part shadow demon. Whatever it is, it probably makes it easier to be the Yorel."

"I'm not the Yorel."

"And I'm best friends with the Queen."

I pulled the reins, and Flax stopped with a questioning neigh. Katrin was joking, but that was not something to joke about.

"I'm sorry," she said, "I thought you'd find it amusing that the Queen was peeved with you—I mean the Yorel. Can't figure out a way to catch him. Says he's a cold-blooded murderer. But she knows all about murder." A shadow crossed her face. "You can trust me. I owe you my life."

"Then you understand that I'll not burden you with what could cost you your life."

We reached a fenced farm. A sheepdog ran out to meet us, barking and lapping my hand as I opened the gate.

"Yosyph," called a crinkle-haired woman from the front door, "what a delight to see you. Come have a bite to eat." A smile lit her sunburned face.

I shook my head, "I'm sorry, Sandra, I can stay but a few minutes. Is Devron close by?"

"He's about to sit down to breakfast. Come in. And you," she turned to Katrin, "look as weary as a farmer on the last day of harvest." Sandra offered her arm and Katrin leaned on it with a sigh.

I followed them into the kitchen.

My stocky friend stood at a table spread with bread, goat's cheese, and grapes. The corners of his smile hid beneath his mustache, though his eyes crinkled with concern, "Yosyph, has your father used all the herbs already?" His eyes flicked to Katrin. "And who is this lovely young lady?"

"She needs help to get to Conborner. I'd take her myself, but I have business that cannot wait. I have a request from my father for more herbs, grapes, and cheese. If you could please gather them in the next week. Another will be by to retrieve them."

I pulled a paper from my pocket, listing items and amounts.

Devron took it and traced his fingers along the curling border. His eyes widened when he made it a quarter of the way down. "I'll need help gathering these supplies."

"I can't help you this time, my friend. I'll be back in two months' time, before the last autumn harvest."

Katrin's voice cut in, close behind my ear. "Is that desert script?"

I spun around and locked eyes with her.

"Thunder and lightning," she whispered. "I thought I wanted to see you clearly, but now..."

"Do you know how to read this?" I hoped she couldn't and willed her to tell the truth.

"A little, but I've never seen it written this way." She looked back at the paper, furrowing her brow. "I can make out a few words. Captain—thousand—"

I turned the paper over. What would we do with her? If she could read this, then she could betray everything.

"I can learn to read it. Please, I want to help. I hate how I've been nothing but a burden to you."

"Now dear," Sandra said, "I'm sure you've been nothing of the sort. You come with me and we'll get you out of that muddy dress. Let's leave these men to their business."

"But I want to help," Katrin protested as Sandra led her from the room.

Devron leaned his chin onto his fist as he read the rest of the message. "Do you not trust her? She could help so much if she can read the desert script. I thought only you, Galliard, and I could."

"Have we trusted to teach anyone else?"

"No, but the time is pressing. She knows the script. Is it not God's hand she's here now?"

"She could also be the key to our fall." I rubbed the tight muscles in my neck. "She lived with the Queen for a week of each year and is betrothed to the prince. She wanted to return to him even after the assassins. Who knows if she wouldn't betray us to get in the Queen's favor and still marry the prince? I don't think so, but I'd rather not tempt her."

"Then what do you plan on doing? If you don't trust her, then I cannot keep her here where I'll be keeping records in your script."

I couldn't leave her there with Devron and—bother. I rolled my shoulders to loosen the tightening knots. "Will you lend me a horse for her to ride? Then I could take her to Conborner and still go swiftly on my journey."

Devron raised his eyebrows and turned his mouth down in disapproval. "Is your mission any more important than the one I must accomplish by harvest?"

"Devron, I hope to bring an army from the desert."

He let out a low whistle. "A needed blessing." He thumped the table with his fist. "Take the bloomin' horse and the girl. She may be a help yet. Who knows?"

"So why are *you* taking me to Conborner?" Katrin rode beside me on Flax's brother, a horse a shade lighter and half a hand taller than mine. A brown linen dress hung on her like a bag. It was one of Sandra's finer dresses, not yet patched. She rode astride instead of sidesaddle, which hiked the dress up to her knees, showing her hosen. The gossips at the well would jabber like geese if they saw her.

"Conborner is along my path, and because Devron is busy, he lent me a horse so we can still travel quickly."

"So it has nothing to do with me being able to read the desert script?"

I shrugged.

"I guess I must get used to you not answering." Katrin grinned.

"That means I can make up any story I want. It was a secret message to the emperor of Lashina, asking for his daughter's hand in marriage. But you are jealous of letting me know of your love for her, so you sought to frighten me from reading any more. And you must race to reach their land before another asks for her hand—"

I choked back a laugh.

"Oh, I've struck close to the truth."

"Close enough for today." I coughed again, a smile twitching at the corners of my mouth.

"If you are in such a hurry, why are you going around the Wilderlands?" she pointed to the road curving westward ahead of us. "Why not go through? We'd be to Conborner in less than a week, rather than a couple weeks."

"You've crossed them before?" I turned in my saddle as I studied Katrin yet again.

"No." She smiled lopsidedly. "But I've always wanted to. I hear it is beautiful."

"Do you know the way?"

"Naven said to head north-north-east, using the sun, and to always build a good fire to keep the wolves away. He said it only took four days to cross, though I don't know how far south he entered."

I rode in silence as the road turned more and more westward. I'd studied the maps. The Wilderlands sat as a wild patch of woods in the north-east corner of Lansimetsa. Its stories of ghosts and beasts kept it free of travelers. The Wilderlands were supposed to be difficult to cross, and I wanted them that way. We didn't need anyone to find the path we'd cut half a day's ride north of the road. Even I'd never gone deeper than that.

But it would take a full two weeks to go around them. What if we did cross? The route would not be as easy as a road, but I needed to travel as fast as possible and Katrin sounded confident. I looked at the sky and spread my hands. When did I start to listen to her advice? When she tried to kick me at the brigand's hut, or when she told me to "move over fool" and tossed my dagger? Maybe it had been once she showed she could read my mother's script, which no one else knew. No, I couldn't say I trusted her yet, but we needed to hurry. I nudged Flax with my knee and turned into the forest.

6

I AM YOUR FUTURE KING — WHAT MORE NEEDS BE SAID

HALAVANT

Being a prince should have certain privileges—including not having my bride stolen. Two whole days and none of the soldiers found her. Incompetent fools! And worse yet, Mother called them back from the search, saying it's a waste of resources since we weren't even 'officially' engaged yet.

Of course, we'll get a ransom note. Why else would have they stolen Katrin away? She's worth a queen's ransom. I would pay it if I were king yet, but Mother says she'll not have it. Oh, how I itch under her regency. Six more months, and then she'll have to step down. But six months is too long to wait to rescue Katrin.

I scratched at the coarse, flea-ridden tunic, and wondered for the hundredth time why I chose to disguise myself as a stable boy. I'd gladly take back the blow to his head and return his infested clothing. But getting out of the palace without a bodyguard required certain sacrifices of dignity and comfort. They hadn't even looked twice while I led a cart horse out the porter's gate, pulling that dratted wine wagon. Even under a floppy leather hat and manure-stained clothes, I would have thought they'd recognize their prince. I'll give them a well-deserved beating when I return.

Ugh, I hated the itch. Why must I sneak out like this? I'll soon be king. I should be able to do whatever I want. What difference does it make to be a few months shy of eighteen? Oh, things will change when I return. Maybe when I find Katrin, I'll wait to return until after my birthday, and then I won't have to deal with any more inconsiderate pomps, including Mother. She's forgotten her place. She is not queen, just regent, and should show me due respect.

I scratched at the tunic again. Night approached, and I'd ridden the cart horse all day. I'd left the wagon on the roadside as soon as I was out of sight of the palace, hoping for a quicker journey. What a mistake that was. This cart horse wasn't a smooth-striding thoroughbred. Its jarring lopsided gait sent a shock up my back with each step. My legs hurt from half standing in the saddle to lessen the shock, and my back ached worse than after any fight. I'd make this horse into glue as soon as I found another.

Fairhaven stood hours behind me, a pleasant memory of times before this irritation of a search. How would I find her? It's not like I could knock on everyone's door and ask. Maybe an inn. People talk at inns, right? At least that was why I was never to visit one. Too much loose talk, inappropriate for my royal ears. Yes, I'll find what I need at an inn.

After hours of uncomfortable riding, I finally came upon a town—little more than a few paint-peeling buildings on either side of the road. One building had two levels and glass windows, and a white sign swinging from its porch. The Thirsty Stallion, it proclaimed under a sloppily drawn horse. It had to be an inn. This would be where I'd start.

I slid from the horse's back. "Glue for you." I half-hoped he would wander off while I was in the Thirsty Stallion. I'd rather walk than get back on him. I pushed my way into the inn. Ugh. And I thought the clothes I'd taken smelled bad. Vomit, sweat, ale, beer, and all the other smells of the barracks were packed into one room. I thought the soldiers were gross, but this—no wonder Mother called the people dirty, miserable animals.

But they could talk, even though they smelled like animals. A fat man scampered up to me. At last, someone who recognized my worth.

"Good day," I said. "Have you seen a young woman with long, red hair and pale skin?"

"Yes, yes, poor child," the man boomed. "Came and paid good gold for a room."

I would kill the search party of soldiers. They should have found her if all I had to do was ask the first inn-keeper. "Who was with her? Where did she go? When did she leave?"

"She was alone, all scratched up and her clothing torn, a fine lady. I sent the village herbalist to tend to her, but she disappeared. Maybe brigands. The Yorel's note told us where to find the brigand's hideaway. But no lady. Not to worry, that Yorel is always watching out for us poor folk. He'll take care of her. I hope. Poor child."

Wait, what? I couldn't follow his rambling. Brigands, Yorel. She was here, and now she was gone. She must have escaped and found refuge at this inn. But why didn't she tell the innkeeper who she was and get help? I kicked a table and winced. The stable boy's shoes were not hardened leather like my boots.

"Boy!" a thin man with a dirty yellow cap called, "you looking for that red-haired lovely?"

I strode to the man. He leaned on a table nursing a beer.

"Do you know where she's gone?"

"Maybe. Maybe not. What is it worth to you?"

"I'll pay you well for any information you can give." I sat down at the table and then scooted the chair back a foot. He was half the smell in the room.

"Well. That's different, now, isn't it?"

I pulled out a gold piece from my hidden pouch and held it up to catch the light. I knew what to do. Those soldiers scared away all the informants. Gold always loosened tongues.

"Put that down before everyone comes over." He snatched it from my fingers, his black fingernails scratching me. I'd have to scrub with lye when I left this place. He bit the coin, nodded, and slipped it into his tunic. "I know the prince sent out guards to search for his betrothed and the Queen called them back. They were a nuisance enough yesterday."

I leaped to my feet. "I'll kill them. They knew she was here, and they didn't tell me!"

"Quiet, fool. The men never made it to this town, so sit down. Do you want to know more or not? I can't believe the prince sent such a fool of a spy as you. But perhaps it's the best he could do against the Queen's order." He paused and rubbed his fingers together. More gold.

I sat down and took a deep breath. He would pay for his insults, but for now, I would swallow my pride if he could tell me more. I pulled out two more gold coins and placed them on the table. "Ten more of these, if you can tell me where she is." Many people were looking our way; some shifted closer.

The man fingered the coins. "Fair enough. If I'd known she was the prince's bride when she showed up two days ago—but then, if wishes were horses, we'd all get to ride."

"Get on with it, fool!" I tried to control my voice.

He leaned forward and breathed in my face. I gagged on the rotten fumes. He grinned. "Tell your prince the girl is with the Yorel. Your prince will need all the luck he can to catch up to that devil. Especially since she went willingly with him."

"You dirty, filthy liar! I'll cut out your tongue!"

"Take it outside," the innkeeper yelled.

Three or four hands pushed me out the door. I stumbled across the threshold, surrounded by a knot of men. I couldn't tell faces apart in the falling evening light.

"He has gold," said a nasal voice.

"And too brash a tongue," said a deeper voice.

I jerked away from one set of hands, and another set grasped me.

"You owe me at least ten gold," said a gravelly voice. "Plus twenty more for the trouble. Hand it over, and we'll let you off with a knock over the head."

"Never!" I crouched, then sprang forward, breaking their hold. I swung my fist and connected with someone's nose. A satisfying crunch.

Then stars. The side of my head exploded with pain. I fell sideways as a club came down again. I raised my arm, and a blow shivered up my forearm to my shoulder. A fist caved in my side, and I couldn't breathe. I doubled over, and a boot connected with the back of my legs. The ground met my face and I couldn't tell one blow from the next. A gray haze spread over me and the blows faded away.

A pounding in my head brought me out of a thick, foggy sleep. It pulsated from the side of my head to my eyes before washing through the rest of me. I groaned as I turned over. Everything hurt.

"Marcus, get me a hot bath and be quick about it," I groaned, my eyes still shut.

A deep voice laughed off to my side. "Well, I'm not Marcus, but I agree a hot bath would do you good, my lad."

A stranger's voice. There was a dry chuckle, followed by the sound of dripping water. I startled as a warm, damp cloth was pressed to my forehead, and the stranger chuckled again.

"Who are you?" I croaked, my voice sounding like the grinding of wheels on cobbles. Whatever I was lying on—definitely not my bed—creaked in protest as I tried to move. Unfamiliar scents assaulted my nose: wood smoke, damp wool, and... animals? "Why am I not at the palace? Where am I?"

"Why don't you open your eyes and find out?"

I squinted one eye open. The other seemed to be glued shut. Variegated blurs of brown solidified into roughly hewn rafters speckled white with the bird droppings.

I've been taken prisoner! I will not be held for ransom. Escape! I lunged from the bed only to crumple to the floor. Waves of pain radiated from both my head and my right arm, which was trapped by tight bandages.

"That was foolish of you," the stranger remarked.

I groaned in response.

"Come along, lad." He put his shoulder under my unbound arm and helped me back onto a low cot.

I looked with my one open eye down my nose at him. "Do not address me in such a familiar manner, peasant."

He stared back. The man stood tall and sun-baked, topped with an untamed mop of sandy hair. His right hand was missing the pointer finger at the first knuckle. He wore clothes which at one time may have been fine, but had since become patched and threadbare. He made no response.

The silence drew out. I would not let this mere peasant get the better of me. "Who are you? Why have you kidnapped me?"

The man laughed. "Kidnap you? Do you remember nothing, boy?"

I wrinkled my brow and winced at the pain. Everything was foggy. "I don't seem to be able to think well."

"I am not surprised, considering the rather large bump on your head. Don't worry, I didn't kidnap you. As for who I am, I am known as Galliard the Wanderer. Who are you?"

"It is no business of yours who I am. I demand you return me to the palace. I—"

"Palace? Who do you think you are—the prince?" Galliard slapped his leg and laughed again.

"Yes, I am!"

"Look here, that fight must have rattled your brains more than I thought. I don't know who you are, but you are not the prince. A group of men beat you up yesterday. Obviously, your oh-so-charming ways did not sit well with them. It was ten against one. You had no chance. They took your purse and left you in an alley. I nabbed you when they wandered off. Sorry I couldn't stop them earlier, but remember, it was ten against one."

Remember. I wish I could. How did I end up here? Katrin was stolen away, and then, and then what? Everything was blank, as if I had heard the news of Katrin's disappearance and then woken in this stable. I had to get back to the palace, or things would go more wrong than they already had.

"I am the prince," I insisted. "My bride-to-be has been kidnapped. I cannot search for her in such a state as this. It is important I return to the palace. I must convince my mother to send men to search for her. I promise you, return me to the palace, and you shall be richly rewarded."

Galliard snorted. "I will do nothing of the sort. I make it my business to stay away from there. Besides, I am headed west."

"Stubborn peasant, I will give you proof. My ring. Where is my ring? I am never without—" I stopped. Memories rushed back. Mother had ordered a stop to the search and forbade me to bother her about it again. I'd hidden my ring in my room, then disguised myself as a stable boy. The town, the innkeeper and the thin man—then the drunken men and the beating. Then the memory of blackness.

If I returned to the palace, no one would seek Katrin. She'd die. "I can't return to the palace!"

"I'm glad to see you come to your senses."

"No, I must find Katrin. I shall travel with you. You said west? As good a direction as any. You will help me find her."

"Wait, lad. I have my own plans, and they do not include a wild goose chase after some girl. You stay here. You won't be left helpless. The good farmer and his wife have agreed to look after you."

"I will not stay here! I will go west with you. I am your prince and future king. I command you to take me."

Galliard stifled a laugh and turned a stern face toward me, "You'd better watch your tongue. Who knows what these folk would do if they knew they had a Royal Highness in their midst?"

"They would be a great deal more respectful than you."

"They would hang the madman's placard about your neck."

I couldn't tell if he was joking or serious.

"When do we leave?"

"*I* leave in four days—as soon as the summer harvest is over. *You* are staying here."

7

MUDDY CAMPFIRES DON'T BURN

YOSYPH

Katrin was right, the Wilderlands were passable. Not easily, but still, we were making a good distance each day. Steep hills lay in a northwest line like an undulating set of walls across our path, always rising more than they fell so we were a little higher each day. We broke a back-and-forth path, traveling up and over and down, repeated for hours on end, with only the trees for variety—willows at the low streams, and pines at the top. We heard birds and squirrels and saw the occasional deer. Katrin scared most off with her persistent chattering—pointing out this animal, that tree—mindless prattle.

I began to long for her sulky muttering. It was easier to ignore. Could I safely leave her in Conborner? I grew worried after she commented halfway through the first day, '*Oh! What's a road doing here? A pity it's not going in our direction.*' Should I take her into the desert with me? No, she'd slow me down. But what then? Could she keep quiet about what she'd seen and heard? How much did she know?

"Yosyph," Katrin said as we made camp on the second evening. "Look! Isn't this a wonderful fire I've built?" She pointed to a compact pile of branches in the middle of a partly cleared spot of ground. She got the dried moss to take fire, but the flames struggled to take hold of the branches. The moss turned black, fell apart, and even the thin stream of smoke disappeared.

I shook my head and pulled the stack of branches off to the side, then pulled up the other plant matter.

"What?" Katrin thrust out her lower lip.

"The ground needs to be completely free of vegetation so we don't set this whole forest on fire. The wood is too tightly packed for air to feed the fire. And you need bark and small dry wood to burn after the moss before the fire can catch on the large pieces."

Her lip trembled, and instead of crying she laughed. She ripped out the grass, giggling the whole time. Then she stacked the branches in an open-air tower and brought over bark she'd set to the side. She struck the flint and blew on the moss to urge the sparks to take hold.

"You already knew all this, didn't you?"

"Maybe." She paused her gentle blowing on the fire. "You spoke more there than you did all day."

"I have nothing to say."

"Then I'll keep seeking your instruction."

"Even if you don't need it?"

"Certainly. Unless you talk without me almost burning down the woods."

I set a pot of water in the fire. "Very well. I have some questions."

"I bet the first one is, where did I learn to read the desert language?"

I looked up from pulling dried herbs and meat from the saddlebag. She was perceptive under all her mindless chatter.

"Naven taught me," she continued.

"Who's this Naven?"

"He is—was—my father's personal servant. He was a messenger and bodyguard from the desert. He taught me to read and write his language so we could communicate in secret. He taught me to build fires and what plants to eat in the wild. And he even taught me to throw knives to defend myself. That is why —it's because of—" she stuttered to a stop. "He is no longer a servant in our household. Father didn't like his daughter learning such skills. I miss him."

"Your father?"

"No, Naven! I'll never miss my father." She shoved a stick in the fire and sent up a rain of sparks. The light danced across thinned lips and fisted hands.

The third morning, I woke to water dripping through my canvas tent. Rain beat against it, and the wind whistled a ghostly melody to the rhythm. I pulled on my boots and crawled out. My tent only came up to my waist, but it kept me dry and warm—except in a storm like this. Katrin had my oilskin tent, and it looked like it was holding out against the water.

No fire this morning. After a cold and damp breakfast, we huddled in our cloaks and rode off. By noon, the hills grew a skin of slick mud, and even the plants had a hard time keeping the water from running in streams down the hill. Katrin's horse skittered sideways as we climbed yet another steep face.

"We'll have to walk them for now." I dismounted Flax. Katrin slid from Barley. Though Flax had been through plenty more than most farm horses, he was still a horse and not a sure-footed donkey. Barley was a complete novice to this.

I'd taken three steps forward when I heard a quiet *oof*. Katrin sprawled on the ground. She pulled on Barley's reins to help her rise before limping and slipping onward. She must have twisted her ankle again.

"You ride Flax." I helped her to mount. "I'll lead."

I took Flax's reins and trusted Barley would follow. We climbed to the top of the hill and down again. Flax never fell, but he skittered enough to keep me tight with worry. My feet slipped out from under me about once per hill, and by evening, my calves were as knotted as my shoulders. My clothes were as covered in mud as if I'd rolled down a hill in them—which, I suppose, I had in small parts throughout the day.

The evening faded into another wet night. I crawled into a damp tent in mud-encrusted clothes. I couldn't imagine Katrin had a much more pleasant sleep, though hopefully, her tent was dry. She didn't say, but she hadn't complained at all since we'd entered the woods, about the cold or her foot or anything. She had steel in her. Not only steel but a joyful brightness. I must have been such a dismal traveling companion for her in my quietness. Perhaps I could lighten up like she'd suggested, but I'd most likely say something else foolish. No, best to remain the mute unless it became necessary to talk.

By morning, the rain had stopped, but everything was still soaked. I sat up to put on my boots, and every muscle in my body complained. *Stop your grumbling*, I told them. *Even the girl muddles through, why shouldn't you?*

My muscles continued their muttering as I attempted a fire. Katrin pulled dry tinder from the saddlebag and urged the semi-dry wood into a flame. It smoked more than it flamed.

"Well, my muddy man." Katrin stretched as she stood up from the fire. "I suppose we should go."

We trudged into the gray morning, up yet another hill. Flax's skittering and Katrin's almost silent gasps were part of the forest sounds now, as familiar as the scolding of the squirrels. I dug my toes into the slick hillside, seeking roots to hold, and climbed upward. A branch served as a staff and helped me keep my footing. Hours later, the sun dipped below the gray clouds and lit the land before it slipped behind the further hill.

Down one more hill, and then we'd camp. I started the downward climb, which was more of a sideways shuffle and slide. I dug in the staff and slid, then dug in the staff again. Then Flax really skittered. He slid into me and threw me forward. Katrin's scream overlapped my yelp. I launched forward and spun heels over head. I put out my arms to keep my head from striking the ground, launching myself into another spin instead. I caught the branch of a tree. My feet slipped from beneath me, and I landed on my back, smacking my head on the ground. Though I had stopped, the world still flipped around me. Distantly, I registered the slipping scramble of Katrin.

She slid to a stop beside me, then gently touched the back of my head. She sucked in her breath before tearing off a piece of her petticoat. I turned to see what she was doing and saw blood on her fingers.

"We have bandages in the saddlebag." I closed my eyes and urged my stomach to stop churning.

"Sorry, sorry, sorry," she muttered as she led Flax to where I lay. She opened the saddlebag and pulled out a bandage.

"Don't fret. It was just a stumble." The world stilled slightly. I opened my eyes and pushed myself into sitting position. Things blurred for a moment and then came back into focus.

"You're bleeding, and your speech is slurred. I have every reason to fret," she shot back.

My head pounded with each word. "Quietly, please."

"Sorry," she muttered again. "We need someplace dry." She glanced around, wiping her dirty hands on her skirt. "There." She pointed to a rocky protrusion a little to our left. We crawled and slipped to it, our horses following the best they could. We found a cave, about three men deep, two wide, and three tall—and it was dry. Along one side stood a good pile of seasoned wood, like someone had left it for future use.

Katrin quickly created a fire, then tended to my head.

"You have too much hair," she muttered as her fingers gently probed the back of my head.

A sharp pain stabbed through my skull. "That's it," I winced.

"Well, it seems to have stopped bleeding. And you are speaking without a slur, so I suppose you are all right."

"I'm fine." I brushed her hands away from my head and stood to get food from the saddlebags. The world spun for a moment and then stilled. My stomach did one more somersault to the rhythm of my pounding head.

Katrin went to the back of the cave to get more fuel for the fire. She returned carrying an armful of wood, a torn pack, and a quizzical expression. She sat down beside me and opened it, the leather cracking from age and disuse. Inside we found stone-hard bread, a blanket, and six thin daggers set in a belt.

"Throwing daggers." Katrin pulled one out and balanced it in her hand. "These are finely crafted, not something a person would purposely leave behind."

Wolves. As if my thoughts called them, a mournful howl quavered in the distance. "We best prepare for a long night," I said. "You take the throwing knives." My shoulder still stung from her all-too-accurate throw a few days before. "I'll keep to my sword."

Her voice quavered. "Do you think the fire will keep them away?"

I didn't answer. "I'll take first watch tonight."

"No." She latched the belt of throwing knives around her waist. "I'll take first watch. You are still pale from that fall."

"No, Katrin..."

"I'll wake you when I get too tired. Go to sleep, Yosyph." I knew I'd get nowhere in an argument.

I shouldn't let her stand watch. Yes, I trusted her now. She'd not fall asleep on the watch, but she needed me. I sat with my sword in my lap and my back against the wall near the mouth of the cave. I needed to stay awake. I needed to stay...

8

PROMISE BROKEN, PROMISE KEPT

YOSYPH

It seemed I'd been asleep only seconds when I heard horses scream and Katrin's sharp cry. She stood close to the low burning fire, feet braced and a dagger in her hand. A dark shape growled at the mouth of the cave. Its eyes glowed, and the firelight glinted from long, yellow fangs. Behind the leader slunk two more great beasts. I lunged to my feet, my stiff muscles slowing me and my head pounding. The foremost wolf sprang toward me.

Katrin screamed.

The wolf lunged at my neck. I raised my arm to shield myself while slashing at him with the sword in my other hand. Pain shot up my arm as teeth punctured through my sleeve. My sword bit into his side. With a howl of pain, the wolf dropped back, only to be replaced by two more.

I looked quickly for Katrin, but couldn't see her in the dim cave. *Please be alive!*

One wolf snapped at my leg. I danced aside, swinging my weapon as the other wolf lunged. He dropped short, pulled back, and sprang again. The first wolf snagged my boot with its teeth. I drove my blade into the chest of the lunging wolf and fell under its weight. My sword was trapped in the beast. I pushed against the limp body, keenly aware of the teeth gnawing at my boot, worrying it back and forth, but not yet puncturing it. The pressure of the teeth released. I pushed again on the dead wolf on my chest, rolling the carcass off me with my sword still embedded. I rolled to my knees and fell flat to my face as two great paws struck my back. Hot breath panted against my neck.

I arched my back against the weight, tense against the expected bite.

The beast jerked back with a howl. I sprang to my feet, yanked my sword from the carcass and turned around, thrusting the blood-coated metal into the wolf. He went limp. Two slim daggers protruded from behind the creature's neck. Similar weapons were buried in the back of another still mound of fur. Three wolves lay dead in the cave.

"Katrin!" I spun about looking for her.

"Over here." Her shaking voice came from above and to the right.

Looking up, I found her perched on a rocky ledge in the cave, about seven feet above the ground.

"Are you hurt?" I put out my arms for her to jump into. Her homespun dress hung halfway off one shoulder, and the skirt gapped a few inches from the bodice, but I saw no blood.

"Nothing a needle and thread won't fix." Her voice squeaked.

She jumped, and I caught her about the waist. My arm throbbed in protest, and she slipped from my grasp, tumbling to the ground.

"I'm sorry." I reached down to help her up. "And thank you."

Katrin took my hand. "For what? For climbing up the wall, while you fought three massive wolves? I should thank you."

"You saved my life."

She blushed and quirked up one eyebrow. "Then I only have two more times before I've repaid my debt to you. All I did was throw some daggers from the safety of that shelf. It's a mercy they all went after you. I suppose they truly do prefer man flesh."

I chuckled. "Seems to be." I pulled off my tunic. "'Tis more a mercy there were only three. Packs are usually much larger. These must have been outcasts and much more foolhardy than the usual pack to attack in the face of fire." I pulled off my linen shirt. My chuckle changed to a groan as I pulled the sleeve away from the punctures. Fresh blood coated my arm.

"You let me tend to that." Color rose in her cheeks as she averted her eyes from my whip-scarred back.

She pulled herbs and vinegars from the saddlebag.

Saddlebag. Barley and Flax! I stumbled to the mouth of the cave. The two horses stood quivering. Their ropes had worn rings of bark from the trees where I'd tied them. Why had the wolves attacked us and not our horses?

Katrin came beside me. "Thank providence, they are still here. Now let me tend to that arm."

As she mixed herbs into a vinegar, she hummed a military tune, one popular for when the soldiers marched by. She moved her lithe body in rhythm to the tune. She pressed the herbal vinegar to my wounds, and I hissed through gritted teeth.

"Come now," she laughed. "You didn't flinch when the wolf bit you. What's a little medicine?"

"You must not have been listening, because I'm sure I bellowed." The words came out lightly.

"I must not have heard it over my own thudding heart," she

quipped back. “We’re quite the team, facing off bandits and wolves, carrying secret messages, traveling over treacherous land.” She hummed again as she leaned over to apply vinegar to another puncture. A necklace slipped from her dress. Firelight flashed off a curious design of twists and swirls in gold. She quickly tucked it back.

“Who made your necklace? It almost looks like the desert script.”

She stopped humming and bit her lip. “My mother gave it to me.” Her voice almost dropped below the crackling of the fire.

“She’s must be proud to have a daughter like you.”

“She’s dead.” Her voice fell flat. She turned away and rummaged in the pack.

I placed a hand on her trembling shoulder. “What happened?”

She kept her back to me but didn’t shake off my touch. Her voice continued in a monotone, though with a slight tremor. “I dashed into the street to get my kitten. My mother pushed me out of the way, and the carriage hit her instead. I was ten.”

I patted her back awkwardly.

For long moments she trembled, then she took a shaky breath and turned to face me. “Yosyph. Why are you so good to me?”

Why? I stared into the fire. At first, it was because of duty and she needed to be saved, despite how proud and unbearable she was. Her beauty had also struck me at first, but I hadn’t thought about that so much lately. She was travel-stained, had hair like a rat’s nest, and was as smelly as a sheep at the end of winter. I looked at her, but only saw—eyes full of question and hurt, a face firm with determination, a tongue quick to bring humor, and a soul brimming with bravery.

“Because you are good.”

“But I’m not. I was horrible to you when you first saved my

life. My mother is dead because of my impulsiveness." She sniffed then clenched her fists. "The Queen was right. I killed my mother, and I have no right to their promise."

Promise? My confusion must have been plain because she laughed, her face lost its tightness. "I'm rambling. I get that way when I think too much about the past. Too melancholy. Forget I said anything."

"Too late. Now I'll be wondering what this promise is."

Katrin scooted closer, and I stiffened for a moment before relaxing and letting her knees touch mine. Her eyebrows shifted back to seriousness. "It's not a happy story." She took a deep breath. "My mother was the Lady Susanne of Conborner and best friend to the Queen, even before she was the Queen. They both were noble women. Both strong-willed and did what they wanted, despite custom. One married the king, the other married a commoner. But they remained best friends and spent a month together every year at the seaside or in the hunting lodge or sometimes even the palace." She twisted one of her tresses around a finger as she spoke, her gaze unfocused.

"When they both were pregnant with their first child, they decided if one was a girl and one was a boy, those children would marry. They swore a blood oath. I think even the king agreed to it. But even if he hadn't, our mothers always got their ways. Halavant and I started our lives together, destined to marry." She laughed, a bitter sound. "But destinies change. The King died, and the Queen changed. At least that is what Mother told me. It was before I could remember. Still, the Queen made Mother smile, and that was more and more rare around Father."

I added a branch to the fire, and it flared.

Katrin leaned closer the fire. "Then my mother died. Before she did, she wrote a letter to the Queen. Father read it to me before he sent it off, to make sure I knew my duty. That is when I found out I was promised to the prince. The letter begged the

Queen to remember their friendship and show the same kindness to me. She pleaded to let me still spend time with the prince each year, if not come live in the palace permanently. Mother ended by evoking their blood oath that Halavant and I marry. I didn't want any blood oath to marry the prince. He was a silly boy. I wanted my mother back." Katrin looked up at me, hurt etched in the corners of her eyes. "My father read the letter twice. Then he smacked me. He told me I killed his wife, and the only reason he didn't sell me as a slave was because I would be queen someday, and I'd give him lands and riches ten times what he had now."

I clenched my hands. How could any father say or do that? The cur!

"The Queen honored my mother's wishes—partly. I visited the palace for a week each year. I'm sure Halavant didn't know of the promise. But still, we grew to love each other. He's sweet, if a bit spoiled. So am I. My week with him was always the best part of the year, despite the Queen becoming more and more difficult. But her discourtesy was nothing compared to Father—" Her lips thinned, and she was quiet.

I set out bread, and she chewed on a crust thoughtfully as I cleaned my sword.

"Father was always unpredictable," she said. "He became a rich merchant after marrying Mother. He'd lavish us with gifts, or throw books at my head, depending on his mood. After Mother died, the book throwing turned into fists and feet." Katrin stopped and pulled her cloak tighter around her shoulders.

"Naven was the only one who stayed kind, besides Halavant. After Mother died, Naven taught me knife throwing, I think mostly to protect myself from Father. By the time I turned twelve, Father had risen to great riches and sunk to great violence. One day, I saw him coming with an inkwell. I threw a knife at him, nicked his ear, and ran.

"Naven helped me escape. We made it four days into the desert before my father's men caught us. They flogged Naven until his back was ribbons of flesh, took all his water, and left him there to die. I got off lighter. My fingers all healed straight, though I can still hear the loud cracks as he broke them one by one. I don't know what he was thinking, because if I'd ever married Halavant, Father would be hanged for his offense. But I don't think he's sane. He thought his threatening would keep me from telling Halavant. I'm not sure why I didn't. But now it doesn't matter. I won't marry the prince. The Queen wants me dead. So the safest place for me is to return to my Father. He'll protect me from the Queen, if only to marry me off to someone who will pay the highest bride price."

I closed my eyes. My fingers flickered in agitated anger. Why! Why do the strong hurt the weak? A ruler to the land, a father to a child? This will all change. When we overthrow the monarchy, we will have a rule of law and not a whim. A law that will protect the weak and give everyone access to justice. Soon, soon.

"You cannot return to that man," I stated.

"But where else can I go?" She twined her hair around both hands then untwisted it. "Father hasn't hurt me since that time. He was angry. But he knows I can defend myself now. I need to bury my love for—." She stopped and took a shuddering breath. "I need to forget the prince. When I am eighteen, I will legally come into a portion of my inheritance, and I can open a shop or something, make myself useful. I've survived seventeen years with my father. I can endure a year more."

She fell silent again.

I wished I had words to make it better. Words to heal her world. I glanced at the knives in the backs of the wolves. "You could become a bodyguard. I am glad you were not trying to kill me back in the royal forest."

Her harsh bark of laughter echoed around the small cave.

The sun rose into a clear sky, and the ground had dried enough we could ride. The hills were less steep, and by evening we'd exited the Wilderlands. A day more, and Katrin recognized the countryside. She grew quiet as we drew closer to her father's house.

"You don't have to go back to him," I told her. I would find a safe place for her, if she would let me.

She bit her lip, looked down, and shook her head. Her hands were white fists around Barley's reins.

A large manor, surrounded by a stone wall, rose on the horizon. Golden fields spread all around it. A servant let us in the gate. He looked at Katrin in her torn and muddy clothes. He ran to the manor, disdain lay heavy on his lips. Two hounds bounded out and barked at the heels of Flax and Barley. The manor door slammed open as we reached the end of the drive. Out stepped a large man with graying red hair, an appliqued coat, gold chains, and ink-smudged fingers.

"Katrin!" he boomed, raising his fist, "come here."

Katrin trembled as she started to slide off Barley.

"No," I said. "He can say what he wants to say with you up here."

"It will only make him angrier." She slid to the ground.

I dismounted to follow her. She shook her head and walked toward the man, with her chin held high.

"Bow that proud little head," he roared. "You've wasted enough of my money. Do you know how much I've spent to outfit you for a week at the palace each year, just to have you throw it away? You were engaged to the prince! And now what? I gave you everything! Everything! And you throw it away!"

Katrin held a hand out to him. "Father, let me explain."

"Quiet! Oh, why did God take my wife instead of you? But I'll be rid of you soon enough. The old Baron still wants to marry you. He'll keep you in line. He's not as forgiving as I am. And with his offered bride price, I'll at least get a return on my wasted money."

"Katrin." I stepped forward and place my hand on her shoulder. "We are leaving. There is nothing for you here."

The man drew back a moment, as if he'd just realized I was there, then his face grew redder than Katrin's hair. "You! You are the reason she ran away from the Prince! I'll have you flogged! And quartered!"

I turned my back on his blustering and guided Katrin back to her horse. I saw a flash of movement out of the corner of my eye. I shifted my weight and prepared to grab his hand as he struck me. But it wasn't aimed at me.

Katrin stumbled with a sharp cry as a fist drove into her shoulder. I whipped about as the man threw another fist at Katrin's back. Lunging sideways, I pulled Katrin to the ground, rolled, and stood between her and her father with sword drawn.

The merchant dropped his fists and stepped back.

"I will cut you down like a dog if you strike her again," I challenged. By now, several servants stood watching, but none moved to the merchant's defense.

I kept the sword between her and her father while she mounted Barley. Once she was safely on, I mounted Flax.

As we reached the gate the merchant bellowed, "Never come through these gates again. You'll die a starved pauper. And don't think you'll find anyone else to help you. No one will take you in. I'll make sure of that!"

"I'll find you a place with a farmer," I said, after we'd gone a good pace from the manor. "They are usually good folk, and you'll always have enough to eat." The sun still sat near the center of the sky. I'd find her a place to work, get supplies, then start into the desert early tomorrow. She wasn't the first refugee I'd found a new home for.

"No one will take me." Katrin twisted her hair about one hand. "At least not in Conborner. Father holds shares in all the businesses and owns all the farmland. All the farmers are tenants. You might find me a place, but when Father finds out either they will lose their employment or dismiss me."

"How about your other family?"

"My grandparents are dead. My parents had no siblings."

I shook my head. I could take her with me. But she'd burn to a crisp in the desert, and the map said *the way is difficult.* On the other hand, she was resilient, and she knew how to read the desert script. She could be useful. Plus, it would solve the problem of her potentially revealing our rebellion. But she'd slow me down.

"Your fingers are fluttering again," Katrin said. "Do you have a plan?"

I shifted in my saddle and studied her. She was still riding tall and strong, even after everything. Yes, she was twisting her hair around one hand, but it was a small gesture of worry when she could be slumped over in despair. She would do well in the desert, and maybe she wouldn't slow me down.

"If you will, I'll take you to my people. You can make your home with them."

Katrin brought her hand to her mouth, and her eyes grew wide. "Do you mean the people of the desert? Naven's people?"

"I don't know if it's Naven's people, but yes, they are in the desert."

"Please, take me! I have nothing here. I know I'd love it there. And I promise I wouldn't be a burden. I can help. Naven taught me all about the desert. We even made it four days in. I know how to survive there."

I looked up and sent a prayer heavenward, my hands forming each silent pleading word. *Bless this crazy journey. Bless us to make it safely to my mother's people and find Katrin a home. Bless them to send an army so this land can be free. Bless us—*

"Will you teach me your hand language?" Katrin asked.

I stopped my prayer and half-smiled. This would be a learning experience for both of us.

9

I TRAVEL WITH A MAN WHO IS FIT FOR A DUNG HEAP

HALAVANT

I doubt even four days of listening to Minister Chase drone on about crops and taxes could have been more boring than my four days spent waiting for Galliard to finish working for this farmer. Besides, it was the dead center of summer. What farmer harvests in the summertime? I suppose it was good I had to wait, because that first day I could hardly get out of bed, let alone sit astride a gentle horse. Though the farmer galled me to get moving.

That first day, when he came in to milk his noisy cows—they'd been lowing and kept me from resting—he looked at me like a poor invalid, muttering things like, 'poor lad', and 'what a pity.'

I'd show him. I was not a baby. I swung my legs down from

the cot and tried to walk. They wobbled beneath me, and my feet didn't want to lift. I stumbled to my knees.

The farmer stopped milking and watched me, his eyebrows raised and the corners of his mouth twitching. So he thought he could laugh at me.

I'd show him. I pulled myself to standing again.

"You be as shaky as a new colt, though your hair is white as an old man," the farmer commented. "You certain you be going on at the end of the harvest? We could use an extra set of hands around here. Seeing you lost your memory and all, you need a home, too."

Let him laugh at my weakness and my bleached hair. It meant nothing more than a yapping dog. A dog to be kicked when I had the strength. But for now, I needed to lie down. I ignored him as I shuffled through a layer of hay and muck to the back of the barn where my cot was. My head pounded and my body shook with the effort of lowering myself onto it.

"You be a determined lad," the farmer nodded.

I scoffed. I didn't need his approval.

"So, you're at it again." Galliard's laughing voice startled me into a stumble and I fell, zinging my bound arm on the floor. "What is this? The third time you've snuck out of bed today."

"Tenth." I pulled myself to stand again and rubbed my arm. I didn't think it was broken, but still, it stung any time I bumped it. "And I wasn't sneaking. I'm preparing to travel. I must find Katrin, and she is getting farther and farther from me each day."

"I see you can lift your feet a bit better than you did this morning. Still, you are not coming with me."

"Insufferable fool," I muttered.

He raised his eyebrows, then took a basket and sat down on a bench. He pulled out a thick slice of warm bread and slathered on butter. The rich scent wove between the stench of the barn. My stomach grumbled. But it was all the way across the barn. *Insufferable and inconsiderate!*

I slowly walked over, each muscle complaining it couldn't move an inch more. I knew better. I'd forced them to make this walk nine times today, and they would do it until they stopped complaining.

When I reached the bench, Galliard nodded and handed me warm bread and soft cheese. It was better than anything served in the palace. "I shall have our baker get the recipe for this bread when I return to the palace."

Galliard didn't look at me, but I could see the amusement hidden in his crinkled eyes.

On the fifth morning, for it took five days instead of four for Galliard to finish helping with the harvest, I rose when the farmer came to milk his cows. I walked through several miles of farm and returned with the rising sun. My lungs tingled with the cold air, and my muscles only complained a little, except my arm in the sling, and my beating head. I was now ready to find my Katrin.

I met Galliard as I returned to the barn. He carried two packs and a walking staff.

"We leave today," I ordered.

"I am." He tossed one pack to me. "And since you seem determined to leave these good folk, here's a pack to start you on your journey."

"You'll help me?" I stumbled to a stop. What was I saying? I didn't have to ask his permission for anything. He had to take me.

He laughed and shouldered his pack. "You can follow me if you can keep up." He turned and walked up the road.

My stomach grumbled. I'd not eaten breakfast yet. Maybe I'd lighten my pack, then follow him. I glanced up. He was already a good distance from me. Insolence! But I wouldn't give him the satisfaction of calling him back. I swung the pack over my shoulder. It was awkward to do without hurting my arm, but finally, I got it settled and jogged after Galliard.

"Where do we go from here?" I asked after I'd caught up to him.

"About five day's walk from here lies a farm of a friend of mine."

"Huh! Another farm!"

Galliard was suddenly stern, and while his voice was not exactly threatening, neither was it gentle. "Where I am going, you'd be wise to make no mention you believe you are the prince."

"I am the prince! Just because you don't believe me doesn't mean..."

"Hush! Around here, the names of royalty are not loved."

"Are you saying these people hate the crown?"

"They fear it, and sometimes fear is even more dangerous than hate."

"But if they do not know I am the prince, how will they know how to treat me?"

Galliard thumped his forehead with his hand. "Are you dense, boy? These are good, kind people who would offer all they have to a stranger in need. Yet you demand of them what you have no right to."

"No right? *I* am the prince. *I* decide what is right."

"Look, if you act this way to my friend, he is likely to toss you headfirst in the dung heap."

"He wouldn't dare."

"Yes, he would and could. He was once a soldier for the King and is a mountain of a man. Watch your tongue where he is concerned, and I warn you: don't make eyes at his daughter, or what you'll get will be worse than the dung heap."

Dung heap! I kicked a stone. It bounced off a stump and ricocheted against my shin. I stumbled and winced. If he didn't watch it, I'd have him thrown in a dung heap, as soon as I found Katrin. But for now, I'd put up with the Wanderer's insolence.

10

EVEN THE WIND CANNOT RIP AWAY THE STORIES WE TELL

YOSYPH

Long grasses filled the land between the caravan town of Gankin and the desert. In the distance, a ridge of hills humped across the horizon, separating the grasslands from the desert sand.

I studied the map one more time and checked the heavy water bags slung over Flax's and Barley's backs. The water would only last us three days, or four if we skimped. The map showed wells every day or two, after the first three day stretch. Those first three days worried me. We'd be fine if we kept to our path. Perhaps we could bring more water and walk instead of ride through the desert. It would take longer. Did I have the time to take longer? I'd already spent ten days, and the autumn harvest would come in little more than two months. I traced my finger along the *King's Trial*:

Dunes—three days and no water.

Stone Forest—three to four days with water every day, if we could find the wells.

Devil's Teeth—two days.

That many days by horse. Twice as long by foot. And if we got lost, forever.

Katrin bent over the map, the end of her turban trailing down beside her face. "The map won't change, no matter how much you glare at it."

She was right.

I rolled up the map, slipped it inside a waterproof pouch, and tucked it back inside my robe. The recently purchased desert robes hung loosely from my shoulders to my feet. I considered taking them off and wearing my regular clothing, something easier to mount with. Yet the map had warned to wear desert robes to keep the body from losing too much water. How that worked was beyond me. They seemed to add to the heat of the day. I hooked one foot in the stirrup and swung my other leg over Flax's back. My leg tangled in the robe and stopped halfway, leaving me sprawled across the saddle.

"You've never ridden in robes before?" Katrin's eyes crinkled with amusement.

I shook my head as I slid to the ground. The robes fell back straight around me, as if they hadn't had the perverse amusement of stopping me mid-mount.

Katrin looked at me as if waiting for my full attention. She stepped into the stirrup and in one fluid motion, flew into her saddle, her robes flowing out and settling around her. She nodded. "The robes are not all that different from my riding dress."

"Which I've never had the pleasure of wearing," I muttered.

Her eyes danced with laughter. "So you do have a sense of

humor." She watched as I semi-successfully mounted Flax. "Does that mean we are going?"

I flickered my fingers in a yes.

"Must mean we are." She tried repeating the finger motion.

"Almost. You signed 'thirsty' instead of 'yes.' This is 'yes.'" I touched my thumb to the middle of my forefinger.

"Well, 'thirsty' is good to know, too." She practiced both words.

We rode through the long grasses and crested a ridge as the sun set behind us. The hills cast long shadows over and against the dunes, which piled one after another into the distance, their high ridges flowing north and south and bowing into the west.

"It looks like my shadow is already on the journey ahead of us," Katrin laughed as her shadow stretched beside mine far down the first dune. "I'll race you to see who can catch the front of our shadow first."

"We'll not be racing anywhere." I shook my head, still perturbed by the robe incident.

"Yosyph, I was joking! Come now, where's that humor from before? This journey will be ten times the tedium if you can't laugh." She slid from her horse and opened her saddlebag.

I also dismounted and pulled out food for dinner. "We will die if I am not serious."

"Can't you take the journey seriously and not yourself?" She poked me in the side. A shiver ran up my back. I clamped down my arm and coughed.

"Oh, you're ticklish!" She grinned, her eyes dancing. "I'll keep that in mind."

"I'll take you right back to the Wilderlands if you abuse that knowledge," I growled, as the corners of my mouth twitched up.

Katrin grinned wider and set up her tent on the sheltered side of the hill.

Later, I lay in my tent running over the problems of finding my mother's people and raising an army, but the thought of Katrin's finger prickling my side interrupted the worries. *What will she do now she knows I'm ticklish?* I shook my head, rolled over, and let the worries go for the night.

The next morning, we stepped off the hill's crest and climbed down into the first reaches of the desert. The dry morning air burned with each breath. By the time we'd reached the bottom, it seemed we'd entered an oven. A hot wind whipped up to meet us, casting gritty sand in our eyes and mouths. The desert had swallowed us whole, and the other world of grass and trees no longer existed.

I reviewed the directions for this part of the journey. *Travel three days, directly east from the town Gankin, across the great dunes. Be wary of yellow-banded snakes and scorpions the size of your thumb. Their sting is death.*

I wiped sweat from my brow.

"I'm glad I'm not the only one," Katrin said.

"We'll get used to it... eventually."

"Oh, I remember how it was. Still, I feel like a butter cookie woman, slowly baking in the oven. Soon I'll be all toasty brown, maybe as brown as you."

The day rolled on with Katrin chattering about all the things Naven had taught her: riding bareback, throwing knives, speaking his native language, and learning how to wrap a turban. She told about her childhood both with the prince and at home. "—and so I fell asleep in the pile of carpets and wasn't discovered until the merchant had gone half a day's distance from our estate. He threatened to sell me as a slave, and I fell into hysterics, not even realizing he'd turned around and was taking me back home. Father laughed, and Mother smothered me in kisses—" She'd finish one topic only to start on a new one.

I half listened, rarely said anything, and found her company a pleasant distraction from things I had no control over as yet. I wondered if she knew her chatter quieted my worries or at least made them harder to hear.

Evening painted a fire of colors across the western sky. The sun slipped behind the dunes and let in the night. The heat slipped away with the sun, and the wind's strength grew twofold.

I shivered as I fought against the wind to get even one tent set up. The soft sand wouldn't hold the stakes, and the canvas kept blowing over. Finally, I gave up and wrapped one canvas around Katrin. The wind caught at the canvas, trying to jerk it away as I tucked the ends around her.

A corner came untucked and slapped against her face. She grabbed at it at the same time, and I caught her hand, instead. Her sun-roughened skin was warm against mine and the heat ran up my arm.

"Are you going to just stand there and become a sandman?" Katrin yelled over the wind.

I blushed hot and dropped her hand. Once I'd wrapped the second canvas about me, I settled down next to her. Both of us leaned against Flax, while Barley lay across from us. The two horses provided some barrier to the whipping wind and a little heat, but it was still cold.

Katrin pulled the canvas a little back from her face and yelled over the wind, "Yosyph, why are we traveling through the desert?"

What would I tell her? She'd accepted not knowing for so long and still followed. "I am the Yorel."

She leaned closer. "I know," she said with slight laughter in her voice.

I turned to face her and got a blast of sand to the side of my face. I pulled the canvas forward and leaned close enough that her breath brushed against my face. "At the end of the autumn harvest, the Queen will enslave all those who are not of pure Lansimetsian blood, a full third of the people."

"She can't!" Katrin cried.

"She won't," I replied. "I go to my mother's land to gather an army. I've already gathered many to fight in our own land, but we are not enough yet. However, with my mother's people, we will overthrow her tyranny."

Katrin pulled at a lock of her hair and twisted it around her finger, staring into the distance, her forehead ridged with thought. Her lips moved. I leaned in, straining to hear her voice.

"—her gone, I could return to Halavant, and—" she stopped and looked at me. "You won't hurt him?" she asked, her voice shriller than before.

How could she love someone so selfish and shallow? What would happen to him? Was he innocent of the crimes of the crown, or had he already been initiated into the dark workings of the monarchy? At the least, he'd lose his right to rule. The people would not leave that blood-tainted line over them. Katrin kept her large eyes on me, waiting for an answer.

"If he survives the war, he will come to trial like his mother and be judged by his people."

"Oh." She brought her hand to her mouth. The wind ripped the canvas away from her face again. She caught it in a white fist. "You don't know him like I do. He's innocent. I'll return when you do and plead his case."

I bit back a retort. I would not take her back to a battlefield. But I did not want that argument tonight. The wind's howling and sand's scouring was more than enough.

Katrin didn't speak again. I nestled deeper against Flax and closed my eyes.

"Please tell a story. It will help pass the time." I almost didn't hear her above the wind.

"I have none I care to tell."

"You've said that before. Surely as the Yorel, carrying secret messages, slipping through the dark like a shadow, rescuing stubborn girls, you have some story worth telling. I need something to think about other than what you told me. Don't you?"

Something to think about other than what filled my thoughts? I could allow that luxury for a moment.

"There is one my mother told me." I leaned my head near her ear so I wouldn't have to yell. Her hair tickled my face and smelled of the sunlight and sand. "There is a fire demon."

"A fire demon?"

I cast my mind back to a tale told in stolen moments on the pirate ship, Mother's voice in the soft, singing tones of a storyteller. I tried to mimic the tones. "Yes, a fire demon. She lives in the desert, feasting on lost travelers. Her hair burns with a flame hotter than the sun upon the sand at noonday. This she conceals under a turban. Her eyes are the cool green of a moss-covered rock, entrancing and singing of water and life. A traveler, seeking water, falls into her arms, and then she consumes him with the flames from her fiery hair."

Katrin shivered. "Naven told me a similar story and said I could pass for such a demon."

I thought about how she'd looked this evening as the sun set, her hair frizzy from the turban. "So you could."

Why was it always coldest before the sun rose? I woke to my breath forming white clouds, water lost with each breath. I wanted to gather it up again and store it away for the heat that was sure to come. Sand itched in every fold of my skin. I pulled the canvas closer and got sand down my back for my trouble. At least the wind had stopped.

Katrin stirred and immediately scratched.

"Blast all this sand! What I would give for a nice hot bath.

And," she added as she re-wrapped the turban about her head, "lots and lots of soap."

By mid-morning, I couldn't recall how cold I'd been at dawn. I knew I'd shivered like winter time, but it seemed like something pleasant read in a book. The dunes stretched out in ever sameness, and the sun marched across the sky.

Unlike the previous day, Katrin sat silently, her eyes staring into the distance. Perhaps the knowledge of my quest had quieted her tongue. The hours rolled on under the burning sun. And the longer the silence continued, the more I worried over what to do when we reached my mother's people, and what would happen if I didn't succeed. Each minute, another thought of failure marched until I slumped under the weight.

"Do you know why I love the desert?" Her voice sliced through the silence and brought me upright.

I glanced over and shook my head.

"Because it is so open and bright. Yes, dangerous, but I can see the dangers. Nothing is hidden. I want to be more like the desert."

"Dangerous? I think you already are."

She chuckled. "There you go with that humor. Wish you'd pull it out to air more often. I want to have someone I can trust enough to share anything with. I guess I wasn't that way with Halavant. I never told him about Father or his mother's threats."

But she'd told me those, and so much more. Yesterday, I'd heard much of her life. Did she trust me like that? Was I her new confidant and protector, like that man-servant Naven she was always talking about? Maybe I could trust her more. I coughed and ah-hemmed, and finally said, "Do you want to know about my life?"

She looked over and locked eyes with me, then nodded, her eyes crinkling to show the smile hidden behind the turban.

"I was born on a pirate ship."

"Oh! Is your father a pirate?"

"No, he was an Ura-ubiya, an honorable man of the Lansimetsa. He is dead."

She nodded and waited silently, our horses treading up yet another dune.

I turned Flax directly east. "Mother was a slave to the pirates. I was, well, I was a lot of things to them—a slave, entertainment, and sometimes an apprentice. I learned to sword fight from Big Nose. He was kinder than most, or at least he wanted me to watch his back. He had bad luck with cards and was always in debt. Even for a pirate that is dangerous. The others—I think they saw me like the captain's monkey, something to make do tricks and mock. They made me walk along the yardarm on the lowest sail, and when I didn't fall, they made me do it higher and higher until I walked along the highest sail. I learned to climb the rigging hand over hand, dance along the bowsprit, and take flying leaps from the crow's nest to the yard. My dinner depended on it, and I often got something sweet if I did well. Yes, I was like a well-trained monkey. Mother prayed each morning and evening for my safety, but there was little else she could do to protect me."

We crested the dune. "It wasn't bad. I didn't know anything different. I had plenty to occupy a little boy's imagination and energy. At night, I basked in my mother's love and in learning—writing, reading, signing, my people's history, stories."

"But it wasn't all good either, was it? Your back tells of many a whipping."

I shrugged. "The captain was a bit like your father. When in a good mood, he shared his finest delicacies, and even his wine once. Though I've never tasted wine or other alcohol since. I became ill all over his silk dressing gown, one of his favorite spoils of pirating, and got my worst beating for that. He'd cuff or whip me whenever he was angry at the wind for not blowing where he wanted or the bread getting maggots. I learned to be silent and the whipping would be less, but when I cried, he'd beat me until I passed out."

Katrin rode closer. "How did you escape?"

"When I was seven, Mother threw us overboard one night when we were in port. The captain planned to sell me as a slave. But it was winter, and the water chilled her so much she died a few days later." I rushed on, not wanting to stop on that note. "A kind man took me in as his son, and I began my life on land."

"All by seven." She whistled. "And I thought I had life hard. I'm so sorry."

We rode through several more dunes. I let the silence walk beside us, and my thoughts for once were quiet.

"How did you learn to shadow walk?"

"What do you mean, shadow walk?" I wrinkled my forehead.

"Didn't your mother tell you about shadow walking? Naven told me among his people there are a few with special talents that allow them to blend in with the shadows. Those who developed the talent—Naven said it took years of practice—can walk through an open square at noonday and be unseen. The Lansimetsians call them shadow demons."

Mother hadn't told me about shadow walking. But now other things made more sense.

"Mother taught me to shadow walk," I said, "but she didn't call it by that name. She taught me not to be noticed. By the last year with the pirates, they'd stopped asking me to do tricks, and only the captain still kept note of me."

"That's probably why he wanted to sell you as a slave," she mused. "You became difficult to discern, and thus an uncertainty he didn't want around."

If mother had taught me more, I could have walked into the palace and taken out the tyrant. I still could if I returned now, at least after we found water and replenished our supply. But I wasn't trained in shadow walking. I didn't have that level of skill yet, and I didn't have years to practice. No, we'd proceed forward. But why didn't she teach me?

Katrin didn't ask me any more questions, and I didn't feel up to talking more about myself. It was more than I'd ever told anyone. I'd learned to not talk around the pirates, and my role as Yorel had only cemented that habit. Talking so much now felt strange, with my tongue clicking against my teeth in the consonants and curling around the vowels. Yet my whole body felt lighter for what I'd told her.

Traveling due east across the dunes proved to be as hard as traveling north across the Wilderlands. The dunes stretched north and south, so we were constantly still going up and over and down. Except instead of mud to slip on, we trudged through soft sand that fell away with each step. Most the time Flax and Barley handled it well enough, but they were going through the water quicker than I anticipated. I checked our water bags when we camped. Two days in, and they already hung limply behind the saddles. Only the slumped ends contained water. According to the map, we could find the well late tomorrow or early the next day. I fervently hoped for the former.

"Please, could I have more?" Katrin asked the next morning, after drinking the half cup of water I'd handed her.

"In a few hours. We'll have to ration now. When we get to the well, you can have all you want."

She licked her cracked lips and half smiled. "Well, at least we could set up the tents last night." She started wrapping her turban and gasped, flinging the cloth away from her. A scorpion scuttled away from the fabric's folds.

"Are you stung?" I tried to keep my voice level.

"No," she stammered.

Relief flooded through me, washing the sudden tension from my body. I turned my eyes upward and signed. *Thank you for protecting her, please let us find the well tonight.* Always another request, but we were putting in the work, so I supposed it was acceptable. To live in a time when I didn't always have to be asking God for help would be glorious.

"I caught some of that." Katrin cautiously shook out her turban. "Thanks, protect, well. Was it for me or the water?"

"Both."

Neither of us talked much that day. Both of us were too parched. Each word dried our throats a little more. We marked the hours by taking a swallow of water. Four hours, four swallows. Rest through the hottest part of the day, if only so our horses wouldn't use more water. Two swallows. Six more hours, six swallows.

We crested another sand dune as the sun set behind us. Katrin's gasp overlapped mine. A land of stone spread before us: spears, columns, mounds, walls, and narrow canyons of stone to the north, south, and east, as far as I could see. The Stone Forest. Even in the muted colors of evening, the rocks ranged in shades of red, pink, and orange. The stretched shadows blurred where one rock formation stopped and another started. Some looked linked at the top. Others seemed to be stacks of cottage-sized boulders, but that couldn't be. How would they have gotten stacked in the first place?

"I thought the stories exaggerated." Katrin licked her cracked lips. "So where is that well? Can you tell me the landmarks again?"

I scanned the landscape as I recited the instructions. I'd studied the map so often over the last three days, that each word echoed in the back of my thoughts. "Stand between the giant's staff and the five balancing brothers. Dismount your horse and walk eastward, reciting the Mage's Sorrow, beginning with the first step. Turn as the tale tells you, keeping pace with your words. Keep each step the width of a horseman's turban. As you finish, you will see the King's throne surrounded by his counselors' seats. Climb upon the Minister of Horses' seat. He is saving refreshment for you."

But which ones were the giant's staff and the balancing brothers? There were too many formations and the deepening evening shadows blended together, making it impossible to pick out distinct shapes. We'd have to wait until morning. We each took one more swallow of water and gave the last to Flax and Barley. They nosed around for more. We made a thirsty camp on the edge of the stone forest, and morning stretched hours away.

11

A VILLAGE SANG WITH THE SONG OF THE CONTENT AND GRATEFUL

YOSYPH

"Ready?" Katrin croaked the question as the sky lightened enough for us to see.

We'd packed the tents an hour before and sucked on dried fruit to help alleviate our thirst. But I dared not start until we could see enough to know we were in the right starting point. We stood between a spear of maroon stone stretching hundreds of feet into the air and a haphazard stack of five wagon-sized boulders balancing like a child's abandoned toys. In every direction towered red stones in arches, pillars, piles, walls, and crevices—a maze to be navigated by a story.

"Oi," Katrin whispered. "This is a maze. Your mother really didn't want someone else to find her people. You can do it though?"

I nodded. I had to. Not only our lives hung in the balance. We had to get an army and return to Lansimetsa.

I measured the width of my turban, about the length of a large step, then tied a piece of twine around my ankles that was exactly the length when stretched out fully. The clothing hawker in Gankin had assured me my turban was a horseman's turban. Hopefully, the dimensions did not change between my mother's time and now. And, hopefully, I didn't trip. But this would keep my tread to the right length better than if I tried to judge the step in my thirst-clouded mind.

It was time to recite the Mage's Sorrow. Now I understood why Mother had told it every night, never changing a word. She told many other stories, but always this one first and always I repeated it back to her until I could tell it without missing a word. It was a strange story and the key to finding our way through this land. The four borders of the map told the story again, each word cramped beside the next. *Mage's Sorrow* marked a blank part of the map, land we'd traverse today, with no more symbols to guide us than those words. "Ready."

Katrin grasped my hand. She looked up at me with more trust than I deserved. No stumbling on the words. I had to get this correct. I took a step to the east, speaking the lyrical tongue of the desert in a dry rasp. "*Long ago, right,*" I turned right, "*at the beginning of the world.*" We now faced the balancing brothers and headed straight for them. Orange boulders littered the ground. Many rocks were my height, but none stood in our path directly ahead.

"A village sang with the song of the content and grateful. Everyone believed God had blessed them to have rich soil, healthy animals, happy families, and they spent their lives blessing those around them until not one poor man was left."

I turned left and found a crack in a boulder, wide enough for our horses to pass through. It blended in with the dark bands of stone striping the boulder for ten feet on either side. The crack opened immediately into another field of boulders, crevices, spires, and arches. Ten paths opened before us. But only one stood directly in front of us.

"The village never grew to be a city." I stepped to the full length of the twine, one step for each word. *"They lived far from others, a forested oasis in the middle of a desert. None ever passed through from the other lands, and none of the villagers left."* Turn. *"And so like a place caught in time, with only the people changing from generation to generation, they lived with rightness."* I paused. Should I turn on that one? I'd thought over it every night since we entered the desert. Before me, the path still continued clear. To the right, it dropped three feet and continued straight.

A squeeze to my hand brought my thoughts back to Katrin by my side. She looked up and smiled. Her lips cracked, and a trickle of blood ran down to her chin.

I dabbed the blood with the corner of my turban, then turned right, leaping down. I stumbled as I landed and the twine around my ankles snapped.

"Queen's wrath!" I cursed.

Katrin's dry chuckle turned to a cough, "I've not heard that curse before." She stood where I'd jumped and held out another length of twine, one of ten extra I'd cut. She had the presence of mind to mark my last step. At least she was keeping her head.

I bent over to tie it about my ankles and fell to my knees. My head felt like it floated above my neck. I took several deep breaths. The cotton cleared from my mind, but my throat burned even more. It took several tries before I could get my trembling hands to tie the delicate knots. I stood, leaning my hand against a rose-colored column.

"Rightness." Katrin reminded me of the last word I'd said. She pronounced it with the lisp of a Lansimetsian, and it brought me back to the urgent need to go forward before I couldn't keep the story straight. I placed the heel of one foot against the base of the drop off and recited the story again.

"It seemed all were content," I chanted. I heard Katrin grunt as she jumped down, and then the anxious neighs of Flax and Barley as they followed. I wanted to go back and help her, but to lose my place might kill both of us. So I stepped forward again.

"But one young man, filled with curiosity to know life beyond what has always been, journeyed into the desert. The village gathered to watch him go, some calling out their last warnings that it was wrong for him to leave, and he would go to his death. But his mother defended his name, saying what has never been done before can still be right." I turned under an archway which stood as wide as I could reach but rose thirty feet in the air.

"Days rolled into years, and the old mother hoped someday her only son would return. The others in the village tried to comfort her, including her in their work and their celebrations, but it left her empty. Finally, in her last days, she pleaded with God, if it was right in his wisdom, to send her son home."

I turned into a narrow channel of pink rock and then out again into a lane of marbled black columns. I stumbled again. Katrin caught at my hand, and my fingers slipped through hers. I looked back. She stood where I'd last stepped, swaying as she held onto Barley's reins. She had circles under her eyes, dark beneath the sunburn. Her wan smile did little to reassure me she wouldn't pass out on the next step. We needed to get to water soon. Yet the story stretched on.

"As she lay on her bed, weakly breathing her last, a shadow fell across her. 'Mother', a man said, 'I've returned as the dreams have bidden me.' The mother turned and saw her son was now grown into a powerful man and wrapped in a robe glittering with silver stitchings of stars. 'It is good you have not left me alone as I pass into the next world.'" I turned left but a black column stood in front of me. A step to the right or left allowed me to pass.

I chose the left. If I was wrong, we could die of thirst. One part of my mind detachedly wondered what would it be like? I couldn't imagine being any more thirsty than I was now. Stories told of people who lived days without water. Would we wander this maze in search of water for days? Would we grow so tired we'd sleep away our last breaths?

"'But you need not die.' Her son pulled vials from his robes. 'I've learned powerful magic. Ones to heal the sick, ones to make a man stronger, even ones to stop aging.' The mother reached up and touched her son's face, smiled, and let out a slow breath. Her hand fell limp. 'No!' cried the son, putting his hand to her neck and feeling for the pulsing of blood, but life had left her." I turned a step before a black monolith.

'No,' he cried, wringing his hands, 'I cannot bring you back from the dead! Why didn't you live longer? I could have saved you!'

"He turned and noticed the village woman sitting in the corner. 'You!' He roared. 'You, and all the villagers, talk so much about doing what is right, yet you left my mother to fend for herself and now she is dead. Your hearts are as hard as stone.'"

I turned into a narrow slot canyon, crunching over crystals, the sky a narrow band of blue above us. At least I didn't have to worry if I was on the right path: only one was available. I placed my hand against the stone walls, keeping my balance as I stretched each step out to the full length of the twine. My legs trembled with the long strides.

"The son stepped out the door, looked upon the orchards and the river, and at the village women who were gathering outside his mother's home. He felt his heart break with grief, and anger boiled up from the pieces.

"'You could have saved my mother. It would have been little enough for you when you have so much.' He raised his right hand. 'So now you shall be left in a land as hard as your hearts.' He raised his left hand and clapped both hands together."

I zig-zagged around two columns and beneath an archway. My head grew light again, and I grasped at the words to the rest of the story as it slipped from my mind like sand. The land darkened and narrowed in around me and then turned sideways.

"Yosyph!" Katrin's sharp cry broke through a fog. Hot sand pressed against one cheek and a warm hand against the other cheek.

"Yosyph?"

I pulled my gritty eyes open. She knelt beside me, her face tight with worry and cheeks shrunken with lack of water. Yet I was the one who passed out.

How could you? I accused my body.

"The last word," I rasped, pulling myself to kneeling.

She let out a long breath and helped pull me to my feet, her arms trembling in harmony with mine. "It was something about clapping hands together." Her voice came a grating whisper. She pointed to her necklace, sparkling in a sunny indent of the sand. "There is where you stood last."

I wobbled over to the necklace and placed it in her hand.

She clasped my hand and nodded, still showing trust even though my body had betrayed us. I had to try. She'd not die out here because I was too woolen-headed to go forward. I rehearsed the story in my head until I came back to where I'd been, the words coming like a song and piercing the fog of thirst. I stumbled forward, pulling my stride to full length again, trembling between each step.

"The village stream silenced. The women gasped as they saw it now filled with crystal. He pointed to the right, and the trees in the orchards grew to an immense height and then hardened into marble and glass. The men who had been working in the orchards ran into

the village, shouting warnings to their families. But it was too late. The man pulled his robes about him and disappeared. Years turned to generations. Empty huts and gardens left barren. The trees shimmered in glass and marble, a mage's sorrow, the starvation of a people."

We passed beneath an archway and into an area almost completely ringed by stones. Finally, two words from the end, I ran into a white marble wall. Gold zig-zagged like lightning across its face.

Katrin coughed beside me. "The king's throne?"

If it wasn't, I'd retrace my steps to where the story said 'rightness' and walk the story from there. If I could retrace them. My body shook as I stood.

"It has to be the king's throne." I tried to keep the worry out of my voice. I stepped back and looked around. Like everywhere else, pillars and boulders spotted the ground, most of them taller than us. I cut the twine between my legs and mounted Flax. He sighed a whispering neigh, his head hanging almost to the ground. From his back, I could see the marble wall reached upward into a chair shape. But which stone represented the minister of the horse? None of the stone looked like a horse. Or a man. *Which one?* My fingers signed.

Katrin pulled herself onto Barley and swayed on his saddle. She put her hand to shade her eyes in the morning light and looked about, turning in the saddle. She slipped as she turned sideways, but caught herself before I could reach out for her.

"That one!" Her voice cracked with excitement. She pointed to a knobby, loaf-shaped rock of gray stone. Nothing about it made it stand out from the others. "Can't you see? Its shadow."

I looked to the shadow cast to the side of the rock. A blocky splotch of dark on the pale ground, and one bright sun spot shaped like a rearing stallion. Could it be we'd only see this at this time of day and year? Or were there other horse-shaped holes in the rock that showed with the passing of the sun?

"It's it, isn't it?" Katrin stared at the bright horse shape. I shook my head to bring my thoughts back from their dazed wandering. The lack of water scattered my thoughts like grain for the chickens. After sliding off Flax, I cast my robes aside to stand in loose, flowing leggings—I wouldn't attempt to climb in those accident-producing robes—and slung a water sack over my shoulders. I struggled up the rock. Its sides were smooth, but with enough pockets to make it almost like climbing a ladder, which was good because I could barely step from pocket to pocket. My arms ached as I reached for each spot.

Twenty feet up, I reached a flat top about thirty feet across. My thoughts rambled as I lay panting on the top. Holes in various shapes of horses pitted the top and flowed out in all directions to the walls of the rock. No matter which way the sun shone, one of them would have appeared in the shadow outside. Right in the center of all this sat a perfectly circular hole. I crawled over to it. A coolness brushed my face as I leaned over it. Rounded ridges, almost like a ladder, ringed the walls of the hole. I slipped down, my feet barely slowing me from a free fall as my toes caught and slipped off each ridge. I grasped at the indents with weak fingers and then let them slide to the next. The air rushed past me in cool promise, then I jarred against a sandy ground. I crumpled to my knees and huddled, gasping.

My eyes adjusted to the dimness. I found myself in a small room, lit by the sun bouncing off the white walls of the hole above me. Three pools of water nested against each other like the three petals of a moon blossom. One pool's sides rose about a foot above the floor. It bubbled up and overflowed its sides into the other two. These two sat level with the floor and must have had small holes in the bottom, for they did not overflow. So much water, clean and fresh, rising and draining, cut off from the desert outside. I crawled over and plunged my face into the closest pool and gulped down water. It washed down my throat like a salve. I plunged my face in again and again.

"Yosyph?"

Katrin's head silhouetted in the sky at the top of the shaft.

"We have water!" I shouted up, my voice bouncing off the walls.

"Thank Providence," she murmured and descended the walls. She'd pulled the robes up and around her legs and tied them about her waist, giving her billowy leggings down to her knees. Her slender legs were covered in fine red hair. *Women had hairy legs, too?* The ridiculous question echoed through my muddled mind. I shook my head as she jumped down the last few feet and ran over to one of the pools, plunging her face into the water. She came up gasping and grinning, water pouring from her face and hair.

I leaned over to get another drink, and cold water splashed over my head, followed by a giggle. I looked up and got a face full of water. I sputtered and saw Katrin's grinning face through streams of muddy water.

"You need a bath." She splashed me again.

I put up my hands, but too late, and got another faceful of water. I slapped the water sideways with one hand and sent a spray that showered Katrin from head to toe.

She laughed, the tinkling tones dancing off the walls.

"How do you still have the energy to laugh?" I shook from the effort of that one sideways slap of water. I lay down and drank some more.

Katrin tilted her head, her eyebrows scrunched with thought. "I think it is because you always gave me as much water to drink as you took for yourself. But I'm only half your size and the water lasted me longer. But never again. You will drink twice as much as me, starting now." She pushed her hands into the water again to splash me.

An insistent neigh stopped us both.

"Flax and Barley!" Katrin brought her hands to her mouth. "We forgot them!"

My chest tightened. I had to get them water. I climbed down the outside of the Minister of the Horse with a half-full water sack over my shoulders. Flax and Barley neighed as I poured water into a stone trough at the base of the rock. Minutes later, they'd emptied the trough and nosed around for more. It took an hour to satisfy everyone's thirst, filling the stone trough and all the water sacks. It was a delightful hour, clambering into the coolness and back out into the sun, splashing in the water, and drying out in the open air.

"Now for that bath!" Katrin said. "Make sure Barley doesn't peek." She held her chin up with the air of a regal lady.

"He can't even climb the rock."

Katrin put a hand over her mouth. A snorting laugh slipped through. She grabbed the extra desert robe and a bar of soap, both purchased on her insistence when we gathered supplies in Gankin, and scurried easily up the wall. I could see how she'd made it up the wall of the cave on the night of the wolves. I passed the next hour getting our horses grain; setting out a meal of dried dates, jerky, and flatbread; and currying the horses. How long could a bath take?

Finally, Katrin appeared over the edge of the rock, her wet hair braided loosely and hanging to her knees, her face scrubbed until it shone. Over the last three days, her face had reddened around the eyes where the turban hadn't covered, and now it had a slight brown tint and the freckles had multiplied until they covered half her face. It made her green eyes stand out even more than before.

"Your turn, my muddy man." She tossed the wet soap at me.

It slipped through my fingers and fell to the sand. I picked up the gritty bar of soap along with my own change of robes. I was glad she insisted on that purchase, too. The pleasure of a bath and clean clothes was only second to the taste of the crisp, life-giving water. I sank into one of the lower pools and soaked there until the water ran clean and my skin prickled with cold.

I emerged to the early afternoon sun. Katrin lay on the top of the rock with her hair fanned out about her like the rays of the sun, her face covered with part of her turban. She whistled softly in her sleep. Flax and Barley stood patiently at the base of the rock. The sun pleasantly heated my wet skin, and I gave into the urge to lie down and sleep, too. Just for an hour.

The chill wind of evening woke me. I sat up, my muscles stiff from lying on the rock.

"Good, you're awake. I wondered if you'd sleep through the day and night." Katrin sat to the side of me with a couple of plates of food, one half empty and the other untouched.

I leaped to my feet. "Why didn't you wake me?"

She sniffed and raised her chin. "If you snap at me, I'll go keep the horses company." Her hair glowed in the setting sun. She looked beautiful, regal, every bit as intimidating as a fire demon. And I wanted to fall into her arms, just like the travelers of the stories. Instead, I drew back a step, angry at my weakness in the desert and my weakness for her.

"Yosyph, why do you stare?" She dropped her chin and laughed a little, "I've not grown a third eye or a second nose, have I? I didn't mean it. You were so tired, and you've not slept much since I first met you."

I slowly inhaled through my nose to clear my anger. "I'm

sorry. It's just I'd hoped we could have traveled half a day more today. I spoke thoughtlessly."

"It's nice to not be the only one apologizing." She half-smiled. "We'll get a good start tomorrow. Flax and Barley needed the rest as much as we did, so it is no time lost."

"Yes... but we may not always be as lucky as we were today. The way to my mother's people was not meant to be found by the outsider." The sun dipped into the horizon, and wind poured in howling agreement.

12

CURSES! CURSES ON THE FATES THAT THUS TORTURE ME!

HALAVANT

I learned something over four days of travel: Galliard was wrongly named. He wasn't Galliard the Wanderer but Galliard the Obstinate. I'd never had to endure a more mulish man, and there were plenty of them that sat in council with my mother. When I became king, I'd place him as the lead donkey in our luggage train, and he could put his talents to use.

I panted as I ran up the dusty road, reaching his shadow long before I caught him. The sun slipped behind trees, and color drained from the land until it was gray.

Galliard turned his head as I came level with him and smiled that disarming and completely disingenuous smile. "Any luck this time?" he asked.

As if he cared. I'd stopped at every ramshackle dwelling we

passed to seek news of Katrin. But did he ever stop and wait for me? Not even once.

"You are a—a—rude man," I muttered. If only I could remember curses, I could say something biting. But ever since that blow to my head, words escaped me when I needed them most. It seemed to get worse each day, words slipping away when I wanted to speak, though I could think them plenty well enough. Maybe it was the travel—sleeping in the dry ditches, eating stale bread, and drinking water from a village fountain while the women washed their clothes at my elbow. I'm sure I got soap in the last mouthful.

"Then why do you keep my company?" he replied after several steps.

Why, indeed! As if I had any other choice. He shared his food with me and let me travel with him. It was more than I could expect from any of these other peasants. If they knew I was the prince, they'd help me right back to the palace for a reward, and Mother would lock me up for running off. But because they didn't know I was the prince, there was no reason they'd help me at all. I had to find Katrin, and if I returned to the palace, no one would look for her. I rubbed the side of my head where a deep ache persisted.

"I think I shall stop for the day," Galliard said into the air. He turned from the road and sat under an elm.

I followed, my gut tight with worry. Four days of asking, and no one had seen any girl with red hair. No one had heard of her. Four days—no eleven. She'd disappeared eleven days ago. This was the only major road from the inn where she'd been seen. Someone should have seen her.

Galliard opened his pack and pulled out half a loaf of bread. Even if my gut wasn't strung taut, I couldn't stomach another mouth full of that stale mass. Then he pulled out an apple. Wait!

An apple? They weren't even in season yet. We never had apples at the palace until early fall.

"What would his highness think of poor man's cake?" he asked in a mild tone.

I looked closer. The green apple was as wrinkled as Councilor Korhonen, who must be as old as the kingdom. Galliard quartered the apple and a tart scent lilted into the air. He set two of the pieces on a cloth on the ground next to him and put two in his lap. He bit into a piece, closed his eyes and made smacking sounds with his lips. My mouth watered against my will. No way would I eat something that old. It must have been from the last harvest. Old and moldy.

He relished his second piece and reached for one of the pieces set to the side. Without thinking, I shoved it into my mouth. The flavor hit me first, sharply tart with undertones of mellow sweetness. It mushed pleasantly between my teeth. I licked at the juice that ran down the side of my lip.

"I take it, it pleases you." He laughed and pulled out another apple, just as wrinkly as the first. I didn't know how something that old could taste that good, but I did not refuse it again.

He stood and broke off a few narrow branches from the elm. "Now, if it also pleases you, it would do your arm good to get exercise so the muscles don't seize up." He tossed one stick to me.

I caught it with my right hand, my arm slipping from the sling and crying out in protest. He was right. I needed to get my arm fit again so I could best Katrin's kidnappers, even if it was the Yorel himself.

I stretched out my arm, rolling my shoulder and rotating my wrist. The stick felt good in my hand. A sword would feel better. My forearm ached, but that I could ignore as much as I ignored the aching in my head. I bounced on my toes and began a basic training routine: step forward, overhand stroke, step back, underhand. Tension melted from my body as I fell into the rhythm of the steps. Swish, swish, THWAK! Galliard's stick crossed with mine, and my forearm zinged as my wrist only partly absorbed the impact. A satisfying thwack. I struck his stick twice in quick succession, and the second one snapped his stick in half.

Galliard stood opposite me, holding the broken wood in his hand, his eyes wide under high eyebrows.

I smiled, and his eyebrows rose higher. *Yes, I know how to fence. I'm the prince, after all,* I thought. All that came out was, "I'm the prince."

"I'm beginning to wonder." He shook his head. "You have grace in sword skill. Shall we continue with stouter wood?"

We sparred with stouter branches. I savored the deliciousness of dancing about the road, attacking, driving the Wanderer back. Feeling him put more force behind his swings and meeting them. Evading his guard and striking him upon his shoulder. Hearing him grunt. Then feeling his branch slide up mine and snap against my fingers, but not losing my grip.

He swapped to his left hand, and then I had to work. I'd never fought someone left-handed, and the guard and attack were all backward. He rallied forward with a rain of blows, but he softened each before it struck me.

I adjusted my stance, turning sideways to keep my branch between me and him. It worked to give me back some of my advantage. We sparred until the sky peppered with stars and an almost full moon lit the road. Galliard finally held up his hand to stop.

My whole body glowed with sweat and the cool evening breeze caressed my stinging hand. My arm ached with sore muscles instead of injured ones, as if the fight had loosened the knots in it. If only my head would stop its infernal pounding.

"If I'd known how you could fence, I'd have kept to the

lighter wood." Galliard rubbed his side where I'd struck him. "But perhaps it is worth it to not have you glowering like a thundercloud. We'll seek shelter tonight and get warm food after such exercise."

I nodded, not feeling like struggling to get the right words out. A bed and warm food would fix my struggle speaking.

Galliard cast his stick aside and strode down the road. I gulped water and trotted after him. This time, he didn't seem to tread as fast. Perhaps he was going easier on me, or perhaps he was tired after our crossing of swords. An owl hooted as we passed down the moonlit lane. Then we saw a light peek out the shutters of a squat, thatched hut. I ran ahead, ready to ask the question I'd asked every place before.

I knocked, and a little girl answered. Her short, curly hair glowed about her head by the firelight, and her face stood in the shadow.

"Henrietta!" cried a woman's voice. "Shut the door!"

"But there's a funny, dirty man." She turned her head to answer. The firelight brought out her pinched features in sharp relief. She wasn't the first scrawny child to answer a door. What did these peasants feed their children? Ashes and wood chips?

The woman yanked the child from the door and faced me. She looked me up and down, her lips thin. "We don't have food for beggars." She started to close the door.

I stopped the door with my hand. "Have—" I tried to ask about Katrin, but my lips wouldn't form the words. "Have—" I halted again. Why could I not speak? I stomped the ground and hit a fist against the door frame. The pounding in my head intensified.

"Get gone, witless." The woman pushed the door against my hand, her eyes darting about like a cornered hare.

"Pardon me." Galliard's mellow voice caused me to jump. He stood beside me with a smile that said, I'm open and innocent, you can trust me. It proved effective on the woman. She stopped trembling and smiled shyly back at him. Women were supposed to do that to me, not some scruffy man missing a finger and a home.

"I'm sorry to intrude on your evening," he said. "But have you seen a young woman with long, curly red hair? My young friend has lost her, and the grief of it has tied his tongue."

Young friend? He's helping me? I felt a tightness in my eyes, and I sniffed fast to catch tears before they humiliated me.

The woman turned sorry eyes on me. I clenched my fists. I didn't want her pity; I wanted to know if she'd seen Katrin.

She spoke, her words softer. "We've had our fill of vagabonds and I never know who I can trust these days. I've not seen anyone of that description. Not in my lifetime. Red hair, now that would be something to see."

Galliard nodded his thanks, and putting a hand on my shoulder, he turned back to the road. I walked beside him, the weight of his hand a solid realness. I tried to speak, "G—" Again! "G—" Again! I had to force myself to speak. Nothing, not even one sound. I wanted to yell curses at the god that would allow my life to fall apart. All that came out was a strangled sound in my throat.

Galliard squeezed my shoulder. "We will be at my friend's house by tomorrow. His wife is a mighty good healer. We'll find help there."

I broke away from Galliard and raced forward. We had to get to this healer woman quickly if she could heal my tongue. I stopped and turned around. I had to get back to the palace physicians. They would know what to do, but it was at least five days back. I turned again and sat down on the ground. Sobs broke through my lips where words would not. How would I find Katrin if I couldn't speak? How could I rule my country? If I couldn't speak, my life was over.

I felt the weight of Galliard's hand on my shoulder again. "This healer woman is a marvel." He pulled me to my feet. "If I were mortally wounded and had the choice between her and the finest surgeon in the land, I'd choose her."

I wiped my hand under my nose and onto my tunic, then jogged forward. If she could help me, I'd not sleep until we found her. Galliard started to say something, probably about stopping someplace to rest, but he shook his head and took up pace beside me. The hours turned as Galliard shared tall tales of men who'd survived amputated limbs or walked after crippling falls. Even as far-fetched as they were, they gave me something to wish for. The deep pain in the side of my head kept rhythm to my step.

"Aiden, I'm worried about him," Galliard said in the darkness. He sat at the table with the farmer, a single candle casting strange shadows on their faces.

We'd traveled on through the night. Galliard did not stop, even though I could hear him panting to keep pace with my forced march. The farmer had answered the door in the wee hours of the morning, his huge frame filling the opening. He held a club in one hand and a candle in the other. He must have recognized Galliard, because he nodded and let us in, without asking a question.

While I lay on a blanket by the fire, they sat discussing me in quiet tones. I strained to hear their words over the crackling of the fire. It felt good knowing Galliard worried about me. But what would he do about it? Where was that healer woman?

"He's not been able to speak since evening. I didn't realize it at first, but he's been speaking less and less with each day."

Galliard explained about finding me beaten, caring for me, and our trek westward.

"How many days ago did you find him?" Aiden asked.

"Ten."

Aiden shook his head and whistled through his teeth. "It is probably too late. He has warrior's blindness. I saw it all too often during the war. A man got cracked on the head with a mace or a two-handed sword, and if he didn't die then, sometimes the man went blind, other times deaf. Once like this boy, a man became mute. Bruising on the brain. But if we can bring the pressure down, he may regain his speech."

The man rose, his head brushing against the dried herbs hanging from the beams. He strode into another room and minutes later returned with a woman. She carried a lantern that bathed the room in a warm light. She stood only to the chest of her husband, a slight woman with black hair in a loose braid over one shoulder.

I leaped to my feet. That must be the healer woman. *Please,* I wanted to say, *please cure my tongue. Whatever you need to do, do it.* I held my hands together in the universal pleading gesture, a motion I'd never done in my whole life.

She placed a hand on my arm, her eyes darting over me like I was a puzzle to figure out. "Does your head pain you?" She pulled me down to a kneeling position.

I scowled. Of course it pained me. It hadn't stopped hurting since the beating.

"Where?" she asked, as if she'd heard my answer. I motioned to the side of my head, not touching it. She fingered the spot. Her firm, probing touch sent lightning pain through my skull into my spine. I'd lived with it for ten days now, yet her touch stole my breath. I jerked away.

"Aiden," she said, "I need boiling water, Monk's Sleep, Yarrow, White Elm, Devils Claw, and my drill." I jumped at the last word. What would she do with the drill? But she held my arm. "Lie down," she ordered, motioning to the long table in the middle of the room.

I looked into her eyes. They were stern, but not unkind. Still, I wouldn't let her do anything until she told me what she would do. I shook my head.

Aiden knelt down by me. "Son, if we don't take down the pressure in your head, you may lose more than your speech. My wife served as a healer in the war. She's done this several times and never lost a man who wasn't dying already. And that you are not."

I shook my head again. They had to tell me what she would do.

Galliard laughed as he lit several more lamps, causing me to squint in the brightness. "Boy, are you afraid of a little healer woman? You've faced a mob of men and survived. I'll make sure you come out of this even better than that. Besides, if you don't let us help, how do you intend on finding your Katrin?"

Fine. I glared at the woman, trying to hide the fear that trembled through my body. *You do whatever you need to do.* I lay down upon the table and let her shave my head where the pounding was worst. I bit my lip to silence a moan, both at the pressure of the razor against my skin and at the locks falling past my face. She then bathed my head with sweet-smelling waters and wine.

She held a warm tea to my mouth. "Drink all of it." I half sat to drink, puckering around the bitterness. "Now lie down." Her voice sounded fuzzy in my ears. I lay down and drifted into a warm drowsiness. Later, I didn't know how long, she said, "Hold him fast. He must not move." Why would I move when everything was so deliciously warm and comfortable? Then came the pain: searing, piercing pain.

13

FOLLOW THE STREAM OF CRYSTAL

YOSYPH

Follow the stream of crystal until you reach the mother nursing her child. Pay respect at her feet and she will quench your thirst.

The rising sun warmed my back as I sat on top of the *Minister of Horse* rock. Katrin had disappeared down to the spring for another bath before we set off again. Though the map showed where to find water each day, there was no telling if it was a muddy flat, a small bubbling basin, or the delightful pools within the *Minister of Horse*. Still with fresh water, a bath, and a full night's sleep, I felt ready to meet any challenge. Surely yesterday was the worst, the gateway before an easier journey.

I studied the map. The instructions were different from yesterday. No setting pace by a story. Today's instruction: Follow the stream of crystal until you reach the mother nursing her child. Pay respect at her feet and she will quench your thirst.

I read further and paused on the instructions for two days from now. Fear no padded-foot hunter if you bring the Whistle of Gamaclies. Another part of the mystery. Who was this padded-foot hunter and what good would this whistle do? I pulled out a wooden whistle: a straight tube with a bulb at the end and a split-wedged mouth. "A child's toy," the Gankin vendor had said. "A common caravan trinket, lovely in lines, but with no musical ability." I blew into it. A single purring note poured out.

"A pleasant song to start the day?" Katrin climbed out of the cave, carrying a partly filled water sack over her shoulders.

I'd told her to wait, and I'd do it. I shook my head and smiled, she would do what she wanted. I looked at her again, and my heart continued at its normal pace. Good. I'd bridled my errant emotions. I would only think of her as a sister, to laugh with, counsel together, and brave dangers side by side. Yes, a sister. Yesterday, I was exhausted, that is why I'd felt that way.

"Are you done studying me?" Katrin came to sit next to me. "I have to wonder what pictures you paint in your mind, with your deep gaze and wrinkled forehead. Is that a strange question? Sometimes I paint in my thoughts. If I were an artist, I'd shroud your earthy skin in tones of misty gray and make only your eyes vivid—intense green, as alive as an oak tree in spring."

Heat rose in my face. Why did she do that?

"Oh," she continued laughing, "and I'd add dashes of pink under those eyes."

The heat spread to my ears. I ducked my head. I could take her teasing. She was like a sister. Sisters were supposed to tease. And brothers back. But what if I didn't know how to? Jack and Anna did it with such ease, but they were husband and wife. Enough!

"We better get going," I said gruffly, rolling up the map and taking the water sack from her shoulders. She might as well paint me all pink for the many times she'd pulled the blood to my cheeks.

"Can I see the map?" Katrin held out her hand.

I grunted and handed it to her. While she looked it over, I studied the land, turning in a slow circle. The *King's Throne* stood off to the East, a dark silhouette against the rising sun. Many other boulders sat in a ragged circle about it. Beyond that, the maze of rocks continued in all directions, more columns and arches glowed red in the morning sun. Glints of green, blue, purple and bright white sparkled from many surfaces. To my left, veins of gold and silver marbled a spear of rock towering above the *King's Throne.* On my right, a thin stream of crystal snaked off to the east. I must have been too tired to see it yesterday. If a miner found this place, he could harvest enough precious stones and metals to make him richer than the Queen.

I grimaced at the thought of her and the mines. If I didn't succeed, a good third of the people would be bound as slaves and sent to spend their remaining years chipping away at a place like this. Like this? No, this had to be the mine General Jonstone spoke of! Someone had ventured beyond the bland rocks guarding the perimeter of the forest, discovered the rich interior, and made their way back out. No wonder Mother kept the path so carefully disguised. Mother's people would surely send an army to stop the Queen from ravaging their land. A weight lifted off my shoulders. They would help. We would stop the Queen and overthrow her corrupt rule. All would be well.

"You seem happy." Katrin tapped me on the shoulder with the rolled map. "What changed your mood?"

"I will gather an army and stop the Queen."

"Well, of course." She grinned as she bound up her robes for the climb off the rock. "You are the Yorel, the mighty Shadow

Walker, and liberator of the people. And I am the feared fire demon of the desert. How could we not?"

I chuckled. "We'd better get going. An army waits for us." I pointed to the line sparkling in the sun and snaking off into the East. It started outside the King's Circle. Today would be easy. Follow the crystal stream.

Flax and Barley seemed recovered from the last few days and stepped forward with high steps, their hooves clopping on the stone as if our laughter gave them energy. The crystal stream turned out to be a crack in the stone ground, about five feet wide. Jagged clear stones filled it, each about the size of the tip of my thumb. I pushed my hand through the crystals, trying to find the bottom, and finally, when I lay with my face against the clear stones, my fingers brushed hard rock.

Katrin placed a crystal on a hard surface, then brought down another stone on top of it. The crystal shattered in every direction. "Not diamonds." She brushed the shining shards from her legs. "I didn't expect it to be. Still, even if it were diamonds, I'd rather have water."

I nodded. No stone, however precious, could compare to the spring in the rock behind us, or the green of Lansimetsa. For all its riches, this land was a barren wasteland.

Flax neighed impatiently as if to say, "Are we going?" and we headed into the day. After a few minutes, I realized that traveling along this path would not be without its trial. The sun reflected off the crystals like off a shattered mirror. My eyes ached from the light, and I wrapped my turban over my eye on the side of the blinding path.

"Clever." Katrin re-wrapped her turban as we rode. "Yosyph," Her voice sounded soft over the sharp clop of hooves on stone. "How did you become the Yorel?"

"He's been around long before me."

"I know. He's part of the tales in Mother's old fairy tale book, and that surely is much older than you." She glanced sidelong as if trying to determine my age.

"I'm almost nineteen," I blurted.

She giggled and looked away. "But how did *you* become the Yorel?"

"It's a long story."

"And we have all day following a blindingly clear path."

I took a deep breath, rolled my tongue about my mouth, flexed my jaw, and took another breath.

"Let me get you started." She grinned. "How old were you? What made you take on that role? Who got hurt? When—"

"Ten," I broke in. "I'd stolen into the royal forest. No one ever saw me, so I'd gotten foolhardy and convinced my friend Jack to come with me. I had to show him the prince's oak with the tiny castle. I think the pirates made me stupid regarding danger. I'd already done so many things that no child with any sense would do."

"But it was a good thing, wasn't it?"

"Not then." I loosened my tight fingers on Flax's reins. "I didn't realize Jack would be noticed. We never made it to the oak. Royal soldiers saw us. We sprinted away from them, but a sixteen-year-old and a ten-year-old didn't have a chance against men on horseback. I fell behind. Jack ran back and dragged me forward. Then a boot in Jack's back sent us sprawling. Soon we were both hanging from a branch by a rope about our wrists. The soldiers looked at us like sport to enjoy. 'You know,' one said, 'it costs a broken leg to trespass in the Queen's Forest'. He grabbed my leg with his two meaty hands and began to twist. I'd endured the captain's whipping without a sound, but as my knee began to wrench, I screamed."

Katrin put one hand to her mouth.

"Then a small voice stopped everything. It was the prince, riding on a barrel-chested pony. He was still little then. 'What are you doing to those boys? Let them go!' he said, his voice high and annoyed. He tilted his chin back and looked down his nose at them. If I hadn't been afraid of a broken leg, I would have laughed at his utter contempt."

A small sigh stopped me in my story. I'd forgotten for a moment she still had feelings for the prince.

"I'm sorry. Would you like me to stop?"

"No, I'm happy to hear about the heroics of my—the prince." She smoothed the frown out of her eyebrows and waved a hand for me to continue. The crystal stream slipped between two massive monoliths. The clopping of hoof on stone changed to crunching as Flax and Barley waded into the crystals and back out ten feet further.

"The soldiers let us go. The prince walked us to the forest's edge and warned us to never return. He didn't hide his contempt for us, either, but I could feel nothing but gratitude for him." I didn't add that over the next eight years, I came to see him as an empty-headed, selfish brat.

"So you became the Yorel because of what the soldiers did to you in the forest?"

"It was the start. After that, I became the mute servant to General Jonstone when he visited my Father's ale house. That is when I became the Yorel."

"I'm sure you pulled off the mute part easily. What things did old silver-tongued Jonstone say? Is he as bad as the gossips rumor?"

"If his deeds are only half as bad as he boasted of himself, then he is worse than rumored. He's the reason the assassins came after you."

"Oh."

That thought silenced both of us for a good passage of time. The crystal stream ran through the most open area we'd encountered. It was as if we'd exited the stone forest and entered a stone meadow. The ground bloomed with short-branched stones in all colors of the rainbow, almost like the coral that the pirates sometimes collected. Arches and spears of rocks stood in the distance behind and to either side of us, but ahead, the way stayed clear. We weaved between them and kept roughly to the direction of the crystal stream.

"What do you do as the Yorel? That is, when you are not rescuing unwilling maidens and gathering a desert army?"

I chuckled. "I rescue more willing people in need and gather an army of Lansimetsians. It isn't all that exciting. Lots of sneaking and little fighting. Gathering the army without the Queen finding out is a snakes' nest of troubles, but one that battle will resolve before the year's end."

Katrin gasped "The desert script—on the papers—that farmer! Is that how you spread the word without others knowing?"

I nodded.

We reached the end of the meadow and all thoughts fled of the impending war.

The ground ended in a cliff falling several hundred feet. A stone bridge connected to a pillar that stood like an island about fifty feet out. Alternatively, a wide path wove down the cliff face to more stone forest at the base.

A wide path down the cliff face or a narrow bridge to a solitary island? It should have been an easy decision, except that the stream of crystals led down the middle of the bridge and to the island.

Although I had learned to walk the tops of sails and leap from crow's nest to swinging rope when I was a child, the years between then and now had burned away my foolhardiness. I turned toward the wide path hugging the cliff side. We could find the crystal stream again at the base of the cliff.

"Yosyph!" Katrin said, disapproval sharp in her voice. "We follow the stream."

I shrugged sheepishly and dismounted. The bridge stood narrower than I could reach with my arms, with the crystal stream running down the center. "I'm going first, and then you can come afterward." I stepped into the stream and sank to my knees in the crystals. I looked back to make sure Katrin wasn't following. She'd dismounted but didn't move forward.

I waded to the edge of the cliff and pushed one step beyond it onto the bridge. The wind crashed against me on both sides of the bridge, like waves breaking on sea cliffs, pouring over me with such force it ripped away my breath. The crystals held my legs in place as I crouched low to the ground. Three long seconds. Then the wind changed and, like the receding wave, pulled downward. Another three long seconds, and then the air stilled. Only then did I realize my head stood bare to the sun. I glanced over the side and saw the long white ribbon of my turban twisting and dancing through the air. Glinting gray spears of rock lined the ground far below, where I'd surely fall if I didn't cling to this path. I pushed two steps through the crystals, my heart beating a hundred times in the movement. Then the wind hit again.

Forty feet. Two steps. Waves of wind. Two steps. Clinging, balled up. Two steps. Wind ripping away tears. Two steps.

The bridge narrowed till I slid along sideways, my legs now thigh-deep in crystals. Parts of the crystals overflowed and slipped over the narrow edge of the bridge. No matter where I looked was over the edge. If anything, the ground was farther away. I almost vomited into the void.

Two steps, then another, and another, until the island stood a few feet from me. All I wanted was to leap that last few feet and stand with the solid ground beneath me. I waited for the calm and pushed forward two steps, then collapsed with my face on the island and my legs in the stream. I breathed as the wind ripped up again behind me, but the island remained calm.

I pulled myself from the stream. The island stood oval, about twenty feet across at its widest, and at its center, the stream ended in a pool of crystal.

Now where? We'd followed the stream. Where was the mother nursing her child? I looked down on the land below. Fifty feet out from the cliff side gave me a different angle to see the rocks below. As I gazed, searching, pictures began to take shape. A man holding a lamb on his shoulders. Five women dancing. There! A woman holding a baby to her breast. Her skin was as brown as mine and wrapped in a lighter brown robe. The child was wrapped in white stone, with its black hair peeking out. The mother sat with her back to a red rock, her feet sticking out to one side like she was half-kneeling. She faced the island where I stood, her face upturned and though the features were rough, I could almost see a smile. She was huge, about halfway up to the island, but so were thirty other statues. I doubt I could have picked her out from below.

Thank Providence, I signed.

The return trip left me soaked with sweat and as out of breath as if I'd run from galloping horses. Katrin leaned forward and grasped my hand as I stepped back into the safety of the land. Her hand was also slick with sweat.

"Did you decide to gaze on the vista every few steps?" she said lightly. The tightness about her mouth betrayed her. I must have looked pathetic curled up every half minute.

I gulped water and then explained.

"You are lucky I'm here to keep you on the path," she teased before signing, *thank Providence*.

I chuckled. She was picking up on my mannerisms.

"Well, you could teach me new hand signs."

"After we reach the nursing mother and pay our respects."

We hiked down the wide cliff face path, and an hour later, we stood at the base of the brownstone mother, her feet towering as tall as I was. I was sure it was the right stone, though from here I couldn't see how she was a mother.

"How do you pay respect?" I muttered, feeling around the stone for any fissure.

"By bowing." Katrin dropped to her knees in the sand and lowered her head to the ground in the most complete obeisance I'd ever witnessed. "The sand is cool!" She pushed sand to the side.

I knelt next to her. The sand *was* cool, even with the sun shining on it. I hitched my robes to the side, then dug like a dog, sending sand flying between my legs. Half a foot down, the sand turned damp. I pulled out our tin cups. We shoveled another foot before hitting stone. Icy water bubbled up.

"Do you know how lucky you are that I'm here?"

"Very," I replied, stepping aside to let her take the first drink of fresh spring water.

14

WHO POURED FIRE INSIDE MY HEAD?

HALAVANT

My head burned. My body burned. I lay in flames. Then there was a coolness on my forehead. But still my head lit with fire. A coolness at my lips. A trickle of water cooled my swollen tongue. I opened my mouth, seeking more.

Voices reached from beyond the flames. I fought through the heat to understand them.

"He's too hot again," said a woman's voice. "We have to bring down the fever."

"You said he might never wake if we gave him more," a man's voice replied.

"If we don't bring down the heat, he'll not make through the night."

Please! Stop the fire! But I couldn't form the words in my parched throat.

A liquid trickled into my mouth. Bitter poison! I struck out and met hardness with my hand. The bitter liquid stopped, and I heard a clattering on the floor.

"Hold him," the woman said.

An arm slid around my shoulders; a hand grasped my chin. Another arm clamped my arms to my sides. The coolness in the grip eased the fire and gave me the energy to fight. I struggled as more bitterness dripped into my mouth.

"He's still strong," the man said, his voice close to my ear.

"His will is strong. Let it be enough to carry him through."

Their voices blurred as the heat raged on, then even that dimmed as if smothered by a blanket. I let the thickness envelop me.

15

DELVE WHERE THE THORNY LIZARD HIDES

YOSYPH

Delve where the thorny lizard hides. Light no fire, but keep to the fire rock's glow. Never turn from your path, though wide avenues beckon with freedom's light. Water's delight waits for the one who holds true.

"Which one is a thorny lizard?" Katrin asked as we ate a breakfast of dates, spicy dried meat, and herb crackers. The food had flavor, but eating it day after day dulled its appeal. Several lizards crawled out from holes and lay basking in the early sun. Some were slender with yellow and black bands. One squatted like a dark purple frog. A small green one scurried after a cricket. I'd not noticed any animals before today. The spring must provide enough water for life.

"None of those," I said. "None of them have thorns."

"Maybe we should scout around a bit. The lizards must have a strict generational territory for this to be the clue."

I nodded at her logic. She could add much to our war council when we returned. Then I grimaced. She wasn't returning with me. *Get your head back on deck,* I signed, remembering a pirate's caution.

I circled around the Nursing Mother to the south, and Katrin turned to the north. Halfway around, the rock stuck out right above my head, creating a sunny ledge with a narrow shaded spot below it. I stepped forward to peer onto the ledge, and something pierced the sole of my shoe. I knelt in the red sand and found a reddish, rock-like plant, a hand-span across and about level with the sand. Transparent spines bristled along its surface. I pulled two half-inch needles from my foot and looked around. I spotted a couple more spiny plants, all nestled next to the rock, looking like nothing more than undulations in the sand.

"Katrin," I called out, "Watch out for spiny rock-like plants."

"I know." Her sharp voice carried around the rock. Hopefully, her feet were better off than mine. A tingling radiated from each place I'd pulled out a spine, like when my feet had fallen asleep and didn't want to wake up.

A scuttling sound. I turned about, careful where I stepped. A red lizard, about as big around as my wrist and long as my forearm, sat on the ledge. I took a step closer, and it puffed up, its neck flaring in a ruff edged with spines. A ridge of thorns rose from its back. I took another step, and it flashed around, disappearing into the rock face. I pulled myself onto the ledge and found the shelf angled down into a hollow with two rough doorways hewn into the stone. The two doorways led further into the monolith.

I waited, watching for the thorny lizard. A few minutes later, it poked its head out of the left door. It turned its head toward me, flicked its tail and disappeared again, not even bothering to puff up.

"Katrin," I called. "I found it!"

"Good." Her voice made me jump. She leaned against the bottom of the shelf, holding one foot. "I've had trouble enough with those spiny devil plants."

"That is an apt name for them." I pulled her up to the shelf. Her right foot had six spines poking into her soft-soled shoe. She gritted her teeth as I extracted them, but a low moan slipped through.

"Come now," I joked. "You didn't cry out when the brigands had you."

"They didn't shove needles in me," she growled back, rubbing her foot. Then she looked at the dark openings and moaned again. "We are going in there?"

"Yes." I took her hand and pulled her back to standing.

"Well, we better get going," came her tart reply.

What was up with her? She hadn't been this short-tempered since the royal forest. My foot tingled and stung as I leaped down from the rock to get our horses. That was probably her problem, too. It was an annoying sensation.

I found a lower ledge that our horses could step onto and then onto the shelf. Once there, they easily descended into the space before the hidden doors. The right door had a lovely cool breeze wafting from it. We entered the dry and dusty left door. The ceiling was a foot above Flax's head; we'd be leading our horses yet again. As we went in further, the daylight behind us dimmed. Where was the fire rock? Better yet, what was a fire rock? Would we bumble around in the dark until we came to the end of the path? Right now the floor had only solid, smooth stone, and the clacking of hooves echoed about us. Would it stay that way? The walls were also solid and smooth. I ran my left hand along the wall as I led the way forward, the dimness turning to darkness until I could see nothing ahead. I turned my head and saw a vague outline of Flax, Katrin, and Barley.

"Yosyph?" Katrin's anxious whisper echoed. "I know this a bad time to tell you, but I freeze up in the dark."

"But you did fine at night before now, didn't you?" My shoulders tightened. This could make the day difficult. Not that the other days hadn't been.

"Not really. I didn't tell you, and as long as there was a little light by moon or stars, I could push through. I'm trying, but my legs won't move, and my heart is pounding like I could pass out. I'm sorry, but please, can't you light a torch?"

I had one torch in my bundle of supplies, but the clue said to light no fire. Yesterday, it required I go to the end of the crystal stream to find our way forward. I doubted today's instructions could be ignored. Where were the fire rocks? A scuttling passed by my feet.

"Yosyph!" her voice rose in panic. *Yosyph, yosyph, yosyph,* the tunnel moaned back.

"Do you think you can ride Flax, lying across his back?"

I took her gulp to be a yes. I led Flax back to her and helped her mount. She rigidly fumbled to Flax's back. Her head lay against his neck, the ceiling not high enough for her to sit. I tied Barley to a length of rope behind Flax, then placed my hand against the wall. Pain shot up my arm, followed by a tingling. Katrin had named those spiny plants appropriately—Spiny Devil plants. What were they doing in the cave! My foot still tingled, and if there were more plants, I'd be all full of pins and needles before long. I felt around on my hand to pull out the spines.

Katrin gasped as a glow caught the edge of my vision. The spiny plant I'd touched glowed in the shape of my hand, growing brighter, until it cast enough light to see more of these red plants, the fire rocks, on the walls and floor. They were spaced out enough I could walk between them, almost as if someone had planted them there.

"I'll not light our way with my hand." I pulled out the last spine. In the low glow, I pulled out a cooking pot and rope. I attached the pot to the end of my walking stick and tapped another of the plants with it. After a few seconds a dim light glowed from the plant's depths, growing until it glowed as brightly as the first, though now the first was dying down.

"Thank you." Katrin's eyes were wide as if trying to take in all the light at once.

We spent the next hours playing hopscotch in a cactus bed. The fire rock must like the dark, because the deeper we went, the denser they grew. It didn't seem to bother our horses. Their hooves crashed down upon the plants, causing the tunnel to light up like a bonfire. I kept my eyes trained to the ground, but I still stepped on another pincushion, causing both my feet to tingle and throb. I saw several thorny lizards, including one munching on the fire rock. If I tapped it, would it also glow? Chances are, it would fly in my face and bite me instead.

The tunnel continued straight and slightly downward. Katrin clung silently to Flax's neck, and when I placed my hand on hers, it was icy and slick with sweat. It wasn't just the dark she was trembling about, because we had plenty of light. Was it the cave itself?

Then the light changed. A dim white light showed up ahead. We drew closer, and a side tunnel led upward toward the light. It would be an easy climb, even with horses. Maybe it would be worth it to take a break in the sunlight and then return to our path. If Katrin passed out among the fire rocks, who knew what it would do to her? She was so cold already, and the shock of it could... I shook my head.

"Could we?" Katrin faced the sunlit path, her face tight with a longing, almost like the light was air to her.

The warning *Never turn from your path* echoed in my mind, but if we didn't, what would happen to Katrin? Could a person die of fear? "I'll scout it out first to make sure it's safe."

I tied a rope about my waist with the other end through two iron rings on the side of Flax's saddle. "Let it out as I go, but don't give me too much slack," I told Katrin. "If the rope suddenly jerks, pull back until the iron rings grip the rope, then have Flax back up."

She nodded and gripped the rope. "You don't have to do this. I'll—I'll be all right."

"I'll be all right too. See you soon."

The path grew steeper as I climbed toward the light. I pushed my walking stick against the sandy floor to give me additional grip. I could see an opening fifty yards ahead. Then thirty yards.

I thrust my walking stick into the sand again, and it dropped through the floor. I fell forward, my hands slipping through the floor. Sand engulfed my face. I couldn't breathe. Sand sucked me downward, and then a tug at my middle stopped me. I coughed out the last of my breath as I disappeared under the sand.

The tug grew stronger. I was pulled slowly, oh too slowly, from the sand. At last, my head emerged.

I gasped as the rope dragged me back to firm ground.

"What happened?" Katrin asked as I stumbled back into the main tunnel. Tears ran down her face. Her hands gripped a knotted mess of rope.

"I'm fine." I brushed the sand out of my hair.

"What happened?" Her voice grew shrill. *Happened, happened, happened.*

"I ignored my mother's warning and almost drowned in sand."

"I shouldn't have come. I promised I wouldn't be a burden, but I almost got you killed because I couldn't wait for sunlight."

"It's not your fault." My voice echoed in the tunnel, *fault, fault, fault.* "I made the choice to go," I said in a quieter voice. "I'm fine. We should go."

Katrin allowed me to tie her to the saddle in case she did pass out, and we proceeded down the fire rock tunnel. Five more times we passed side tunnels, lit with white light. But the light was much dimmer in the last one, as if the sun were low in the sky. Another hour passed beyond that, and then a bluish light glowed up ahead.

"Must be the moon tempting us now," she said. She'd not passed out yet, but every time I touched her hand, I wondered how she could be any colder.

The blue light grew brighter, and the fire rocks grew further apart, until at last we reached the end of the tunnel. It opened to a land dotted with scrubby trees, lit by a full moon. A sheer cliff rose behind us, at least five hundred feet tall, maybe a thousand. It was hard to tell in this light. A fountain bubbled in a stone basin ten steps from the tunnel.

I whipped around at the sound of weeping. Katrin lay on Flax, sobbing and shuddering. I'd never seen her fall apart like that, not with the brigands or the wolves. I untied her from Flax, wrapped her in a blanket, and held her while her body grew warm and her breathing finally fell into the even pace of sleep.

"Never again," I vowed, "will I take you through that tunnel." I brushed her hair from her face and kissed her forehead to seal the promise.

16

THE KING WILL LEAD YOU TO THE LAST RESPITE

YOSYPH

Lion's roar and waterfall silent. Walk between the tumbled trees deeper to the mountain's cleft. Fear no padded-foot hunter if you bring the Whistle of Gamaclies. The king will lead you to the last respite before entering Devil's Teeth.

I carried a great weight. And though weariness hung on my arms like chains, I did not want to put down the weight. It was something important. But what? Darkness thicker than an unlit cave engulfed me. I couldn't see what I carried or why. I trudged on, the ground swallowing my legs until I pressed thigh-deep through sludge, and still, I carried this weight. Something soft and breathing. Hair tickled my cheek, and a glowing warmth rested against my chest. Someone, not something. I breathed in the scent of sun, sweat and something sweet. Katrin. I clutched her tighter as I pushed forward. I had to get her to safety. I—

A roar ripped me from my dreams.

I leaped to my feet, sending Katrin tumbling to the ground. I scanned the landscape for the source of the sound. Nothing. Flax pranced nervously, and Barley would have bolted if I hadn't tied him to one of the scrubby trees in our camp. Out of the corner of my eye, I saw Katrin push herself up on her hands and knees and glare at me.

"Do you always wake by leaping to your feet?" she asked acidly.

"I heard a roar." I looked around again. Still nothing, and no sound beside the bubbling fountain and the light wind. I looked down, abashed. Perhaps it was part of my dream, and my leaping caused our horses' nervousness. Katrin didn't deserve such a rude awakening, especially after yesterday.

"I'm sorry for that."

She laughed, shaking her head. "Don't take my first words in the morning to heart." She raised her head to look at me. Her eyes shifted over my shoulder. I spun around. I'd forgotten to check the cliff and cave behind us. No beast. Instead, the cliff glistened in the rising sun—a smooth face, rising into the sky, mottled green and brown, and off to one side, a strip of blue stone.

She looked up at the cliff. "Perhaps, you heard the 'Lion's roar', and that blue rock is the waterfall silent. I'll wager the roar is a sound that a special rock makes. The rocks around here have done enough other strange things. Besides, how could you depend on an actual lion to live in this land?"

I nodded at her reasoning. I would much rather a roaring stone than a hunting lion. "If so, then these shrubby trees must be the tumbled trees. They are as twisted as if a child had pulled their branches in all the wrong directions. Though there seems to be no path among their scattering."

"First, where is the mountain cleft?" Katrin scanned the horizon, her hand shading her face from the sun. "We should see any mountain that is within a day's ride."

"Unless it drops again into another cliff." I instantly regretted my words.

"Please, don't let the Devil's Teeth be another tunnel."

"The map shows a canyon." I hurriedly pulled out the map and showed her the picture of a canyon, though like everything else it was little more than a symbol. I had no idea if the canyon went through a mountain or down another cliff.

"As long as it's not another tunnel, I can bear it. We might as well start out going south as that is the direction the map shows. Maybe the trees get more organized?" She quirked up one eyebrow.

I fingered the wooden whistle that hung about my neck. Perhaps they would. We couldn't stay here. Our food and the horses' grain were dwindling. Katrin stood dirty but smiling, the paleness and trembling gone from yesterday. So we headed south.

The land about us stood lush compared to the desert on previous days. The twisted trees bore long silver leaves and stood about as tall as I. Beneath them, sparse grass hinted at green, but more boldly told of yellow and brown. The sun bore down with as much heat as before, clean and welcome after the tunnel.

The trees continued haphazardly, as the land rose in a slight incline. At the top of a hill, the land dropped away again, and our old friends, the rock pillars stood ready to greet us. *Tumbled trees.* They half stood in two lines, each leaning on the next. Each pillar was at least twenty feet tall, even tumbled sideways. What caused them to fall? I shivered at the thought. In the distance a mountain range cut the sky, its ragged peaks sawing into the blueness. Our path stood clear and my fingers moved in thanks. Katrin signed the same. She giggled as I caught her eye.

"You still haven't taught me many hand signs," she reproved. "It isn't as if you've been too busy, just trying to find our way across a path that is determined to kill us."

"I'll teach you the sign for laugh." I flicked my fingers in tiny waves.

"So next time you are too serious I'll sign to you 'Laugh' and you will break out into earth-shattering rumbles." Her voice filled with mischief.

"Like this." I let out a rolling laugh. The sound echoed between the rocks and came back in a roar. Flax reared and spun beneath me. Barley threw Katrin to the ground and bolted.

A lion stood a stone's throw away, between the columns of rocks. His tawny mane flowed about his yellow face. He stared at us with golden eyes. I jumped from Flax, in front of Katrin, and drew my sword. A low rumble of warning vibrated from the lion. He crouched, his muscles tight and ready to pounce.

"The whistle, you fool," Katrin screamed.

I almost stumbled forward at the force of her words. I raised the whistle to my lips and blew. A single purring note poured out. The lion sat back on his haunches. I was a fool. I nearly provoked it to attack.

"Yosyph." Katrin's voice trembled. "Do you think it will leave us alone now?"

The lion watched us, his tail tapping against his side. I blew the whistle again. He turned and walked down the columned path.

"I think," I said, "he's the king to lead us."

"I'd rather follow a wolf." Katrin laughed shakily.

Laughter warbled from the stones. "I'm certain you would," said a tenor voice. A tall man stepped from below one column twenty feet in front of us. He wore white robes and a turban, only revealing his dark eyes and nearly black skin around them. "I'm also certain you'd like to retrieve your horses." He switched to the desert tongue. "I'll wait for your return." He sat next to the lion and rubbed his hands through its mane.

"Naven?" Katrin's voice broke on the name.

"Yes, that is my name, little one. How came you to know it?"

"Naven!" Katrin darted toward the man.

The lion jerked up its head as I ran and caught her hand. That was still a lion.

"Let me go," Katrin cried, pulling against my grasp. "It's Naven."

So that was the man who had protected her, the one she thought had died. He must have survived the whipping and the desert path. And, for some reason, he was here now. The thoughts whipped through my head under one thought, *that's still a lion and I'm not letting her get anywhere near it.*

Katrin stopped tugging against me and called out in desert tongue, "It's me, Katrin." She pulled her turban from her head, letting her red hair spill out in a messy braid.

"Tinder Flower?" The man strode toward us and enfolded her in an embrace. "Little Tinder Flower? What are you doing here?"

"The Queen tried to kill me." Her broken voice was muffled in his robes. "And Yosyph saved me."

Naven reached a hand out to me. "My friend," his voice grew husky, "I am at your service. First, I'll help you gather your horses, for you will want them."

He led the lion further down the path so I could convince Flax and Barley to return. They trembled as I tied them to a tree. Naven stood with Katrin hugging his waist and his arm about her shoulder. She would have family here. Then why did part of me feel forlorn?

"Naven." Katrin bounced on her toes. "How did you survive? Tell me everything."

The tall man unwrapped the turban from his face. Below his black eyes, a large nose and a firm mouth balanced the rest of his face. He could have been in his forties. He smiled, showing missing front teeth. "I will, Tinder Flower, and you must promise to tell your tale, too." He turned to me with a raised eyebrow. "And you carry the shadow walker's blood. Yet you are untrained. I doubt your story will be a short one. Mine, on the other hand, is a tale short enough to drink tea over."

"How do you know I am a shadow walker?" I asked.

Katrin giggled.

I blushed. She'd noticed my ability too. Was it as blatant as a scar for those who knew what to look for?

Naven frowned. "Most would not notice it, or you. But my father was one. I will assume you are more honorable than he was."

In about the time it took me to get lost in the implications of that answer, we sat in the shade of a leaning column, around a fire of fragrant silvery wood, and drank hot tea. My muscles relaxed.

"Don't make me wait longer." Katrin bounced with the impatience of a little child, setting her cup into the sand and leaning toward Naven.

"After they whipped me and took you," Naven said, "I thought I'd die. But horse traders from the Kishkarish saw the buzzards circling and drove them off before I became their breakfast. They took me back to their land—my land, before selling me as a slave to pay my father's debts. When I regained my strength, I begged to be allowed to return for you, my Tinder Flower. But I had a debt to pay to my rescuers, and two years passed before I could return this way."

"You braved this crazy path twice?" Katrin interrupted.

"Oh, no," Naven laughed. "There are much easier ways to and from our land. Only those who desire to prove their courage and honor walk the King's Trial. And even then they have a guide who has gone before. The guide is not to help them beyond advice and leading them safely home if they choose to give up. Fewer than ten in a generation brave it. And of those ten, only one or two make it the whole way in honor. Usually at least one dies. No, I've never braved the path, nor will I. What need have I of foolishly earned honor? And I think most only do it to be found worthy to sit in the Council."

Why, Mother, I looked up at the sky, *did you send me by this path? Do I have to prove my worth for the people to accept me?*

"I traveled back to your father's house and found you gone," Naven continued. "Old Eliza said you were visiting the prince, and all looked to be hopeful for your marriage when you came of age. She also promised me that—that jackal had not touched you since. I knew my presence would only bring wrath down on your head, so I returned to my people, hopeful that your life would bring you great happiness."

"Naven, why didn't you take me?" Katrin said. "I didn't marry Halavant, and everything's a mess."

My shoulders tightened. She still wanted Halavant. Why did I think she favored me?

"Tinder Flower, I think it is good I didn't. This young man here needed you as much as you needed him. He'd have died if you hadn't called out to him to use the whistle. God's hand works in mysterious ways."

I forced a chuckle past my tight throat. "I'd have died many times before that, once even before we entered the King's Trial. Katrin seems determined to keep me around, despite my foolishness."

"And you, my muddy man," her mouth spread in a delighted smile, "are worth each day of it."

The blush extended to the roots of my hair.

Naven clasped both our hands. "Now I know it is a good thing I didn't take you. But please, tell me your tales."

Katrin told hers in a few hours span. She left out her father breaking her fingers, which I thought was wise. Naven looked ready to kill the man even with what she did tell.

"And then we entered that horrible tunnel," Katrin said. "I've never felt so afraid. I thought at first it was my fear of the dark, but even with the fire rocks glowing, I grew so frozen that Yosyph risked going off the path to get me some sunlight."

"And your rope saved me," I interjected.

"Were you not afraid?" Naven turned his searching eyes on me.

"Yes, but no more than is common to man."

"Then you did not prick yourself with the fire rock?"

"That I did plenty. Once on my hand, and twice on my feet. They burned and tingled like I never want to feel again."

"That should not be. The fire rock's poison elevates fear to such an intensity—a heart beats faster and shallower, and then —" Naven stopped and looked down. His face flinched. "Those who tread that tunnel are warned never to touch the fire rocks. There is little the guide can do except get them out of the tunnel quickly. Who would send you on this path with just enough knowledge to get you killed? What map did you follow? How did you survive the tunnel having been poisoned to such an extent?"

"My angel mother sent me." I took the rolled parchment from my pocket and handed it to him. "Here is the map."

Naven took the parchment and scanned over the writing at the top. He stopped and read more slowly. "Tanyeshna, of the Kishkarish tribe. I remember. She walked this path once. She was a few years older than me. A beautiful and gentle woman. One bound to rise to the head of the council, if she hadn't been banned from the land for helping that foreigner escape."

Tell me what happened! my fingers signed, but I held my silence.

Naven continued to read and stopped again, "Prince? I don't understand. We don't have royalty. You cannot be accepted as a prince, for your mother wasn't a queen. Yet—" He stopped and read over the map, nodding at different parts. "Yet, according to the book of law, and I've studied that enough while out here caring for Dooroo." He said the word rolling the "r" so it sounded like a cooing dove.

"What's a Dooroo?" Katrin asked.

Naven laughed.

I'm sure I wore the same puzzled expression as Katrin.

"The lion. Dooroo is the lion. It is my year to care for him. All the older men take a year at this duty, keeping a flock of goats to feed him and reviewing his training with the whistle, but I digress. It is true that as one who travels the King's Trial, according to the directions given in this map and without a guide, you would be accorded the honor equivalent to a king for your valor, wisdom, and strength. But none have dared to. It is pure insanity. And yet you have made it this far."

"I must make it by this path the rest of the way," I said. "I must be trusted enough by the Kishkarish people to raise an army against the Queen of Lansimetsa."

"Halavant's mother?" Naven asked. "Is she that terrible?"

Katrin stuck out her lip. "She tried to kill me."

Naven shook his head, "That is not enough reason, Tinder Flower, to raise an army and start a war where thousands will die."

"She plans to enslave a third of the people and send them to mine the Stone Forest," I said.

Silence met my statement. Naven looked down into his hands and studied the sun-wrinkled lines. He finally looked up, his furrowed brow weighted with sorrow. "That news would raise an army to defend our land, but they will not leave the desert. You must learn to Shadow Walk, and with God's blessing, this war can be averted."

My pulse quickened. Could I stop this bloodshed on my own? "Can you teach me?"

He shook his head. "It is a black art, even among our people. I never had the ability, and even if I had, I hope I would not have sought out instruction. Most who learn it turn evil, for the shadow walking power is corrupting. But there is one honored Shadow Walker, one who's proven honest even at a steep cost to himself. And from what Katrin's told of you, I think you also hold to this honor. Perhaps he will teach you if you prove your worth by traversing the remainder of the King's Trial."

"Then I shall."

"And I will too," Katrin piped up.

"No, child," Naven said. "The Devil's Teeth is the hardest part yet. I will bring you and the horses by another way. If he survives, then I will take him to the Council. Don't sulk, Tinder Flower. God has set this young man's feet on this path and upheld him. I trust we will see him again. It is not a farewell yet. All who walk the path take a few days' respite at the lion's gate."

A few days respite. And then prove my worth to learn to Shadow Walk. Could I spare those few days? I should go as soon as possible.

"You must rest," Naven said, as if he'd read my intentions, "and build your strength. You will climb the Devil's Teeth."

Climb? Mother left no directions other than the title of the canyon. She must have known further direction would come from whoever kept the lion. What were the Devil's Teeth? Whatever they were, I had to pass them, too. Let them not be like the narrow crystal stream over the void.

Naven pulled out smoked goat's meat, "Now Yosyph, tell your story, and I will tell you of your mother."

Katrin wrapped her arms around my waist, clinging tightly. I would have enjoyed it, except it felt all too much like a sailor's frantic grip in the middle of a hurricane. Was I her safety in the storm? And if something happened to me, what would she do? I shook my head. A third of my people would die in slavery if I didn't make it. I could not worry about one.

17

I NEVER THOUGHT PEASANTS COULD BE SO KIND

HALAVANT

Sunlight warmed my face, and a heavy softness lay over me. I turned on my side, stretching out my arms and legs under the covers, feeling the coarsely woven pillowcase under my cheek. It smelled of lavender and lemon balm. My body felt scrubbed clean, as if I'd lived a long time between baths and had finally enjoyed one. The only thing disturbing this luxury was a dull ache on one side of my head, but even that seemed a little thing. I breathed in the sheet's sweetness and yawned. A lovely day to sleep all morning and then go on a romp through the woods with Katrin. Wouldn't she love that?

What dreams I'd had. Vivid as any. Maybe I wouldn't sleep in. I didn't need more dreams like those.

I opened my eyes and groaned. It hadn't been a dream. Herbs covered every inch of the ceiling. An open window let in the sunlight and a gentle breeze. "If I close my eyes, this will all disappear and I'll be back home," I said wistfully.

"Lovely first words," Galliard said with a weary smile. I smiled in return. At least I had him around.

"How do you feel?" He knelt by the side of my bed. Dark circles underscored his eyes.

"Better than I did before." I reached up to touch the side of my head and found a bandage. "What did she do?"

"Lenora drugged you and drilled a hole in your head." Galliard shuddered. "I about ended up on the floor next to you. I never want to see anything like that again. But it worked."

A woman's crisp voice sounded from the doorway. "It wasn't the drilling that did it." The healer woman entered the room. She was older than I'd realized. Gray streaked her black hair, and small wrinkles creased her caramel skin. She carried a tray with a bowl. "It was the herbs. I only drilled the hole so that the herbs could take effect on the swelling of the brain. But no more talking until you've eaten. We've had a hard enough time feeding you these last three days, with you slipping in and out of fevered consciousness. I used more Monk's Sleep than I liked to, but it was the only thing that brought down the fever."

"How big of a hole?" I didn't want to be walking around with a big gaping hole in my head.

She tsked and brought a spoon to me. Savory broth poured onto my tongue. I must have been still a bit drugged, because I didn't realize until that taste how ravenous I was. I slurped it down.

"She was like a mother hen, fussing over you." Galliard took the spoon from her hand and fed me.

"And who sat up beside him day and night, putting his own health at risk, until I threatened him with a dose of Monk's Sleep if he didn't rest?" Dry humor was in her raised eyebrows.

Galliard chuckled and then held up his little finger. "The

hole is only as big as the tip of your smallest finger. And I don't care to know what she packed in there, or pulled out."

"Ten days." She shook her head while crushing herbs with a pestle. "You let ten days of swelling build up. It's a wonder it went down at all. Or that you regained your speech, let alone survived it. But young'uns like yourself are usually hardy."

The door swung open, and a blond giant entered the room. It took me a moment to remember he was the farmer, Aiden. His head brushed against the herbs. "And how is the young patient?" His eyes also showed shadows below.

Had they all three watched over me? Why? Galliard didn't believe I was the prince, so that couldn't have been the reason. The softness of the bed and the warm soup made my eyes heavy. I'd ask them later.

I closed my eyes and sank deeper into the pillow. A thunderstorm of stomps brought me fully awake.

"Papa, Papa!" a child said, echoed by other children's voices. "He's awake. Can we see him now?"

I opened my eyes to see seven children standing in a huddled mass at the door, the little ones pushing against the taller ones to get closer. The tallest, a dark-haired girl not yet grown into curves, wore an appalled look and tugged at them.

"I'm sorry, Papa," she said. "Young Aiden heard he was awake and told the rest. I was out in the garden and didn't know until they'd stormed the room."

These were all his? Seven!

"Children, he needs to rest. Tomorrow perhaps." Aiden shooed them out with gentle swats.

"But he's been asleep for three days," the littlest boy whined. "Hasn't he had enough sleep?"

"Daffyd," Aiden said with a warning tone I knew all too well from my tutors. "Go."

They left with feet dragging on the wood floor. Lenora

smiled and shook her head with a look of bemusement and love. I caught my breath. It was like Mother's when she'd caught me sneaking desserts before a royal banquet. What was that, five years ago? She'd sat down, shared an éclair with me, then sent me back to my boring studies. It was one of the few times we'd been together without a minister hovering. A stolen moment. I sighed.

"Drink this, and then you can sleep again," Lenora said, more warmly than before. I drank a mild tea, not the bitter stuff, and sank back into sleep.

The crisp call of a rooster woke me. My head ached worse than the first time I woke, but I didn't feel so sleepy. The drug must have worn off. But the aching did not pound and pulse like before. I fingered the spot. Yes, definitely less pounding. I could touch the bandage and not feel like I'd hit it with a hammer.

Sunlight slanted in the empty room. No, not empty. A pair of feet stuck out on the floor at the base of the bed. I pushed myself to sit and almost fell back to the pillows with light-headedness. The dizziness passed, and I leaned forward. One of the children, a boy, long and lanky but still with a child's face, lay stretched out on a blanket on the floor, a black mop of hair covering one eye. I shifted onto my hands and knees to see better, and the bed groaned. The boy stirred and opened blurry eyes.

"Oh!" He jumped to his feet. "You're awake! I must tell Mama! Don't go anywhere." He ran from the room, slamming the door behind him.

I chuckled. He was a flighty fellow. From my kneeling position, I could see out the window. A house stood a short distance away with a garden spread about it and fields beyond. This room must be expressly for healing the sick. How often did she do this? I fingered my head again. The boy ran to the house, waving to someone and calling out. He emerged a short time later, carrying a dish. My door slammed open again, and he stood grinning, holding a bowl out to me. The rich smell of oats and sugar tickled my nose.

"Mama will be here soon, but she said I can feed you."

I laughed. "I think I can feed myself."

"No." He shook his head. "You must lie down, like a good patient. I'll be a healer like Mama, and you must listen to me."

I half sat against the pillows, surprised how tired I was from kneeling for a few minutes. He blew on a spoonful of oatmeal and fed me.

"Mama says I shouldn't ask you questions, that you barely survived the surgery, and God be thanked you didn't die, but can I ask one question?"

I nodded while swallowing the buttery, rich cereal.

"How come your hair is white? Did the fight that hurt your head scare you so much your hair turned? Or were you born that way?"

I grinned. "It's a new fashion among the young nobility to bleach their hair. I, being the prince, led out, but perhaps I went too far. Though if you could have seen it all in ringlets and tied with a velvet ribbon, you'd have to agree it looked dashing."

The boy stood with his mouth open. He stuttered, "You're the prince?"

"Yes." My smile dropped. "Not that anyone believes me."

"That's fantastic!" he exclaimed. "You can go tell the Queen to stop taxing us so much and give back our cow."

Lenora strode in carrying a tray. She glanced sharply at the bowl from which I'd only eaten one bite. "Young Aiden, you were supposed to feed him with food, not excited words." Her eyes darted over me, and she nodded as if she liked what she saw. “Good skin tone today,” she muttered. She grasped my wrist and counted, nodding again.

I glanced over at Young Aiden and saw him holding his own wrist and counting. I laughed.

“Laughter is a healthy sign,” she said to herself. “How is your head today?”

“It aches, but it doesn’t pound like it did before.”

“It will ache for a while yet.” She looked me in the eyes. They were kind beneath her brisk manner. “Now to the unpleasant part. I need to change the dressing and make sure the swelling is staying down. Do you think you can hold still, or shall I call in my husband?”

I hesitated. I wanted to say I could stay still, but drugged memories of the pain made me doubt it. I looked down, ashamed at my weakness.

“Papa’s already in the field, and so is Galliard,” Young Aiden said. “I’m strong enough to hold him.”

Lenora smiled at her son and shook her head. “You will grow strong enough soon, but go get Papa.”

He dashed out while Lenora arranged the tray full of towels, several scissors, a small knife, bandages, ointments, and a basin of steaming water. My stomach knotted up, and I looked out the window, trying to control my rapid breathing.

“I’m sorry, dear,” Lenora brushed my hair from my face. “I sometimes forget how frightening those things look. I won’t be cutting you, just looking. It will hurt, but nothing like before. Please eat. You need to build your strength.”

Her cool touch helped calm my nerves, but I kept my eyes riveted on the window and forced down the oatmeal. Young Aiden came running back, not with Aiden but with Galliard.

“What’s this?” Galliard boomed, striding into the room with the smell of soil and sunlight. “You are up with the rooster. If I were you, I’d be lying blissfully asleep for hours yet.”

"That's because you haven't slept for four full days," I replied, a grin pulling at my mouth.

"That doesn't count." He washed his hands in a bucket in the corner. "You weren't really asleep, but burning a cord of wood inside your body."

"That I was. I think that was worse than the pounding head."

Galliard sat on the bed and held my head steady in his hands. I closed my eyes and took shaky breaths.

"So you decided," he said, "to give up the burning, it being summer and all. Wise choice." His chuckle had a tightness to it.

I felt a tug as Lenora cut the bandage and unwrapped my head. The ache increased with the movement. She bathed my head, and I felt a long firm pull in my head.

I couldn't suppress a scream. White spots swam beneath my eyelids. Galliard's firm hold kept me upright. I took a deep breath and opened my eyes. A short, bloody tube of linen lay on the tray.

Lenora dabbed at my wound. It stung like alcohol on bloody knuckles. Then she rubbed an ointment on the wound, and a cool numbness covered the sting. She wiped her hands on a cloth. "Everything looks better than I could have hoped. You will have a soft spot on your head, but nothing more. May I cut the rest of your hair? It will make the daily bandaging easier."

I laughed shakily at the request. She'd saved my life, and now she asked if I worried about saving my hair. "Yes, cut it off. I doubt I'll want to run a comb through it until this heals."

Soon the bed was covered with tangled locks of white hair. I winced as the scissors tugged lightly. Then she bound up my head again. I lay down, covered in sweat, and fell asleep.

Evening painted the sky when I woke again. I'd have to stay awake longer if I was ever to catch up to Katrin. How many days now? I tried to think, but it all blurred together. The inn, the beating, the farm, the travel, the drilling, the fever. She could have gone in any direction. I should head home and hope she'd escape and come back. Maybe the ransom note had come, and I wasn't there to receive it. I shook my head and winced. Sharp movements reminded me why I was still sleeping so much. At least I could repay these kind people. They'd never pay another copper in taxes, and I'd get them ten milk cows. Better yet, when I became king, they'd get a dukedom. And Galliard. What could I do for him? I barely knew him despite all the time I'd spent with him. But he would wander no longer.

A savory aroma brought my thoughts to the bowl sitting by my bedside. I ate, determined to leave in the morning and locate the closest detachment of soldiers. They'd help me back to the palace, and then I could right at least some wrongs.

I'm sorry Katrin. I'll find you. Even if it is after I become king. Wait for me. Stay safe. Stay alive. I love you.

18

CLIMB THE DEVIL'S TEETH OUT OF THE MOUTH OF HELL

YOSYPH

A long path, edged with leaning rocks, stretched behind me. Jagged canyon walls sprang up ahead of me, leading southward. And though the morning sun couldn't reach the narrow enclave, I sweltered in the heat. Thirty feet away, lava bubbled from a primal stew pot and surged in slow molten molasses down the canyon.

"The mouth of Hell." Naven pointed to the lava, then to the canyon walls. "And those are the Devil's Teeth." Vertical knife-like edges, packed together like the folds of a fan, created the hundred-foot-tall boundaries around the lava.

"How do you traverse this?" I hoped for a clear path to follow.

"Goat trails. They criss-cross the walls. I do not know more. If you are lucky, you'll reach the end of the lava river in one day.

If not, you'll need to find a wide enough ledge to sleep on or stand awake all night. Goats, I'm afraid, leap happily where you will have to use fingers and toes to keep hold."

My heart sank deeper the more he spoke. Katrin's parting words rang enticingly in my head. *You've done enough,* she'd said. *Come the rest of the way with Naven and me. Your people will help you when they hear your cause.*

But Naven's eyes spoke a different story. My desert kin cast out my mother and would not accept me unless I completed the trial.

I couldn't come this far to give up now. Others had passed this way and survived. But they had a guide who had gone before, someone to give advice and get them safely home, someone who knew the right path.

I gazed into the distance and saw a few shaggy shapes, leaping along the razor-faced rocks. All I had was a bunch of wily goats to lead me.

"The lava does not flow the full length of the canyon." Naven gazed into the distance. "When the ground within the canyon rises enough, the lava gathers in pools. When it does, you can safely walk the base of the canyon the rest of the way. I will send up my prayers for you. I trust we will see you again. May God guide you." He pressed his forehead to mine, in a gesture that I'd not felt since my mother died. Then he spun about and walked back the path we'd come.

I watched him go, wishing to follow him back to Katrin.

I could still taste her kiss, salty with tears. She'd given me a quick peck on the lips, a tight squeeze, and the threat that she'd never forgive me if I died. If I returned now... but at what cost? Tens of thousands clashing in battle. Even if the Queen's armies lost, how many would die? I could stop it before it happened if I learned to Shadow Walk. I could pick off the leaders and end the madness.

I turned to face the Devil's Teeth. Two narrow paths ascended to the right of the cauldron, and one to the left. Naven's last words, *May God guide you,* echoed through my mind. If I'd ever needed guidance, it was now. My fingers flickered in prayer. *Please help me. I need to choose the correct one.* I studied each path, three narrow ledges leading off in different directions. Nothing made one look better than another.

I pulled myself onto the higher of the two on the right to keep me farthest from the lava. I edged onto it, grasping at the wall with my fingers. A feeling descended. It wasn't fear, but rather a not-rightness. I edged back and tried the lower path. Again, this same feeling. Was this the answer I'd prayed for, or were my emotions playing with me?

I started on the left trail with no weighted feeling. Was this the right one? I couldn't wait forever. I edged along the trail, the ledge growing smaller until my toes clung to the edge. The lava popped fifty feet below. I sought firmer finger holds in the slick obsidian rock. The trail came to the edge of one of the vertical rock folds, and I couldn't see if it continued along the other side. I wanted to pray again, but my fingers were occupied hugging me to the rock.

I spoke, stuttering out my plea. "Oh, God of my mother and my people, I know I haven't ever spoken out loud to you before. But then, I haven't spoken much to anyone until recently. Please help me get around this blind corner."

I waited a moment, then slipped my right hand around the edge. The fold was not as sharp as it appeared from a distance, but rather a rounded point about the width of my arm. I felt around on the other side for something, anything, and caught a hole at waist level. Clinging tightly, I leaned around the edge. The path continued about two feet lower, wide enough to bear my full foot. I stepped onto it, my legs trembled from bearing all my weight on my toes. Only minutes in. A day remaining. I shuddered again.

The hours passed in like manner. I edged along, sometimes on a sliver of a trail. Sometimes the trail continued fifty steps before it came to another fold in the rock, other times only ten.

These vertical folds in the rock frightened me the most. I couldn't see around them, and the blind groping around the edge for a hold left me panting and trembling. I'd stop and look, pray and look, feel about and pray more. But I got no more directions or impressions. Did God guide me to choose this path? If so, why wasn't he helping me more?

My fingers ached, and my toes cramped as I inched along yet another narrow ledge, to yet another blind corner. I reached my hand around and could find nothing. Tears of frustration and exhaustion trailed down my cheeks. "Please help me!" I cried out. "I can't do this on my own!"

A peaceful feeling, an assurance, whispered over me. My limbs shook but my heart quieted. "I can do this," I whispered, and the feeling fled. "Sorry," I modified. "With your help, I can do this. Thank you."

A memory sounded on the wind. Words Mother spoke in the rocking of the pirate ship. *God preserved you for a great purpose. Keep close to Him, and He will keep you.*

"I will try." I pressed my hands against the rock, my fingers seeking non-existent cracks, and took a clinging step around a blind corner. My toes found a tiny lip. I placed my weight on that foot to bring around my body and slipped!

My fingers scrambled against the rock, catching nothing.

My feet slid against the obsidian.

I hugged my body around the corner, trying to squeeze the rock fold between my hands, arms, and legs.

Shards of rock broke away, ripping into my clothes and laying open my cheek.

I slowed to a gripping, slipping, inching descent.

Leap to the right! The thought yelled as strongly as Katrin's warning to use the whistle. But if I let go, I'd quickly fall the rest of the way.

Leap to the right!

I slid another inch downward. My arms shuddered as I applied more pressure to stay there. I could hear the bubbling of the lava under my beating heart. Soon, I'd lose the strength to hold my position. Did I trust that God had guided me thus far? I slid another inch.

Leap to the right? I took a deep breath, pushed with my right hand and leg against the rock while letting go with my left.

I lost contact with the rock.

Air rushed about me.

Then a strong wind, like that on the crystal stream bridge, pushed against me, flattening me against the rock face. My feet touched solid ground, enough to bear their full length.

I glanced down. I stood on a ledge, about two feet wide and eight long. Lava bubbled twenty feet below. I crumpled to the ground.

"Thank you," I prayed, my voice trembling with my body. "I'll not doubt you again. But," I paused, uncertain if it was reverent to go on, "if it pleases you, don't test me like that again."

A large bubble of lava popped and splattered the cliff a few feet below. My trembling tripled. I would have been a charred mass by now, if not for His hand. He'd saved me, despite my doubting and my pride. My pride! I sucked in my breath. How many times had I taken credit for fulfilling the prayed-for blessings, acting like I had to do it because God wouldn't, and ignored the miracles that made each action possible? Giving Him a silent cursory thanks?

He should have left me to fall, but He didn't. I pressed my head against the rock and let tears fall. "I'm sorry for being an ungrateful, proud fool," I cried. "Thank you for preserving me and for always helping me."

My tears stung my right cheek. I touched a flap of skin, my fingers came away thick with blood and a warmth flowed down my chin to my neck. I'd have to stanch it before I grew light-headed. I bound a strip of cloth about my face. My cheek throbbed under the fabric.

Then I glanced up at the sky. I still needed to keep going forward. At least that part of my mistaken thinking was true. God wouldn't work miracles unless I also put forth the effort.

The afternoon passed better than the morning, with fewer toe-hanging ledges. As the sky darkened overhead, the bubbling sound increased. The river gathered below in a large pool, popping and bubbling, glowing red. A little more, and I'd be beyond it.

But the path ended. Nothing. There was a sheer cliff and a seven-stride leap before dropping several men's height to solid ground.

"Shall I leap again," I almost jokingly prayed. Probably not. Faith didn't mean foolishness.

A "naaa, naaaa" sound brought my eyes up. A goat stood seemingly on a sheer face, inches out of reach. It shook its head and bleated at me. I stood on my toes. A bit more. I stretched. One foot slipped. I pressed myself to the rock and dropped back to my feet, panting.

"Naaa, naaa," the goat bleated.

"I'm trying," I growled. The path under my feet was wide enough for me to stand with my heels hanging over the edge. I half-crouched, pressed myself against the cliff face and sprang upward, reaching for where the goat stood.

My hands caught a deep lip in the rock face. I slid my hands sideways, and the lip continued. The goat naaa'd one last time and bounded off.

I scooted sideways the last twenty feet by my hands, my feet dangling. Then I slid along the crevice another ten feet to increase the distance between the lava and me. My arms shook. I let go and crunched to the ground, rolling to absorb the impact.

I lay there panting. I stared up at the star-studded sky and the panting turned to laughter. I'd climbed out of the mouth of hell by the devil's teeth and God's mercy. When my shuddering laugh died away into a sigh, I rolled to my knees and prayed, raising my voice long and loud in the undulating chants of praise that my mother once whispered in lullaby to me.

I woke huddled on my knees, the sky overhead lightening with morning. Rolling lava popped close by, and I shuddered. Before I stood or even took a drink, I lifted my voice in gratitude.

Then I stood and almost fell over as blood rushed like a thousand fire rock stings through my numbed legs. I marched about, biting my tongue until the pain dulled to the throb of yesterday's climb. I'd never put my legs through such rigors, not even as a small boy on the pirate ship, leaping from rigging to rigging.

But I was uninjured. I reached up and touched the blood-crusted cloth on my cheek. Well, besides that. I stretched, grateful for firm ground. I pulled out a date cake and headed down the canyon, away from the lava.

The canyon walls continued their fan-like folds, and the occasional goat leaped about. I trod along in the silence. And the silence echoed with emptiness. I'd always gone in silence; why did it bother me now?

Katrin. I missed her voice, her words, her questions, her joyfulness, her courage. I missed *her*.

One more day and I'd see her again. I blushed. She was making me glow even when she wasn't there. That kiss. What if it meant more than goodbye? What if she felt something for me?

No! I was nothing more to her than a brother and protector. She had no tender words for me, only teasing and light-hearted jests. She still loved Halavant. I'd caught her sighs and looks. I couldn't let my thoughts linger. *Think about Naven's story of my mother,* I signed to myself. *That will keep my mind occupied.* I pulled Naven's words forward in my thoughts, words of my mother and a glimpse of my father.

Your mother passed the King's Trial and stood in the Council for five years. She wasn't the first woman to pass this trial and stand in the Council, but she was the most vocal. Everyone concerned her. She spoke for the shepherd whose sheep died of disease. She spoke for the family of the man deep in gambling debt. If someone was in need and justice was against them, she'd eloquently show how both mercy and justice could help them. She championed the downtrodden, the prisoner, the crazy. Even the foreigner.

I smiled as I listened to Naven's words again in my mind.

I'm certain I'd never have been sold as a slave for my father's debts if she had still been in Council when the case came before them. But her sense of goodness and mercy was also her downfall. A prisoner, a madman, was brought before the Council. He promised great riches for his safe return to his people. But he'd been caught trespassing in our most sacred temple. And worse, he'd drunk from the seraphim's fountain. Death is the sentence for all who drink of it, our people or foreign.

Your mother listened to his plea and argued for his freedom. But the Council held to tradition stronger than to mercy. The night before his beheading, your mother drugged the guards, freed the man, and fled the desert with him. The Council proclaimed her dead. If she returned, she would be sent into the next life swiftly.

Parts of Mother's letter came to mind. She gave up everything for my father, for I was sure that man was the man whom she had married. That must be why she sent me by the King's Trial. She must have guessed what the Council's reaction would be to her actions. Naven thought this would "purge me of my mother's sins in the council's eyes."

I needed the council's help, or at least the help of the Honored Shadow Walker who sat in counsel with them. Would I have to deny my mother? Never! I'd find another way. But why had she prepared a way for me to go back to her people if they were so close-minded and cruel? What did she know that she hadn't been able to write?

I pulled out her letter and read it again as I walked. *The sage gave me his blessing, promising that you would bring peace to a torn land, but only after you had walked through deep shadow. Thus far, his prophecy is too true. He also warned me that—* And the line ended in an ink splatter.

I would bring peace to a torn land. That had to be Lansimetsa. I walk through deep shadow. Maybe it also meant me being a shadow walker. But what had the sage warned her about?

The canyon dropped away into a lush grassland—my mother's lands. The hidden green in the desert. A people removed and separate. The sides of the canyon spread wide and stretched into the distance as protecting walls. If they continued with their fan-like folds, this land would be nigh impossible to attack save by the entrance. The afternoon sun was bright, and a cool breeze washed against my face.

I closed my eyes. I'd made it.

A voice rang out. "Enemy or friend, reveal yourself."

I stiffened and opened my eyes. An old man, with deep-set wrinkles in sun-blackened skin, held a spear prepared to thrust at my midsection.

"I am Yosyph of the Kishkarish tribe," I replied in his language. "I've braved the King's Trial and seek refuge."

The man lowered the spear slightly, his eyes wide with surprise. "They did not tell me that one had started on the King's Trial. Where is your guide?"

"I had no guide save my mother's map and God's guidance." I brought out my map for him. "Have Naven and Katrin arrived yet? I left them two days ago at the Tumbled Trees."

The man took my map, glanced at it with wondering eyes, then looked back to me. "They will not arrive for another two days, for that path is longer. Come, my friend."

He led me into a room carved into the cliff face. It was cool and dimly lit. The wafting scents of hot tea and roasted meat spread on a low table set my mouth watering.

"Come. Eat. And then tell me your story." The man motioned to a cushion by the table.

I grabbed a slice of goat meat, and as the rich grease dripped down my chin, I wondered, which parts of my story could I tell him? Which parts did I even understand myself?

19

WHEN I RISK MY LIFE FOR SOME CLOTHES

HALAVANT

I glanced out the window of the healing room. The last child ran into the main house to the call of dinner. I had to be quick. I'd vowed to leave two days ago. But instead, I slept most of the time, ate a little, endured the changing of the bandages, and slept more. Last night, Lenora sewed up my scalp, and I hadn't needed to nap much today. I was ready, but I had to be quick.

I exited the room, my legs unsteady after being in bed so long. Clothes hung on the line stretched between the house and the healing room. I pulled down rough woolen trousers and a coarse shirt. The large nightshirt flapped about me. It must be one of Aiden's, for it could fit two of me and went down to my ankles. The clothes I was pulling on were also his, but none of his family's would have fit me. If only Galliard had clothes hanging there. I'd repay the family with a dukedom as soon as I could, but I had to go. They wouldn't understand. To them, I was still the invalid who almost died.

"Mother!" Young Aiden's clear voice called. "He's out of bed." I turned to see him standing at the window and grinning.

Lenora rushed out the door, followed by Galliard and Aiden. Her face was a storm. "What do you think you are doing!" She took my arm. "I didn't save your life for you to go sneaking off. Now get back into bed."

"But," I said plaintively, "I'm healed. You sewed my scalp closed yesterday. You said everything is good. I'm going."

"Elise!" Lenora called. Her eldest daughter pushed her way through the knot of children standing at the house door. "Get my looking glass."

Elise disappeared and came back with a simple glass oval framed in oak.

Lenora held up the mirror. "Look."

I looked. The face reflected my surprise. It wasn't my face. Yellowish bruising covered most of it, blending with a scruffy yellow beard. My eyes and cheeks were sunken and white, and ragged hair sprang out in all directions beneath bandages.

"You should have seen yourself after the fight." Galliard took the mirror from Lenora's hands and handed it back to Elise. "You were a mass of blacks and blues. Did you ever wonder why people drew away from you as we traveled? Then that fever left you like a death mask."

I shuddered.

"Are you ready to lie down again," Galliard asked, "or shall I keep describing?"

"I may look like death." I raised my chin, trying to exude confidence. "But I'm alive. I need to get back to the palace. They must worry about me. If you won't let me go alone, then help me. I need to get to the closest detachment of soldiers. They'll take me the rest of the way."

Galliard's jaw worked in and out. "Son." His voice shook, and not with laughter. "You'll get yourself killed claiming to be the prince. It's treason."

My shoulders slumped. He'd never believe me. I'd have to sneak away, but it could take days before they stopped watching me closely. As much as it grated me, I'd have to pretend I didn't want to go. "You're right. It seems so real, all those dreams and nightmares. It makes me almost believe that I'm the prince. But I'll listen to your counsel."

Galliard raised his eyebrows. "The fox always pleads innocent to the farmer. I think it is time you come eat and sleep in the house with the rest of us. Aiden?"

Aiden nodded and placed a big hand on my shoulder. "Please, join us for dinner."

"Can I at least wear clothes?" I pulled at the nightshirt.

"No," Lenora said. "Now come sit down before I send you back to bed."

The family poured back into the house, a jumbled, pushing, laughing mass. Aiden kept his hand on my shoulder, either to hold me until the doorway cleared or to keep me from running. Not that I'd have made it far.

The large room we entered had a brick fireplace, one long table, two large open windows, and herbs scenting the ceiling. But the cabinets! Cabinets lined all the walls. Each one had been painted brightly by children's fingers—thumbprint flowers, handprint sunshine, and the smeared lines of nine smiling stick figures in front of a house. Beneath that was a detailed brushwork of fields and rivers and trees. I'd have lost sparring privileges for a month to have thus defaced furniture in the palace, but here it felt—

"Do you like my paintings?" a little girl asked amidst the

noise, tugging on my hand. "Mama lets me add to it when I'm done with my chores. But only in my seventh year." She subdued a little then perked up. "That means I still have a month to add to it."

"Malsa." Lenora touched her cheek. "By then you'll be old enough to help create other beautiful art, and you must leave space for Daffyd."

Here, I decided, it was warmth and joy. I let the color and noise wash over me.

"Steady there." Galliard caught my arm as I swayed.

"Everybody sit!" boomed Aiden, cupping his hand around his mouth, and in loud seconds of scraping benches, almost everyone took a place around the long trestle table.

The littlest one, Daffyd, took my hand in his little pudgy one. "I'll give you my dessert if you sit with me," he said, his green eyes earnest.

I didn't know what dessert would be, but the lay of bread, greens, corn, berries and a couple of roast ducks filled me to bursting as I ate. I groaned with fullness as I leaned away from the table, wishing the bench had a back.

Conversation flew about me like a whirlwind. Reports on the fields and garden. A boy boasting how he snared the ducks. A few of the younger children laughing about a trick they'd played on the sheep that day. Young Aiden teasing Elise about a neighbor boy.

Aiden stood taller than any soldier I'd known. Even seated, he was tall as his wife standing. Did he have northern giant blood in him? Yet he was as fair and blue-eyed as any true Lansimetsian, with a beard to rival the one on the statue of my grandfather. Lenora stood opposite in appearance, though equal in wit, small and slender as a heron, with long black hair, caramel skin, and deep brown eyes. She wasn't of the desert. Maybe the islands? The children mixed and matched their parents; some fair with black hair, some caramel with blond, and some replicas in miniature.

If only I had brothers and sisters, perhaps life would not have been so dreadfully dull at the palace. I couldn't miss my father—he'd been dead for longer than I could remember—but if he'd not died, maybe I'd have siblings like this. I shook my head. Not that Mother would have brought this large of a brood into the world. I drive her crazy enough on my own. I chuckled.

Aiden stood up from the head of the table and announced, "Time for dishes and bed. Plenty of work tomorrow." He turned to me. "Do you think you can climb the ladder?" A brightly painted ladder led through a hole in the ceiling. That must be where the children slept.

"He'll sleep on the main floor," Galliard said.

My hopes rose. I could sneak out tonight.

Then he added, "Next to me."

I sat to the side, watching a flurry of dishes, flicked dishrags, and clanking pewter, and then the hugs good night. The children hugged their father and mother, and Galliard. Then Daffyd dove into my lap and wrapped his arms around my neck. "Good night. Don't let the bedbugs bite. But if they do, tell Mama and she'll get rid of them."

I gasped in a forgotten breath as Lenora picked him up and sent him up the ladder.

"You look like love has smitten you." Galliard laid two pallets along one wall. "Those little ones do pull at the heart."

"Are they always this way?" I touched my neck where Daffyd had clung.

"Most children are. Now go to sleep before I ask Lenora to brew up another dose of Monk's Sleep."

Now I knew why they kept the healing house separate from the main. The night was cobbled together with noises. The ceiling creaked under a restless sleeper. Someone climbed down the ladder to use the outhouse. Snores poured from the next room—surely Aiden. Finally, I fell asleep.

I awoke to the clanking of a spoon in a pot and the smell of porridge. I yawned and stretched, sleep still lying heavy on my lids.

"Sorry, dear, to wake you." Lenora interrupted her quiet humming. "Go back to sleep. You'll learn to sleep through the noise. I know at least half my children have no trouble sleeping through even the breakfast bell."

"Please, may I have clothes today?" I tried to look innocent.

"Not yet. Now if you won't go back to sleep, come keep me company." She spooned berry-studded porridge into a bowl. I sat in a chair next to her and ate. I didn't know how she made everything so good. Her herb knowledge wasn't only in healing. I sighed contentedly as I scraped the bottom of the bowl.

"How did you learn to be a healer?" I held out my bowl for more.

Lenora paused in serving me. Her face took on a faraway look.

"In the time of King Luukas," she began, "before he married, Lansimetsa faced bitter enemies from across the sea. When the old king died and the new king was only a young man, no more than sixteen, the Carani attacked. King Luukas led our armies, riding out in the front ranks." Lenora's face glowed as she recalled, "He was wounded thrice over the next two years. But he never gave up. And we followed him. How could we not?"

I sat up straighter to hear every word. Mother never told the wars like this. Just dry facts. And she never talked about Father.

"I learned the healing art from my mother, and she from

hers. We brought the knowledge of the Truven Islands and of Lansimetsa to the battlefield. I learned more as I treated hundreds of wounded beside my mother. Then she died." Lenora paused, her lips tight. "And I continued her work."

"Did you ever meet the king?" I forgot about the bowl of porridge in my lap.

"Once." She grated nutmeg into the pot. "I was only thirteen. He, eighteen. We'd—"

"What did he look like?" I interrupted. I'd seen the painting —tall and lean, serious eyes under curling brown locks. But what was he like in life?

She tilted her head a moment. "He was tall and strong— though nothing compared to my Aiden—with stormy eyes and mouth quick to smile. What stood out most about him was his powerful will. He'd walk through the army encampment with such confidence that we knew we'd win, even with cries of the wounded filling the healing tents and heaped mounds of the dead."

I closed my eyes and saw my father walking with his head held high, a golden crown upon his brow, and armor shining like the sun. But then other parts of her story infringed: howls and cries and limp bodies. I shuddered. Was war like that?

"We'd been at war for two years, and the tide was turning in our favor. Then he fell in battle, pierced through the side by a spear. His standard-bearer was dead, his knights scattered. Aiden, a common sergeant, carried him from the field to me."

"Why you? You were just a girl."

She blushed. "Aiden and I, we'd an understanding between us." Then she briskly added, "And I was better than the king's healers, even then. When his healers found him in a tent packed with wounded commoners, they carried him away, but I'd already saved his life. The king never knew that."

She gave the pot a vigorous stir. "I should have sought him

out later and told him. I could have taken a position in the royal courts and slowed the progression of his illness. Maybe I could have helped his first wife overcome her barrenness. Then she'd not have died seeking a cure, and he'd not have married that woman. Things would be different."

"Ay." Galliard sat up on his pallet. "That they would be. However, we can but choose how we will act in what is now. Speaking of now," he quirked up one side of his mouth, "where is that breakfast bell? I'll hide it so I can eat all of this before the rest get here."

Lenora tapped him on the head with the handle of her long wooden spoon. "Go ring the bell, or else you'll not be getting any."

Breakfast echoed dinner in the confusion of noise, though less intensely as tousled-headed children and a tangle-bearded father wolfed down the porridge. Then they scattered to the four corners of the farm: field, barn, sheep herd, garden. The kitchen was empty, except for little Daffyd.

"Mama said I could stay with you." He climbed into my lap and snuggled against me. The sun poured in the window, and I leaned back against the pillows of the chair. My eyes drooped. No, I couldn't fall asleep. Did she drug me again?

"Do you want to play a game?" I asked Daffyd, gathering up ten pretty stones that lined one window. He nodded and watched wide-eyed as I took ash from the fireplace and drew a grid on the hearthstones. If Lenora let the children paint on her cupboards, she'd surely not mind a little ash to wash off this bench.

Daffyd watched as I lined up two rows of stones and then his face brightened. "We're playing Frogs and Toads?" he asked. "You go first, 'cause the person who goes second always wins."

I'd had another game in mind, but followed his instructions of hopping stones and croaking. And indeed, it seemed the second person always won, but perhaps it was because I did not understand the rules. Sometimes he leaped his stone over one space, sometimes four. If he'd been any older, I might have challenged his strategy, but his pure delight in beating me was worth much more than any win.

I paused at a light touch on my shoulder. Galliard looked down at us, his face creased with dirt and a smile. "We are eating a cold lunch under the apple tree. You coming?"

Our cold lunch turned out to be cider and bread fresh from an outdoor oven, thickly spread with butter and soft cheese. I could get used to this peasant fare and the company.

"Do you want to come sit in the garden this afternoon?" asked one of Lenora's middle daughters, her face blushing under her caramel skin. "Our hazel berry bush is full ripe, and if you've never tasted them sun-warmed off the bush, you have to."

I caught Lenora nodding. How much had she orchestrated? Keeping me off my feet but my mind busy? This was much more pleasant than boring tutors, long meetings, and formal dinners. I didn't know if I wanted to go back, but I had to find Katrin.

The afternoon and evening passed with the sweetness of the sun-warmed hazel berry. Tonight. I'd go tonight.

The middle of the night was toe-stubbing dark. I bit my lip to stop crying out as my little toe bent sideways around the leg of a chair. If I woke Galliard, then I'd never get away, not in months. I glanced at his pallet and couldn't see anything, but I didn't hear him move. I held in a breath of relief. Now if I could get his clothes and shoes. I felt around. Nothing, they were gone. I carefully touched his blankets, trying to find them. His pallet was empty! Where was Galliard?

I'd go anyway, even in this nightshirt. I had to. Everyone else was asleep. Galliard was gone—somewhere. I'd find him again, soon, and give him my thanks. Give them all my thanks. I slipped out the door. The pleasant coolness of evening had turned to midnight chill. I shivered in my bare feet.

Which way? I glanced about and stopped. The house stood dark behind me, but light glowed between the shutters of the healing house. I scampered over, my feet finding all the twigs in the grass. Voices murmured indistinctly. I brought my eye up to the shutter. Aiden, Galliard, and another man sat around a small table. Galliard's back was to me, and I did not recognize the third man with the gray mustache over his lip like a fuzzy caterpillar.

"You are a hard man to find," the mustached man said.

"As it should be," Galliard said.

The mustached man leaned forward. "The time for hiding is over. We must gather. And you must lead."

What were they talking about? Why was Galliard in hiding? I pressed my ear against the shutter.

"Me? But where is the Shadow?"

"He is bringing other help. We will need it to stop the enslavement. It is only—"

Aiden thumped his hand onto the table. His words carried clearly. "Even without him, no one will take my wife!"

The other man shook his head. "Not just her, but your children, too. They have her blood."

Aiden clenched his fists. "They have my blood, too. What does it matter that she came to this land more recently than I? Thirty years or three hundred years, we all entered this land at some point. It was underwater, for pity's sake. Are the only pure-blooded Lansimetsians mer-people?"

Who would take them? Surely a prejudiced lord, wanting their land. I'd not let him!

Galliard's voice cut in, so sharp I hardly recognized it. "Did my noble blood stop them from slaying my brothers?"

No! Who did that? They would pay with a long and painful death!

I turned from the window and ran down the road, the partial moon lighting the way in blues. I would return to the palace. I'd stop the villains from taking Aiden's family. I'd restore Galliard to his rights—a sob caught in my throat—and adopt him as my brother! Tears blurred the way as I stumbled forward. One foot caught a stone and warm wetness spread. I ran on, the hours bleeding together.

A stone wall rose beside the road, blocking the setting moon. Finally, one of the military forts! Thank goodness mother ordered them placed every day's walk throughout the land. I held my side, gasping. Then I pounded on the wooden door. Nothing. I pounded again.

"Quit yer pounding," a gruff voice said from the wall above me. "State yer business or begone."

"I am," I paused, my breath still coming in pants, "I am Prince Halavant. You must let me in!"

"And I am King Luukas," the voice jeered. "Begone, before I get annoyed."

"I am the prince," I cried. "I order you."

No answer. I pounded on the door again. They had to let me in! A large stone sat in the dirt by the door. I gripped it, to pound the door louder, but I swayed and dropped it back to the ground. I was still so weak. I screamed, "Curse you. You'll all hang for this."

The door slid open. Lantern light blinded me. A hand grabbed me about the neck and threw me to the ground within the fort.

"What is this thing?" the gruff-voiced man said. The toe of a boot nudged my stomach. I curled up in a ball, praying he wouldn't kick me.

"It looks like a madman. Needs to be chained up where it can't bother the good people," said a reedy voice.

The two grabbed me under the arms. I stumbled down a set of stairs. A door opened into a dark room. They shoved me and I stumbled forward. The door slammed shut, and a key grated in the lock. I vomited, adding to the already thick smell of human waste.

A prisoner! By my own men! When they found out who I was, they'd grovel, they'd plead, but I'd—and I had not the stomach to think about it further. I crawled over to a wall and curled up, shivering on the stones in the thin nightshirt.

I huddled in the small patch of waning sunlight. A whole day! No one came, not when I screamed, nor when I pounded the door. I moved as the light moved, except once when it fell on a pile of human refuse. My head and the rest of me ached. I moved from the late afternoon sunlight and thumped against the door, re-opening knuckles split from earlier banging.

My thoughts ran tired circles. Galliard would come for me. But he didn't know where I was. Some soldier would recognize me. But I hadn't recognized myself in the mirror. I'd break myself free when they came with food. But my body trembled with weakness and cold. I was the prince! I shouldn't be in a cell!

A key turned in the lock.

"Son!"

I jerked up my head at the voice. Aiden fell to his knees, swooping me into his arms. Warmth engulfed me, and I fell into a fit of shivering.

"He's yours?" a lanky soldier asked in a reedy voice. "You'll have to pay a fine for him disturbing the peace."

Aiden shifted me to one arm, pulled out a purse of coins and handed it to the man. The soldier counted the coins, simple coppers, but a lot of them, and nodded. "I'll not write up a report on him."

"I'd appreciate that," Aiden said. "We men of the sword don't bother with the paperwork."

"Right you are, Aiden. Makes me wonder why you gave it up to farm. But having a crazy boy—well, I can understand now. It sometimes happens with the mixing of bloodlines. I'm sorry for you."

"We've all our trials in life," Aiden said, his voice tighter than before. "I'd best take mine off your hands."

He carried me up the stairs and out to a waiting wagon, laying me in the back.

"No." I sat up. "You must help me convince them I'm the prince. We have to stop the villain from taking your family!"

Aiden's eyebrows raised in surprise and then lowered in warning. "Hush." He placed a hand over my mouth. "You can tell me later." He wrapped a blanket about me and set off down the road, the wagon jostling and the horse tack jangling. When we were a good distance from the fort, Aiden spoke over his shoulder. "You overheard something from the healing house last night." It was a statement.

"Part of it." I crawled forward to sit beside him on the driver's bench. "A villain plots to take your wife and children because they are not Lansimetsian. And the same villain killed Galliard's family. But I'm the prince. I can stop him."

"Her," Aiden said.

"Her? A woman did this?"

Aiden didn't explain. Instead, he said, "Galliard will give you a tanning for leaving like that. Took us half the day to find out where you'd gone. And then he couldn't come get you himself—too dangerous. It took all my words to convince him of that. Yes, a villain killed his family. He's a wanted man for not dying with them. He'd have died for you, though. He talks about you like you were his little brother brought back to life."

Questions swirled in my head. Who did this? What happened? Why? I spoke one. "Who's her?"

"The Queen."

My questions clashed together in a thunderclap. My mother! They had to be mistaken. She couldn't have.

Aiden's deep voice rumbled through the storm in my head. "Now are you ready to stop pretending you're the prince?"

20

A MARK FOR COURAGE

YOSYPH

Long dark lines circled my left arm, starting at my shoulder and continuing to my elbow. Thorny lizards and a lion wove between sharp canyon walls and a maze of rocks. My mother had a similar tattoo running down her right arm, as had anyone who passed the King's Trial.

I sat on a stone outside Qadir's abode, the Devil's Teeth behind me and miles of grasslands surrounded by ridged obsidian cliffs before me. The black dots of herds, probably goats or sheep, maybe horses, milled about in the distance. Beyond what I could see, small villages and a large city nestled in this fertile haven in the middle of the desert. My mother's land. And I sat at the doorway.

Qadir was the keeper, both of the King's Doorway and the records of all who passed the King's Trial—chronicling it on paper and in skin. Needles and ink pots spread in a semicircle around me. The old man pricked the last of a lion's mane near my shoulder.

"The left," whistled Qadir through a gap in his teeth. "No one has ever passed the Devil's Teeth on the left. Not since the great sage, Akram, first created the King's Trial to test the courage of our people. Oh, many have tried, but they died."

"I would have died, too." I winced as he needled in the design of lava in red. The new ink reminded me all too much of the fire rock's sting.

"But the winds stopped your fall and lifted you to a safe shelf." His voice dropped to an awed whisper, though I'd told him my tale two days previous. I didn't blame him. What happened felt like a dream.

"My mother said God preserved me for a wise purpose. Will you help me?"

The old man harrumphed. "What do you think I'm doing? This tattoo, on your left arm, will admit you into the Council and give you the right to speak. They may even make you the head of the Council. They should, but I doubt Jarrah will willingly part with that power. Still, he's not the one you have to watch out for. It's Farid."

"Who is Farid?"

"He's the Honored Shadow Walker—as if there could be such a thing. I wouldn't trust him to come within a furlong of me."

His vehemence startled me. Naven had spoken of the Honored Shadow Walker with respectful tones. Why did Qadir distrust Farid? It was good I'd not mentioned my shadow ability, and that he'd not seemed to notice it.

"He's the one I must speak with." I sat taller.

Qadir hissed for me to stay still. "So you need him to kill the

Queen you've been talking about. You can ask, but you must be careful around him."

"Why?"

"He was your mother's guide through the King's Trial. And," he paused, lifting his eyebrows as if he found something amusing, "she refused his offer of marriage. Of course she did. No one would marry into that curse."

Ouch! No wonder I'd have to be careful about him. My mother's rejected suitor could be difficult to work with. I mentally ran through all I could say to convince him to teach me. Better yet, what if I could convince him to take out the Queen and her generals himself? That would be ideal. I'd not have to learn the "dreaded curse" of shadow walking, which could take years to learn. An experienced, honorable shadow walker could take care of it. And war would be averted.

"Why do they call it the King's Trial," I asked after an hour's quiet, "when the Kishkarish have never had a king?"

Qadir laughed. "You ask that like a foreigner. Tanyeshna didn't teach you much."

"We were slaves on a pirate ship," I said sharply, "and she died when I was seven. She taught me more than anyone could have hoped."

"I'm sorry," Qadir soothed, tracing along my forearm in ash, lines of wind pushing a figure upward. "You are right. She taught you enough to bring you through the reaches of the trial without a guide. That has never happened before. Your question. Why the King's Trial?" He paused in his ash drawing. "God is our king. This is His trial for those who seek to gain wisdom and draw closer to Him."

I closed my eyes and sent up a silent prayer. *Thank you for training me in the King's Trial. I hope I've learned to listen. Please let Farid help us stop this war. But if not, then please let him teach me.*

"Yosyph!"

I jerked open my eyes as Katrin ran across the stones, her turban trailing half off her, and a red braid banging against her shoulder. I stood and froze.

"So this is Katrin." Qadir grinned gap-toothed and pulled his ink pots to the side. It was good he did because Katrin didn't stop until she tumbled into me, wrapping her arms around my neck.

"Yosyph," she cried, breathless and flushed. "You're here! Naven promised you'd be, but you are really here!" She pulled back and touched my cheek where a line of stitches ran. "But what did you do? Are you hurt elsewhere?" She stepped back and looked me up and down, her eyes stopping for a moment on my tattooed arm.

"I'm unhurt."

She looked at me expectantly. What should I say? Should I tell her my feelings? What *were* my feelings for her? Finally, I settled on a safe response. "Have you and Naven decided yet where you will stay?"

"'Where I'll stay? Didn't you miss me at all?" Katrin huffed.

"You'd better hug that wildcat," Naven said in the desert language, coming up with our horses, "before she tears out your tongue."

"Losing his tongue wouldn't change him much." Katrin changed to speak in the rolling, lilting tones of my mother's language. She no longer halted on the words.

I laughed inwardly at the torrent of chatter Naven must have endured the last four days.

"He doesn't use it much," she continued.

I can speak with my hands, I signed.

She laced her fingers through mine, silencing my muttering, and turned to Qadir. "And you must be Qadir. Has old tight-mouth been civil to you?"

The man shook with silent laughter. "He's as cold as you are bright. My grandson needs a wife. If Naven hasn't already planned a husband for you, then I would be happy to have such a firebrand for a granddaughter."

I clenched my hands at his suggestion, and Katrin's hand responded in kind. She'd arrived moments ago, and he was already trying to arrange a marriage for her. I could almost hear the words she was about to bury Qadir with, none of them pleasant.

Before she spoke, Naven bowed to Qadir. "Honored Keeper of the King's Gate, Katrin is like a daughter to me. I will make sure she is well provided for and protected. But she is not used to our ways. Let's give her time."

Katrin grip loosened slightly. She wouldn't let herself be forced into anything.

But just the same, I was glad Naven was there to speak up for her.

21

I STOP PRETENDING TO BE A PRINCE

HALAVANT

I sat in the healing room. Outside the shuttered window, an owl hooted. We'd arrived back at Aiden's farm after dark, and I was exhausted from my day's imprisonment. Yet Aiden insisted I must be at this nighttime meeting with some mysterious person, probably that gray-mustached man from last night. So I sat in the healing room, blankets tucked around me, a steaming mug of tea in my hands, and hot rocks at my stockinged feet. A lamp in the middle of a small table lit the grim faces of Galliard and Aiden.

"What do we do with him?" Aiden asked. "Being crazy doesn't excuse the danger he puts us all in."

"I'm not crazy!" I huffed.

"He ran off to protect us. He has a good heart," Galliard said.

They talked over me like I wasn't there. Why did they even

want me at the meeting if they wouldn't listen to me? I yawned and snuggled deeper into the blankets.

"Galliard," Aiden replied, "you know the cost of a loose mouth."

"I'll not make him pay for another's sins. I'd first—" Galliard halted at a knock, a rapid pattern of shorts and longs.

Aiden opened the door.

I let out a shout as Lord Fredrick stepped over the threshold. He was the dusty-voiced lord who monopolized whole conversations at gala dinners with topics such as wheat weevils. I'd had my share of sitting near him. Twice was enough in a lifetime. What was he doing here?

"Boy!" Galliard grasped my arm as if he were afraid I'd faint. And perhaps I would have.

Lord Fredrick looked at me. Then his eyes widened, and his already sallow face blanched. He grasped the door frame. Aiden jumped to his side, helping him to a chair.

"They said you were ill." Fredrick beckoned me to come closer.

I sat next to him.

He reached out to touch my face, then pulled back. "What happened to you?"

"I went looking for Katrin." I leaned forward eagerly. "You recognize me?"

"You look more like your father than the boy that disappeared weeks ago."

"Fredrick," Galliard's voice rasped with tightness. "Who is this boy?"

Fredrick turned to the two standing men. "This boy is Prince Halavant, the rightful king of Lansimetsa."

Aiden's beard couldn't hide the rounded mouth of surprise. Galliard fell to his knees, grasping my hands in his and pressing his forehead against them.

"My liege," Galliard said.

"Get off your knees," I said with a laugh, "and will you please call me by my name." Now that he finally knew who I was, I could help him and Aiden and anyone else who needed me. Things would change.

Galliard stood, lifting me in the process, and deposited me on the bed. "You must rest and heal."

What? First he pledged his allegiance on bended knee, and the next moment, he was giving me an order. Not much of an obedient subject. I laughed. I didn't want him to become a fawning hypocrite. But neither would I be a puppet king.

"It is no laughing matter." Galliard glared at me. "You're not fully recovered, and today undid much of Lenora's work."

I stuck out my chin and folded my arms. "I won't sleep until you tell me what's happening!"

A look passed between Galliard, Aiden, and Fredrick.

Galliard laughed. "I suppose you haven't died yet. Let's get you comfortable, because this will be a long night."

After arranging pillows in a chair, cocooning me in blankets, and fussing over me like three mother hens, they finally sat down to talk.

"Your Highness," Lord Fredrick began, "what do you wish to know?"

"I want to know who is trying to take Aiden's wife and children. Who killed Galliard's family? And why? And don't you dare tell me it's my mother! She may be a cold and stern woman, but she is no murderer! There has to be another reason!"

"If you get worked up," Galliard laid a hand on my shoulder to keep me from standing, "we'll save this conversation for tomorrow."

It would be a long night if they wouldn't talk. I settled back in the chair and stared at them, daring them to keep quiet.

"Is he this stubborn at the palace?" Galliard asked Lord Fredrick.

"His Highness is being reserved. His travels have brought about needed growth."

"Traitor." But I secretly I felt glad at his comment.

"I'll start," Galliard said, turning to me. "It isn't a tale I care to tell. I am Jonas of Gatchenbrat."

I stifled a snort. Jonas! Mother's lapdog was named Jonas. No wonder he went by Galliard. Gatchenbrat? I'd heard their family name mentioned repeatedly in history, even mixed in with royalty. An old family. He was a noble, as much as Fredrick. Maybe even a distant cousin of mine.

Galliard raised an eyebrow.

"Sorry, carry on." I nestled further in the blankets, prepared for a long story.

"I was once eldest of four sons. Ten years ago, two of my brothers rose in rank until they reached the Queen's Elite guard. An honor for our family." His voice had dropped to stilted bitterness.

Why bitterness? The elite guard was a close-knit group of thirty men that Mother kept for addressing sensitive matters. What those matters were, I'd never asked, but I enjoyed fencing with them when they were around.

"Three months later, in the dead of night, my brothers slipped into the manor and dragged each of us from our beds. 'You have to leave now.' 'They might be here within the hour.' 'They'll kill you.' They stumbled over each other's words as they tried to get us to go. But our sweet mother," Galliard gripped the edge of the table, "was never one to be rushed anywhere. And I, the fool, wouldn't let them manhandle her out the door. So they told us that the Queen's Elite did nothing save carry out dark deeds: killing a duke who'd grown too powerful, poisoning a prying minister of state, silencing a dissident voice."

The words flooded over me, their weight keeping me from speaking. I wanted to come up for air, but Galliard continued.

"Mother still did not believe them. She thought they'd gotten tainted ale and needed to sleep it off. I listened to her and urged my brothers to go to bed. Even when my youngest brother," Galliard glanced at me, his eyes filled with sadness, "said we should listen to them."

"My brothers tried to convince us by sharing more details. They were not initiated immediately, but rather were pampered and praised and urged to indiscretions. Then, when thoroughly integrated into the Queen's Elite sociality, small favors were asked. Testify against a criminal so he could be accused even though they didn't know that he'd done any wrong, weaken the bowstring of a visiting lord so he wouldn't outshine the Queen in hunting. Small things that grew larger."

Stop! I wanted to yell.

"My brothers worked as a seamless team, and that made them doubly valuable. But when they were assigned to murder, they ran. They already knew the consequence of deserting. Not just for them, but their whole family."

Galliard glanced at me. I must have looked pale, for he grasped my hand. "You have no responsibility for what happened. I love you as a brother."

"But what happened?" I forced out the words.

"Eight of the Elite arrived before we could flee. My brothers entrusted our mother to my care, because I was no swordsman." Again his voice cracked with bitterness. "They held them off so we could escape. I should have stayed. Johnny should have gone. He was the youngest." Galliard swallowed hard. "What was left of them was strung up in the trees and the story spread that bandits had done it. Mother died broken two weeks later."

They were right. I should have gone to bed. My chest ached with tightness, my head with the whirlwind of questions. I'd wanted to know what happened to Galliard's family. Now I knew what was happening in mine. I kept asking questions, not waiting for them to answer. "What have you been doing the last ten years? Why hasn't someone revealed the Elite's corruption? How did Fredrick get pulled into it? Or Aiden?"

Over the questions my mind screamed, *my mother is a murderer!* No, she surely hadn't run another through with a sword or stuck a dagger in their gut. But she kept close to her elite guards. She'd talked warmly of how she could trust them to do anything she needed. She'd hinted at things I hadn't understood that now were clear. How many 'accidents' had she orchestrated?

I could hear her instructing me. *A ruler must be strong. Others will take advantage of one's weaknesses. Especially for me, as a woman. Never shy away from what must be done. You will make me proud someday.*

Is that what it meant to be a ruler? To kill those who threaten your power? To silence those who oppose you? To weaken the people of the land so your power is that much greater than theirs?

Never shy away from what must be done. Yes, Mother, I will do what must be done.

"I'll claim my right as king." I threw aside the blankets. "I cannot wait for my eighteenth birthday. My father reigned at sixteen and defended our country from the Carani. I can at least take my duty and right and stop further evils upon the land."

"My king." Lord Fredrick inclined his head. "For I will not call you prince again, I agree that you cannot wait for winter to claim your rule. But it will not be as easy as striding up to the throne and taking the crown from your mother's brow."

"But it's my right!" I sputtered.

"Right or not, you need those who will follow you to support you. She has more than her elite. She has generals who once were in her elite, barons and lords who benefit from her secret works, a huge army sworn to protect the crown, and she is the current ruler."

"But when the people know what's been happening, they'll place me as king despite the barons and lords and generals and..." I trailed off. That was a lot of despites.

"Most people are not eager to fight against their ruler," Aiden said, "even when faced with heavy burdens and injustice."

"It's always been that way," Lord Fredrick continued, his dry logic grating me. "If it were too easy for a people to rise against their monarch, then we'd live in constant anarchy. So the people live with high taxes, the possibility of offending the crown, and other difficulties—because the alternative is war and death."

"So, it will be difficult. I still must do something!"

Galliard put his hand on my shoulder to keep me from standing. "You are right, and we will help you. But there are things you must learn first." He studied my face. "You've earned my trust by your tirelessness in seeking your bride, and by not seeking to deceive me as to who you are, even though I never believed you."

I smiled at the gentle jibe.

He continued. "But that is just my trust. Up to this point, I've only told my story, and I am willing to risk my neck to help you see what is happening. This knowledge I will tell means that we trust you with the lives of Lansimetsa. Can you promise that you'll counsel with us and others who have experience and then act based on sound decision?"

I wasn't reckless! I clenched my jaw to retort, but memories of the last weeks shouted impolitely. I'd rushed off to find Katrin. I'd provoked the men that attacked me. I'd gotten myself arrested as a madman. I was ready to fight for the crown. Could I be trusted to think, counsel, and then act? But wasn't being a man of action part of being a king? Hadn't my father won a war because he'd not back down?

"I think you should have time to think about it," Galliard said. "The morning after tomorrow we'll answer your questions."

I started to protest, but a warning look from Galliard stopped me. Could I show them self-control in this small thing? I swallowed my words and nodded. I could wait. As soon as I thought those words, the heaviness of the day pushed against every inch of my being. I would have to sleep. I crawled into the bed of the healer's room. As sleep dulled my ears, I heard whispered voices.

"Do you trust him?" Aiden asked.

"I doubt not his honor nor his valor," Galliard whispered. "I trust him to fight for what he sees as right. If only we can stem his impulsiveness long enough for him to act like his father."

"Bless his soul," added Lord Fredrick.

22

KING'S BLOOD AND SHADOW'S CURSE

YOSYPH

A hiss woke me from my narrow pallet. I stretched out and touched the cool stone of Qadir's house. I could still feel the beat of the dance last night. Qadir and Naven had punctuated the air with flute and drums late into the night, while Katrin wove her body through the music and air, as beautiful and wild as a flame. I'd watched enthralled until she pulled me to my feet, and I'd provided the rigid counterpoint to her freedom.

"Wake up!" Qadir hissed again. I reluctantly opened my eyes to a gray pre-dawn visible through the open doorway.

"The Honorable Shadow Walker is here, and he wants to see you." Qadir's voice was a mix of contempt and fear.

What was Farid doing here? I threw on my outer robes, and Qadir gave me a firm push out the door. He did not follow. The pre-dawn washed out everything. I looked about for Farid but saw the only ink pots gathered on the ground, the scattered stones, the ridged cliffs, and a grassland stretching away.

Then a deep chuckle resonated to my left. I jerked my head around. A hand's reach away, the shadows formed into a man, wrapped in dark robes, taller than me and about as lean. His craggy face was clean-shaven, and his black hair curled at his neck. He smiled, and his figure took more substance.

A shiver ran down my spine. He hadn't been there a moment before.

"So, you are the reason my dreams are disturbed." He caught my left wrist and pushed up my sleeve. I tried to pull away, but his grip was like iron. He studied the tattoos, rotating my arm, his eyebrows rising higher.

I'd wanted to meet him. I needed his help. But I could hardly stop myself from recoiling.

"You took the left wall?" He released my wrist. "Come, I have much to teach you and not enough time."

"You'll teach me?" My need to follow him and be instructed fought with my instinct to run.

"You came to learn how to shadow walk, did you not?" His rich voice contrasted with his indeterminate form.

How did he know all this? What dreams had I disturbed? My eyes must have spoken my questions for he laughed again, bringing sharpness to his features, then sobered. "You remind me of someone, from long ago. She was also full of questions, though she spoke them, whereas you hold back."

"Do you know who I am?" I followed him to a rock as he sat down.

He watched me and waited. Did he know? If I didn't tell him and he found out later, it could destroy his trust in me. I pulled out my mother's letter and map once more. It seemed her words caused surprised acceptance to each of my desert brothers. What would the words do to my mother's rejected suitor?

He watched as I unrolled the parchment and handed it to him. His eyes scanned the words. His unreadable face became a mix of minute twitching: eyebrows, corners of the mouth, jaw. Nothing large, as if he caught at each emotion before it could betray what he felt. He read the letter, looked over the map, and read the letter again. Then he set it aside with a sigh.

"That is what happened to her." He didn't look up, and his voice caught on the words. "I wish it were otherwise." Then he looked up at me. "You are *his* son. It is God's judgment I should teach you. First, I must tell you who you are. Sit."

His son? I remained standing. I didn't come for a lesson in my lineage. "We don't have much time. I need your help to stop the Queen of Lansimetsa from destroying the land. I must return next week." I told him of the planned enslavement of all the foreign-blooded people in Lansimetsa.

Farid listened, again his face twitching. When I finished, he stood. "You need to know your heritage." He looked down at his hands for a long moment. "I loved your mother, but she wouldn't have me. Five years I persisted, before she ran off with that foreigner. I followed and found her married to him, and she was happy. But I couldn't leave it alone. I returned four years later, and she was gone, drowned at sea, the people said. Her husband had only searched for her for half a year before rushing into another marriage—to have an heir before he died of a bone-crippling illness. I could have brought him death sooner. I could have easily slipped into the palace and strangled him on his throne. But that would not have brought her back."

Throne? Palace? My hands flickered the words before I could still them.

Farid stopped and watched my hands and then my face. "It's been a long time since I taught her to speak with her hands." He paused again, watching me and giving my questions time to pull me into painful knots. I tried to control my features. I doubt I was as successful as the shadow walker. Finally, he nodded and spoke. "Your father was King Luukas. You are the heir and rightful ruler of Lansimetsa."

My legs gave out beneath me and I sat with a thump to the ground. *King!* Mother's letter said my father was dead. She described him as *honorable, kind, gentle, brave.* But she didn't tell me he was a king!

"At first, I didn't know who he was." Farid sat down beside me. "He never told us when he was a prisoner. And when I returned home after following him and your mother, I never told another. I was still too bitter to give any validity to her choice to go with him, so her name is still slandered. This secret is to my dishonor. But today, I will begin to cleanse myself of it as I teach you."

Thoughts formed in the turmoil in my mind. I was the son of a king. I was the rightful king. I could claim my right and end this war. My heart rose in hope and then sank again. But who would believe me? I had no way to prove it. A letter could be forged. The kingdom had forgotten their first queen. They didn't even know she was pregnant with a child when she was lost.

That must be why Mother never told me who my father was. What good would that knowledge be to a child slave on a pirate ship or to a poor orphan, other than getting him killed? Perhaps the pirates would have ransomed us, but for some reason, Mother didn't feel that was safe. Another question I'd never have answered.

That way is closed, I signed.

True, he signed back.

"Will you go with me and stop the enslavement?"

"It is your place and your heritage."

"There is not time to learn. Please come yourself."

Farid shook his head.

Please, I signed.

No, he signed, rising to his feet. *Let us start training.*

So much for my ability of persuasion. Even as indeterminate as he seemed, his 'no' stood solid. I still had to learn the way of the shadow walker and stop the coming war.

I sweated in the afternoon sun. Moving from one rock to another. Not sneaking, but walking, upright and level-headed.

"Larger strides," Farid barked. "Head up higher. A shadow walker is calm and assured. The emotion of sneaking gives you away. You may have gotten away with some things by sneaking, but you cannot enter the palace in front of guards and dogs by that."

I brought my head up and threw back my shoulders. We'd been at this for hours, and still I could do nothing right.

"No," Farid said, "anger will make you visible to even the distracted. Watch."

Farid stood and walked away from me. I watched him closely, taking in his whole person—his back straight, his head high, his stride purposeful, and his whole person a quiet confidence. As he walked, he melted into his surroundings. One moment a black-clad man, and the next only rocks.

Then his voice whispered by my ear.

I hated when he did that. I clenched my body to stop from jumping.

"You must calm your emotions, not hide them. Buried feelings bubble up like lava, hot and bright. You carry many emotions layered upon each other: anger, fear, grief, justice, hope, and love. Yet you must learn to let them flow out of you before you can shadow walk."

How? I signed. *How do I give them up? I've buried them my whole life. Do I stop feeling? Do I stop being human?*

Farid shook his head, "You do not understand. You do not stop being human. You feel intensely now, and you will feel intensely again. But you've always hidden your feelings, buried them deep. Now you must learn to *quawlaar*—to set them down, like a heavy pack, then take them up again."

Quawlaar? Not sever, but set down?

I pictured my mother and all those who had died because I couldn't save them, and the grief welled up. I saw Jack with his foreshortened fingers and shuddered. I pictured General Jonstone plotting, and the soldiers hanging yet another innocent, and anger boiled outward. I thought of the thousands that would die if I didn't learn to shadow walk, and fear shivered through me. I thought of Katrin, watching me intently from the rock, and heat rose to the tips of my fingers.

As each emotion flowed through me, I imagined draining it into an ink pot like the ones Qadir used and setting it to the side. Soon, I found myself surrounded by colors: anguished blue, fierce red, gangrene yellow, brilliant rose, and a slew of other colors. And I felt quiet inside. Cold and quiet.

I looked down at my hands and saw the ground through them. But I didn't feel surprised.

Farid nodded. "You did that faster than I expected. It took me two days to let my emotions flow out the first time, and only after trying for months."

Though my body shivered, I felt nothing. The colors glowed about me. Did I want them back? Wouldn't it be better to not feel? I could do what I needed to and not be distracted. And I'd never have to carry that weight again. Would I come out of the shadow?

“Yosyph.” Farid’s voice took on a commanding force. “Take back your emotions.”

Though I didn’t feel, my mind and my honor were still my own. I reached out for the glowing rose ink pot and poured it over me. I burst with warmth. I wanted to stop there. I could live with that emotion. But the one seemed to open the door for the others. They spilled at my feet. As the warm rose color flowed down, the weight of the others seeped through the soles of my feet and spread upward.

I collapsed to the ground and vomited. A storm of emotions swirled inside my body. I’d thought they’d go back to their hiding places, but each warred freely in my chest and head, darting in and out from my limbs. Anger, anguish, love, fear, duty ripped through me, shredding my skin and organs. My stomach cramped again. If I could drain them away again, I’d never take them back. But I was too weak. I curled up in a ball.

“Help him! Make it stop!” Katrin’s cry pierced the storm. Her arms encircled me and the emotions swirled faster.

“He must carry more weight than any man should.” Farid’s voice came as if from far away. A cool hand lifted my head. “Eat,” he commanded. “It will still them for a time.”

I turned my head away as my stomach spasmed. Farid forced my mouth open and pressed a berry into it. It burst and sweetness coated my tongue. My inner-storm eased. I lay panting in Katrin’s arms.

“Yosyph, Yosyph,” Katrin murmured in my ear, her voice trembling. “Please be all right.”

I tried to gather my strength and tell her I would be fine, but I couldn’t get a word between my teeth.

Farid sat down where I could see him without moving. “Forgive me, Yosyph. I didn’t think you could set all your emotions down on the first try, or I’d have prepared you better.”

I lay mute in Katrin’s arms.

"I'm afraid I burdened you with more emotions," Farid continued. "But I had to test you, see how much you ruled yourself by integrity and how much you allowed emotions to rule you."

I don't think I can shadow walk, I signed weakly. *If I let the emotions go again, I don't think I'll have the strength to take them back.*

That is a choice, Farid signed. *Though one cannot eat or sleep in the shadow. I'll teach you how to sort through the emotions so you don't have to take them all back, and how to put those you should have into their proper places.*

I closed my eyes. His words should have caused a tightness of worry and fear, but numbness from the berry blanketed me. I wanted to sleep.

"Rest now," Farid said. "I'll wake you when the mute-berry should wear off, and then you will be able to enter the shadow again." He added in warning, "You'll want to enter the shadow as soon as you can. When you can speak again, you'll also be fully aware of these emotions and that they are still untamed inside of you."

I shuddered. Even in the mute-berry's fog, his words brought fear to the surface. I would do anything to avoid that storm. Anything honorable. If I was strong enough.

23

HOW TO STEAL A CROWN?

HALAVANT

I thought after the exhaustion of being locked up in a dank cell, that late night meeting would have kept me asleep for a full day. The others expected it. If they knew of my insomnia, Lenora would have forced the bitter Monk's Sleep down my throat.

After sleeping part way into the morning, I woke, and sleep couldn't find its way through my worries and questions. I didn't want any medicine, so I pretended to be asleep whenever anyone entered the healer's room. There was too much I had to figure out before the meeting Galliard had mentioned. How could I claim the throne without bloodshed? It should have been as easy as claiming my right, but after Galliard's tale, I doubted it.

Why, Mother? What have you become? A parade of 'accidents' marched across my thoughts. The duke who'd openly questioned her, only to have the axle break on his carriage, crushing him in the rollover. *A pity,* she'd smiled. A new summer palace under construction on the former lands of a baron, whose whole family died of the dreaded *Yellow Illness*. Or could it have been poison? Mother—no, not mother—*the Queen* graciously accepted the heir-less land back to the custody of the crown. A fire destroyed a milliner's shop shortly after Mother broke out in a rash from a new hat. And Katrin disappeared after an argument with her. Was she dead, too? Oh, please don't let it be.

They expected me to rest? I tried to drown my worries by planning how I'd claim the crown. I rushed through a hundred plans, each more foolish than the last. I searched my memories for every fantastic story of heroics told by my nanny. I dredged up half-heard history lessons, especially the treasonous ones, where one ruler deposed another.

At last, the morning for answers came. Lenora reluctantly gave me clothes and strict instructions to rest as soon as we arrived wherever we were going.

I rode a swaybacked farm horse, not any smoother-trotting than the glue-bound horse from weeks ago, into the Wilderlands that bounded the northern edge of Aiden's farm. Galliard and Aiden rode a horse on either side of me, and any time I bounced particularly high, one of them held out a hand as if to steady me. I suppose I was still a little weak, but not that much. The hour's ride through tangled woods was tiresome more from anticipation than exertion.

We came upon a dense thicket of pines. Galliard led us under and between them. One branch whacked me in the chest, and I almost tumbled from my horse.

"Steady." Galliard caught my arm.

We emerged at the rim of a valley where thick pines

formed a wall around the entire edge. Thatched huts, blackened fire pits, and tents pocked the bottom. What was this place? Had Galliard been working to overthrow the Queen? It needed to happen, but I shuddered to think someone had already started such an uprising. What would have happened if I hadn't left the palace? Would I have been killed by the commoners storming my home? No. The Queen kept too strong of a force in the capital and across the land for such a thing to happen. But that brought me back to my troubled question. How was I to take the crown?

"Son." Galliard leaned over and pulled my straw hat lower over my face. "No one knows who you are other than Lord Fredrick, Aiden, and I. It may be wise to keep it that way."

"You want me to start lying now?" I whispered back.

"Don't go announcing anything yet."

I laughed and bit my lip.

About twenty picketed horses grazed outside a large tent. A man dressed in leather jerkin and breeches stood by the tent door. "You're late," he said. "They've been waiting an hour for you. And who's that?" He pointed a finger at me.

I supposed I was still a sight, with what he could see of my face under the low brim of the hat.

Galliard answered before I could speak. "I vouch for him."

The man shook his head and let us enter. A table made of planking set on stumps took up most of the tent and was edged with benches. Twenty or so men sat around it. I scooted next to Aiden in the middle of one bench. Lord Fredrick sat opposite me. The other men were a mix of nobles in fine hunting clothes and commoners in work clothes. One was the gray-mustached man from two nights ago, the one that had warned Aiden his wife and children would be taken.

Galliard stood at one end and looked over the table. The

hum of conversations stopped. "I know I'm not the man who should stand here. It should be the Yorel—"

I leaped to my feet. "You've stooped to work with that criminal!" I'd heard the stories: people disappearing, whole families killed, an inky demon that no one could catch.

A clamor of voices erupted.

"How dare you insult..."

"—not a criminal, he saved my son—"

"Where is the Yorel, we—"

"Quiet." Galliard's voice took on a level of command that I'd not heard before. The room silenced. He looked to me. "This is one thing you need to learn, so listen quietly. The Yorel is the reason we have any chance to free our land."

The world was turning upside down. The Queen a criminal, and the murderous Yorel a hero? I sank back to my seat, swallowing further questions.

Galliard let his eyes rest on each person at the table. "I never planned to lead the Yorel's army against the throne. It should have been him, or at least Robalon. But the Yorel is doing what only he can do, and Robalon is dead. So this duty falls to me. May God bless our efforts."

A plump noble raised a tentative hand. "Jonas—I mean, Galliard—you are a good man, and I don't doubt you would lead us well. But why do we gather the army now? Why not wait for the Yorel to return?"

"Because," Galliard said, "after the last harvest, a horrible cleansing will sweep the land. All who reported foreign blood on the census will be sent to slave in the mines."

I grasped Aiden's hand and felt the taut tendons. "Lenora and the children!"

He shook his head for me to be silent.

"They can't do that!" a man in a butcher's smock bellowed. He bore the dark skin of at least part desert descent. "How could the Queen's Army imprison a third of the people? Our villages and towns will rise against it. Our soldiers will revolt against the command."

"That is why we are gathering the Yorel's army now," Galliard said. "But we cannot depend on many to stand at our side. Most already view their so-called impure neighbors with suspicion. Haven't you noticed the bias of the traveling minstrels and play-actors these last years? What do they show and sing?"

Galliard began to sing a popular song. His tenor voice carried through the tent.

> I had a sweetheart, pure of blood.
> But never will I see her more.
> For the Truvian cur captured her heart
> And left her flesh to feed the sea.

I hummed along and then stopped myself. It was a lyrical piece from a tragic tale, performed for the court this spring.

Galliard swapped to a rousing march, one sung with vigor by the troops.

> We are Lansimetsa, true-blooded and pure.
> We march for our wives, our children, our lands.
>
> We make no brother pact
> With dusky-skinned desert fiends
> No marriage with the vixen-eyed Truvian
> No northern giant will mar our lands
>
> We are Lansimetsa, true-blooded and pure.
> We march for our wives, our children, our lands.

I'd heard the song daily as the men marched out to duty. I'd whistled it without thinking about what it said. But it had influenced me. Lenora, the healer woman, was the first Truvian I'd taken time to know as a person. And before her? I cringed. All my courtly courtesy disappeared around those of other races. What a fool I'd been. How many others were, too?

"What are we to do?" a noble with a pheasant feather in his red hat whimpered. "Half my servants and surfs have foreign blood. It would ruin me."

"And that's all you care about?" roared the dusky butcher.

"Quiet." Galliard rapped the table. The men swallowed their words, and silence settled over the table again. Galliard turned to the gray-mustached man. "Devron, tell them about the army. They deserve that hope."

Devron swallowed. "But it isn't for certain."

Galliard raised his eyebrows. "Have you ever known the Yorel not carry out his promise?"

I barely caught the muttered "yes." This Devron must know the Yorel personally, and he wasn't as starry-eyed about him as the rest of them seemed to be.

"Tell them," Galliard quietly ordered.

"The Yorel is gathering a desert army to help us fight," said Devron.

A desert army? They were bloodthirsty fiends that showed no mercy in battle. We couldn't fight beside them. Fiends? I shook my head. How much of what I believed stemmed from prejudice, and how much was actually true?

"When?" several voices called out.

"He hopes to be back before the end of the last harvest. It is still a month away. I pray that he will be back long before then."

"Then we are saved!" the pheasant feathered noble cried. "We can all go home and wait for this army."

"No, we can't," Galliard said. "As Devron mentioned, this isn't certain. And even with an army from the desert, we must fight beside them. We must prepare so we can fight as soon as the Yorel sends word. And if we don't get word, we must fight anyway."

"She'll massacre us." The pheasant feathered noble trembled. "We have no soldiers. We have little in the way of weapons. She's made sure over the years that everything is *regulated* by her army."

I was ready to grab this noble by his trembling lip and throw him from the tent. If he had noble blood, it was too thin.

"We have an army and a standard for them to follow." Galliard's voice carried through the tent. "For years, I've traveled under the guise of an itinerant laborer, helping build hidden nests of rebels and reserves of arms, carrying messages from the Yorel. We have an army of men who go about their everyday life but are ready at a day's notice to form and march. Only Devron knows more about the Yorel's plans than I."

"And I am no leader." Devron pulled his straw hat lower over his eyes.

"It should have been Robalon," muttered the dusky butcher.

"Aye, it should have been a lot of things," Galliard said. "But we must work with what we have, not what we should have. And today we have a further advantage." He paused and let silence settle. "Prince Halavant has joined our cause and will be a standard for the people to follow. Many people are still loyal to the memory of the king and will follow his heir. He is a good man."

I steeled myself for their response. After everything they'd endured through the Queen, how would they feel toward me?

One peasant leaped to his feet. He was a wiry man with a mop of orange hair hanging around his eyes. He gripped the table. "Perfect." the man's voice rose in wild hope. "Why do we talk of war when we have the key to change everything by peace? We have the prince, the heir to the throne. We write the Queen that we are holding her son ransom, and unless she changes the laws and gives into our wishes, we will kill her son. She must have some motherly love left in her. She will have to give in."

I shuddered.

"A brilliant plan, but it has a fatal flaw," said an ancient man, his wrinkles accentuating the irony in his voice. "It has been used before. The king of my father's land paid the ransom, got his son back, then punished all the people, driving them into the ground. A quarter of the people were massacred. If she is willing to send a third of us to the mines, I don't see why she wouldn't kill that many."

Silence filled the tent, enough so I could hear the pounding of hooves racing toward the tent, then voices.

"Halt."

"Let me pass!"

Galliard threw open the tent flap. A horse skittered to a stop as the man leaned back on the reins. The tent guard grabbed his foot and pulled him from his horse.

"Let him up," Galliard ordered. "What message is so important that you speak before you dismount?"

The man pushed himself to stand. "The town crier announced that all who reported foreign ancestry on the census must register at the nearest fort on the last day of this month."

That was only ten days away! We had to hide the people. But how do you hide thousands of people? We had to fight. But how could we when we only had a scattering of farmers and merchants and cowardly nobles to fight against trained soldiers with weapons and defenses? A storm of voices, crying out similar questions and worries, swirled about the table.

My mother enslaving our own people? It would have been less bitter if we'd fallen to the Carani when my father was king. If only they would attack again. The royal armies would be forced to turn against the enemy and leave our own people in peace. What if they did? I glanced at Fredrick's right hand. He wore his signet ring. For once, one of my crazy plans didn't seem so crazy. This could work.

"What if the Carani attacked again?" I said.

The storm of voices continued, but Galliard turned to me. "What did you say?"

"What if the Carani attacked again?" I shouted.

Sounds of surprise popped around the table.

"What has that to do with the cost of wool?" Devron asked. "And why should they?"

I gulped and rushed on.

"Lord Fredrick could send letters sealed with his signet, stating that the Carani are attacking along the western coast. He has an estate there, so it would be realistic for him to call for help. And a Carani attack should attract the help of a significant portion of the Queen's Army. They almost overran us last time. If we sent men to make it appear there was an actual invasion, then we could draw a portion of the Queen's Army away, at least from the West, perhaps even from the capital city."

A murmur rippled through the room.

"Who are you?" asked the pudgy noble.

"He is the future king of Lansimetsa." Lord Fredrick spoke for the first time.

If I'd felt noticed before, now I felt the weight of forty eyes. My anonymity evaporated. The murmurs deepened.

"I am Prince Halavant," I said, surprised that my voice didn't shake, "and I will fight beside you. We must not wait a moment longer."

24

PRIDE GOES BEFORE THE DARKNESS

YOSYPH

I lay in cold stillness. I sometimes stayed in the *quawlaar'd* shadow until the sun moved halfway across the sky. But three things always pulled me back: Katrin's soft whisper, "please come back into the light;" my duty to Lansimetsa; and the knowledge that if I stayed in the shadow, I'd die. And so I tried to pull back a tiny part of the muddy storm. Instead, the emotions flooded me. And in spasming pain, I cursed the moment that I'd ever tried to *quawlaar* or shadow walk. Then more mute-berry and sleep. Ad nauseam.

I'd not spoken a word in two days, my hands shook with the effort to sign, and I could no longer sit.

Farid woke me from yet another sleep. "I have been praying and pondering what to do. We must carry our sorrow as well as our joy. But we can give part of the weight to God. For all your courage, you seem to have little faith to trust your burden to God. Has the storm humbled you enough?"

Humbled? I lay helpless. Was that not humbled? It was true, I had not turned to God for help. How had I forgotten? I could trust God to help me sort through my emotions and bring them to order. To strengthen me as He had in the Devil's Teeth.

"Look," Farid commanded.

I focused my blurring eyes on him.

Farid slowly signed, *Give your burden to God and He will give back the portion you should bear.*

As the mute-berry began to wear off, I spasmed in pain, then *quawlaar'd*. The emotions poured from me as from a ripped water sack. Cold silence mixed with my aching body. I lay surrounded by a muddy brown of boiling emotions. The love and hate, hope and anguish were no longer distinguishable.

Please, God, I pled in the silence, *help me be strong enough to carry this burden. Help me sort through them and put them in their proper place.*

Nothing happened. The brown storm of emotions boiled around me as before. I closed my eyes and let the coldness envelop me. I would die here. It was a fact. I couldn't eat while visible. I'd tried. My stomach spasmed with the effort, and even in the mute-berry state I couldn't keep anything down. I couldn't eat when in the shadow walker state. I'd tried that, too, and found Farid correct. I knew I should feel sorrow for the thousands of Lansimetsians who would die. I didn't. The shadow deepened, and I felt as if I were dissolving into it.

My mother's words whispered through my mind. *God preserved you for a great purpose. Keep close to Him, and He will keep you.*

I've tried. I don't have any more strength.

Then let me carry this burden with you. This quiet thought was not from a memory. I opened my mind to the thought. Could God help carry my burden? Is that what Farid meant? I fingered the thin tendrils that kept the boiling emotions tethered to me and let go. The shadow crashed over me like a wave, and I sank into darkness.

At the moment I thought I'd disappear, I felt an emotion, but not my own. A feeling of peace warmed the coldness, then the glows of separate colors swirled about me. I reached out, trembling with the effort, and they slipped one by one through my fingertips and flowed into my chest. A weight and a realness. And suffusing it all—peace.

"Yosyph." Katrin touched my cheek. "You're back."

"You can eat more than that." Katrin coaxed, holding out a spoon of foño. She'd fill me to popping if she had her way. She continued to remind me I was pallid, but after a day of rest, I felt lighter than I ever had before. How had I carried that mass of emotions? I closed my eyes to enjoy the first rays of the rising sun.

The spoon of foño found its way into my mouth, and I choked on a laugh. I'd have to watch myself, or I'd develop a paunch.

"Are you going to share your joke?" Katrin asked, as I pushed away her proffered spoon.

"I'm afraid if you keep feeding me I'll not be able to climb stairs, let alone walls. It's time for me to train."

"Training." Katrin pouted. "You almost died training. Who needs you to learn to shadow walk? Why can't Farid stop the war?"

"I must. Thousands depend on me. You supported me as I went through the King's Trial. Will you support me again?"

She rolled her eyes. "You better not die. And don't you dare stay for more than a few minutes in the shadow."

I hadn't *quawlaar'd* since yesterday's blessing of peace, and I was hesitant to try. But it was time. I walked over to where Farid sat against the canyon wall.

He nodded for me to sit by him. "Are you determined to continue learning?"

"I must, unless you come to end this war yourself."

He studied my face. I didn't bury any emotions but let the peace and determination sit clearly in my features. Then he signed, *To end the war you must learn three lessons. We leave at first light tomorrow.*

So soon? I signed.

I've had another dream. If we wait any longer it will be too late, he signed back.

"Lesson one," Farid led me down a steep trail to the grasslands. "Deeds done in the shadow don't have strong emotions connected to them, even when you let the emotions back. One can do horrible things in the shadow and not have the consequent emotions. That is why I tested you and questioned Katrin so long. I wanted to know if you placed your honor above all else."

He knelt down and parted the grass. A brown bird sat puffed out on a nest, and cheeping rose from beneath her wings. "If I asked you to break the neck of this mother bird, then smash her chicks, you could easily do it. But I doubt you'd want to. Your emotions would hold you back. However, if you were in the shadow, would you do it?"

"I would never do that," I said, surprised he'd even ask. "Life is too precious to destroy without reason."

"Enter the shadow and do it," Farid ordered. "You must know how it feels to kill and not have the emotion afterward."

I stepped back from Farid and the nest, horror rising in my chest.

"If you cannot do this thing, I'll not teach you more."

The mother bird kept her bright eyes on us, and a tremolo of warning rising from her throat, but she would not leave her chicks.

If this was part of the training, then no wonder most of the shadow walkers turned to darkness.

I turned to Farid. "I will not senselessly kill."

Farid raised his eyebrows and disappeared. The mother bird squawked as her neck twisted about. I dove for where Farid must be. An elbow struck me in my gut. I grunted, swung my arm, and hit his head. The bird dropped to the ground and lay limp. Something hooked my foot, and I tumbled to the ground.

"Stop it!" Katrin's scream sounded off to my right, a good distance away. Her steps pounded down the steep path. A fist hit my shoulder and another my chin. I swung at my invisible adversary and met nothing. A weight on my legs kept me from rising while a fist pummeled my stomach. I swung my fist as I tried to inhale. This was the honorable Farid? Qadir had reason for his distrust.

"Disappear!" Katrin shrieked.

I saw her at the edge of my vision, only a stone's throw away.

After days of repeatedly *quawlaar'ing*, it took the simple thought, and my emotions rushed from me. Now we were both in the shadow. But he was no longer completely invisible, or rather, he was, but his emotions glowed about him like fireflies, giving an indistinct outline of where he was. I had one, too, for more blows rained down on me. In the cold of the shadow, I didn't feel anger over him killing the mother bird nor betrayal at his blows, but I knew what he did was wrong.

I blocked a blow to my head and landed one to his midsection. The firefly glow leaped away from me and raced toward Katrin. If he'd kill the bird for a lesson, what would he do to Katrin? She would not be another victim of his teaching.

I leaped after him and brought him down in a smooth tackle. No panic blurred my thoughts. My hands found his throat and squeezed. His hands gripped my wrists, trying to wrest them away. As his hands' struggle grew weaker, I let go. Farid's gasping breaths and coughing pushed waves of air past my face.

I pulled my emotions back in, and they settled into their places. I stood and stepped back. The yellow grass lay flattened under the shadow of Farid. Katrin skittered to a stop, a fist-sized stone in one hand and her eyes flaming. She looked at the flattened grass and then at me and dropped the stone.

"You're hurt." She touched my cheek and chin.

"I'm not really," I said as I realized that none of the blows landed with full force. I'd felt his iron grip on the first day and nothing of that power landed on me. He should have been able to wrest my hands from his neck. But he didn't. What was he trying to teach me?

I knelt by where Farid must be. A hand snatched my wrist and twisted it. I jerked back. Farid appeared sitting on the grass, holding my wrist and looking grim.

"Lesson one," he coughed between words. "What you do in the shadow does not carry the emotion back into the light."

"You're insane." Katrin picked up the stone that she'd let drop.

"I could have killed you," I said to Farid, taking Katrin's stone-grasping hand in mine.

"You thought you could have killed me," Farid amended. "Which is enough to produce strong emotions. Do you feel those?"

I searched inside of me. I felt the anger over the bird and

betrayal at his attack, but that was the extent of my emotions. There was none of the terror or sickness that always accompanied the times I'd killed a man in defense.

"I commend you for your honor with the bird." Farid rubbed his neck. "I didn't know which way you'd go with my command. If you'd killed it, you'd still have learned this lesson, but I believe this way was better."

"I hate your lessons," Katrin muttered, as I pulled the stone from her grasp.

I had to agree.

"Lesson two," Farid said, as we sat down to a mid-day meal of bird. I couldn't stomach it, though it needed to be used for food so it would not be a senseless killing. Katrin brought out foño and goat meat she and Naven had prepared. The four of us now camped a good distance from Qadir's abode. Ever since Qadir found out I was a shadow walker, he'd shunned both Farid and me. Katrin and Naven followed us.

Katrin kept watch over me like a hawk. She was like banked coals, ready to flare up with the slightest wind. Farid may not have been in danger from me this morning, but Katrin could have rendered him unconscious with that stone. Who was the protector now?

Thank you, God, for this food, I signed before eating. *Please protect Katrin and keep her free. And thank you for Farid's instruction, though I don't know how much I trust him now.*

"Lesson two," Farid chuckled lightly, "is not about how much you can trust me. Though all I have done or will do is for a purpose and will help you in your goal to free your father's land. You can trust that. Lesson two is on faith, which is not all that different from trust. What kind of faith do you have in God?"

I turned my thoughts back to the Devil's Teeth and the training to *quawlaar*. Both times, I had to trust the impression I'd received and let go. Both times, I would have died if I hadn't listened, though it felt like I'd die by following the impression. "Is faith to heed God's counsel, knowing He will save me if I do?"

Farid nodded. "Most people say that if they have enough faith, then God will do what they want, save the life of a loved one, heal an illness—even free a kingdom. And that is false. So your answer is better than most. Still, it is not right."

"It's the second part that isn't correct." I tried to figure out how to say what was vaguely forming in my mind. "My faith is to trust God and follow the path He sets for me. But that doesn't mean he will always *save* me. I could still die, even following the impressions from Him."

"And why do you trust God, if it isn't the trust that He will keep you alive or help you in the way you desperately need?"

"I don't know. Maybe because my mother trusted Him, though she died much too young. Maybe out of this honor you talk about. Maybe because it is right."

"This lesson is much too long for the time we have. One day, you will want to study this more. For now, I'd recommend you trust God because you know Him to be good, loving, and just, and that He will do nothing but that which will bless you and those around you, even if that means trials. It's a bit like the training this morning. You hated the teaching, but you learned a valuable lesson. My motives are good, though I'm faulty in my methods. God is perfect in both."

"And why is this lesson two?" I asked.

"Because you'll likely have impressions to do things that go counter to what you've planned. Do you hold to your pride and keep going your way? Or do you listen and change your plans? The choice often isn't between life and death, and so it will be easier to ignore. You need to learn to listen and act."

He pushed his right sleeve up to his shoulder, revealing the familiar tattoos of the King's Trial and beneath them, taut red scars, the garish echoes of deep burning. "And even then, sometimes you may never understand why. What kind of faith do you have in God?"

"Lesson three."

I paused at the top of my thirtieth push-up. The afternoon sun bore down on my bare shoulders and made my palms slick against the stone. My legs burned from sprints and leaps. Before the weakness brought on by the shadow training, I'd have done a hundred push-ups and run for hours. But in my weakened state, Farid could have easily ripped my hands from his throat. He could have anyway. He had strength beyond the normal man, even with the pain of scarring. Still, I had to regain my strength and stamina for the work ahead.

"Don't stop." Farid put slight pressure on my back, making it that much harder. "Ten more while I tell you about your grandfather. When you finish those ten, then you can rest."

I grunted as I lowered my body and prepared to push up again.

"His Kishkarish grandfather?" Katrin lay a damp cloth across the back of my neck.

"No. His Lansimetsian grandfather."

"You know who his father is?" Katrin asked.

I hadn't told her that my father was the king. I hadn't even thought about it since the time I'd decided it wouldn't make any difference in what was coming. I forced my way through another push-up, my arms shaking, about to give out.

"He didn't tell you?" Farid looked from Katrin to me. "She'll learn sometime. But if you'd rather, I can tell this story in the privacy of the shadow so she can't follow us."

Katrin tackled me, grasping me about the middle. I dropped flat. "No!" she said. "You're not going anywhere without me."

"It's all right." My voice muffled against the stone. "You can tell it here."

"Yosyph's grandfather is Edvard, and his father is Luukas. Both were, in their time, king of Lansimetsa."

Katrin's hold on me loosened, and she tumbled off to my side. I turned my head and choked down a laugh. Her face was a mixture of surprise, disbelief, and anger.

"And you didn't consider that important!" she raged, thumping me on the back.

"I didn't even know until Farid told me," I tried to explain.

"Did he tell you that first day? That was three days ago!"

"I'm sorry," I said, not sure if those were the right words to still her firestorm.

"You better be! This changes everything! Didn't you think? You are older than Halavant, and thus the rightful King of Lansimetsa! Go back and take the responsibility that is yours. You don't have to learn to shadow walk. You don't have to risk killing yourself again and again!"

"There's no way to prove it," I said.

Those words stopped her. Her face lost its enraged color, and she sat back on her heels.

"Fine." She thumped me once more on the back, though this time it was only half-hearted. "But you still should have told me. I thought we didn't keep secrets from each other."

I tried not to think of the secret that I'd leave tomorrow with the first light. I didn't know if she'd try to follow me. She'd become protective of me since I started shadow training. Fussing over me and fuming at Farid. She'd hate me for leaving without a goodbye. I rolled over and sat beside her. I hoped she didn't hate me for too long.

Katrin's face brightened. "Do you know what this means? You are Halavant's older brother! You have to protect him."

We were brothers? Two men who were nothing alike—brothers! I doubted that the prince would want to have anything to do with me. I was set to destroy the monarchy, and I'd taken Katrin away to a distant land. And if he was part of the crown's corruption, I would bring him to justice along with the others. For Katrin's sake, I hoped he wasn't.

Farid sat beside us. "When your grandfather was king of Lansimetsa, the Carani attacked, and the war cost the lives of tens of thousands. Your grandfather asked the help of the neighboring lands. Lansimetsa is a fertile land of fields, crops, orchards, and vineyards. It's the most fertile that I know. But that is all of its riches. It has no mines, no other resources that could buy the help of others. So your grandfather didn't ask the help of the rulers, but of the common people, promising them land for their service in battle. And they came, seeking a better life, many fighting and dying, and many others surviving to marry and raise families. When the Carani attacked again in the first year of your father's reign, he used the same tactics as your grandfather. And thus Lansimetsa became a mix of many people."

"And that is what the Queen is trying to destroy," I said.

"Yes, it seems to be. Often people are afraid of what is different from them. And so they hate it, and they teach their children to hate it. Prejudice is a powerful mask for fear."

"Lesson number three is that I must be careful of prejudice?"

"That was not lesson number three. This is." Farid scooped water with his cupped hands from a water jar. "Where is the hole for the water I removed?"

"There isn't any." Where was this lesson going?

"But I removed water. Shouldn't there be a hole?"

"Other water flowed in to fill that space," I said.

"What will happen if you kill the Queen?"

I understand, I signed. "If I kill the Queen, then another will fill her spot. The prince is still too young and some other regent with a love for power would grab the throne. Perhaps General Jonstone or an astute duke. But if left to chance, it will most likely be someone that will be as bad. The same water filling in the hole. I must not only remove the source of misery for my country but also help fill the leadership role with someone who will heal the land."

Farid put his hand back into the water, cupping it around the water, but not removing it, just separating part of the water from the rest. "Another question. How will you remove those people? Kill, sell into slavery, imprison?"

"I want them brought to justice. If I kill the Queen, then she may become an object of pity. But if she's brought to trial and judged of the people, then she becomes a lesson in tyranny, as would any of the others who have committed such crimes against the people."

"And what will stop the people from killing all of the noble blood, your brother included?" Farid picked up a stone, and with the speed of a snake striking, shattered the water jar.

Water spread over the stone ground. "Often revolution ends in anarchy, and there is nothing left to hold a country together. The people go from terror to terror until they beg for another powerful leader, and then tyranny starts again. What will you do to stop that cycle?"

25

SQUATTING FROG PRACTICE

HALAVANT

I didn't know how anyone could be a general or even a captain of men. I barely held myself together as I watched fifty men embrace their families—a husband's gentle kiss to his wife, a son nestled into the teary embrace of a mother, a young man telling his sweetheart not to worry—before finally watching them gallop westward.

It had only been two days since the meeting in the woods, and those men—architects, bridge makers and ditch diggers—volunteered to build facades of war on the western shore. We now had only eight days to detour at least some of the Queen's Army from the registration of all foreign blooded and most likely imprisonment. Two more days, and official letters from Lord Fredrick would be delivered to all forts between here and the capital, letters pleading for help against a Carani invasion.

I wanted to give the facade builders more time, but the longer we waited to inform the Queen's Army of the invasion, the less time we had before the registration to stop the enslavement. At least these builders rode horses, while the Queen's Army would be marching. It would work, if the Queen's spies didn't get there first and see it was all a facade. So many ifs. It was insane. Yet these men went.

Lenora's story of the moaning wounded and the piles of dead sat sullenly in the back of my thoughts. How did my father lead in war?

I saluted the last two men as they galloped into the dusk, then fled to the trampled practice ground on one side of this hidden valley. I picked up my sword, the leather grip still damp with sweat, and lost myself in the familiar patterns of first position, second. We would make this plan work, make their sacrifice worth it.

How much havoc could one lie cause? The news of the invasion spread like wildfire. One day after messengers delivered the message, those same messengers raced back to report that the Queen's Army was mobilizing. Not a small part of the army, nor some spies to double check if the report was real, but half the army.

I grinned at the response. That was far better than I'd expected.

"We're lucky," I said to Galliard. I sat beside him in his tent, looking over a diagram of the palace. It was a shoddy representation, drawn by a kitchen drudge who'd joined our cause. I inked in corridors and rooms.

"I don't know about that." Galliard scratched the back of his neck. "Seems too good. They shouldn't have sent out so large of a force without verifying the attack first. Especially as they were supposed to be rounding up all the partial-blooded in less than a week."

"Maybe they considered the attack more important than gathering up poor Lansimetsians." I scribbled in an underground passageway between the stables and a cellar. I'd used it more than once to sneak out. "They've been training for a Carani attack since before I was born. They could always play slave driver later." A smile spread across my face. "They'll never get the chance."

"I can only hope. If so, this will give us more advantage than we'd planned. I sent a rider to warn our builders. They'll have no chance against this large of a force. They'll have to abandon the facade, but it will still buy us enough time."

It would. The roads grew crowded, as at first a few soldiers, and then hundreds, marched westward, boasting: *The Carani are back, and Lansimetsa will beat them to the ground.*

I stepped from Galliard's tent and stumbled over the Poet, a gray-eyed dreamer and self-appointed chronicler of, as he called it, "*The Rise of the King.*"

"Listen, my liege." He caught my sleeve. "This will inspire the men."

I stopped myself from laughing. A middle-aged rural noble, he'd been educated in the great works but lacked social graces. No one at court would have dared snatch my sleeve.

He didn't seem to notice my bemusement as he read from a scroll. "The armies of the tyrant have marched off to fight the Carani. But when they get there, they will find it but a mist of ghosts and noise. Little do they know, when they return the true king will sit upon the throne.

"The soldiers left behind think we support them as we help build fortifications around our villages. A unity permeates the air. But under this unity, whispered watchwords pass from mouth to mouth. A butcher gathers his wares and goes off to protect his dear old mother in a neighboring town. No one notices that he disappears along the way. The blacksmiths make weapons for the soldiers all day and make plows into swords for the farmers at night. Men go into the forest to chop trees for pickets around their town and learn the fine arts of sword-play before returning with full carts of slender trees.

"Though it has only been five days since the young King Halavant revealed himself—"

I laid my hand across his paper to stop his recitation. "I'm not king yet, and if we are going to win this war, I must go help teach that sword-skill you so eloquently write about. You should come learn."

He bowed. "Yes, my liege, but if you will allow me to first present you with a gift: the finest parchment and blackest coal stick. When you need a diversion from your kingly duties, you might enjoy sketching." He offered a small, square book of papers and a cloth-wrapped coal stick. It fit inside my palm, nothing big enough for even the simplest picture, but I bowed my thanks and tucked it into my jerkin.

The Poet would do better to pick up a sword than a pen. He couldn't even hold his sword when another struck it. I'd only had a few days to teach these men, and too little time left before we must march to take advantage of this window. Maybe we could still avert the war, if we showed enough force, and the people knew I was leading this army—the King's Army, as the men called it—maybe we could change the power peacefully.

Not that I made any of these decisions on my own. They called it the King's Army, but I wasn't leading it. *Stockpile swords and speak softly.* The odd saying muttered by a fire-blackened smith made sense. There wasn't time for me to learn the intricacies of the web of men and plans that had been refined over years. So I sat in on meetings, spoke too often and tried to listen more, and once in a while offered an idea that was useful. Mostly, I taught swordsmanship.

I strode to the trampled training ground. About a hundred peasants whacked at each other with sticks, their enthusiasm far exceeding their skill, and their perspiration driving off any wildlife. When Galliard said they had *an army of men who go about their everyday life but are ready at a day's notice to form and march*, I saw now why he didn't add *and fight*.

"Men," I shouted.

Most of the hundred lowered their sticks, but a few took the opportunity to steal in a last blow.

"Quit it, ye scoundrel!" a burly middle-aged man growled at a younger copy of himself. He rubbed his rump where the blow had landed.

I stifled a laugh. I was supposed to be their esteemed sword-fighting master, but I would fit better as one of the prank-pulling youth.

"Basic position." I showed them the simple stance of legs spread wider than shoulders, one foot forward. The men jumped into approximate stances.

"We still look like squatting frogs," a nasal voice mocked.

"Sir Squatting Frog." I pointed in the general direction that the voice came from. "You get to be my sparring partner this morning."

That won guffaws from the others, but the man who stepped forward glowered at me. He was a slight man, old enough to be my grandfather. His tailor's apron held several needles. What was he doing here? Much too old to fight.

"I'm sorry. I didn't realize," I stumbled. "I'll choose a different partner."

"No," the man responded. "You'll not cheat me of the chance to fight someone who knows what he's doing."

I glanced longingly at the archery range. That teacher had a far easier job, as most of these men had hunted with bow and arrow since they were boys. Arrow after arrow poured into the hand-width circles on the tree trunks.

A sharp rap to my knuckles brought me back to the man before me. He stood in first position—*squatting frog position*—with a rather pleased look on his face. This would be a long practice.

"How I wish I could spar with Galliard," I muttered as I led the men in overhand, backhand, thrust. But Galliard was always tied up in meetings and planning. The King's Army, in this hidden valley, had grown to five hundred as many came from the west. Hundreds more were gathering in small groups along the way to Fairhaven, ready to join up as the King's Army marched by. The organization of so many small groups puzzled and amazed me. How did Galliard keep them all straight, and how had the Yorel kept them from the Queen's knowledge?

Galliard strode up to me as I excused the men from their practice. "How are they doing?"

"I wish I had a year more to train them, or at least a month."

"Wishes and horses, and a year to ride them."

Galliard and his sayings. I let a wry smile break my scowl.

Galliard put his hand on my shoulder. "How are you doing?"

His touch pulled to surface the question that I'd buried deeper with each day. "I don't know what I'll do when I face my mother."

"I'll be beside you when you do." He drew his sword. "A bout of swordplay before we march tonight?"

I vented my fear into my swings, and soon Galliard lay panting and laughing on the ground. "Don't injure me too much. I still have to lead the men. And you do, too."

Aiden held Lenora in his arms, and his children clung to him. I turned away, only to be met by similar scenes around the camp. Those of foreign blood brought their families here and to a hundred other hiding places throughout the Wilderlands.

Let the Queen's soldiers think the people were scared of the Carani invasion and going into hiding. So far, those gossiped words satisfied the remainder of her soldiers, not that they paid much attention to anyone other than those helping to reinforce their fort. They were scared, too.

If we didn't stop the enslavement, then at least it would be difficult for them to find anyone to enslave. But we would succeed and when I was king, I would repair the wrongs done to my people. They'd get their families back, even if I didn't get mine.

I jumped as someone pushed a small bundle into my hands. Aiden's oldest daughter—quiet, responsible Elise—held out a second package, her serious face level with mine. She had her father's height and her mother's looks. "These don't taste like much, but they'll give you energy and help keep away camp sickness. Be careful." She squeezed my hands, then ran off. Perhaps I did have a family, in Aiden's clan and Galliard. Elise just did what any sister would do—right?

The evening grew late as the men bound on their weapons, a blanket roll, and a water pouch.

"We are off to war," stated one weaver, his delicate Truvian features making him look little more than a boy.

"And we shall not return until we have won our cause," returned a blacksmith whose height showed a strong strain of northern giant.

We set off into the dark of night. Thirty-four horses carried supplies. We would not slow ourselves with carts. Scouts ahead kept watch for both friendly and enemy eyes. We marched through the Wilderlands along paths left by woodcutters.

It would take five days to get to the capital. Five days to take back the crown.

26

IN THE SHADOW OF CHOICES

YOSYPH

Sand puffed behind Farid and me, as our horses loped over the desert. The grasslands had disappeared days behind us, and mountains cut the sky before us. Farid's horses were bred for the heat and endurance, and even they were tiring at our constant pace. I found staying in the shadow made the time pass quicker, and the horse didn't seem to mind an invisible rider.

"Does being in the shadow make me lighter for the horse to bear?" I asked.

A voice came from above the other empty horse. "Perhaps."

That was the extent of most of Farid's answers, unless he had a lesson to teach. If I'd been out of the shadow, I'd be annoyed by his taciturnity, and then sorry for my taciturnity with Katrin, which would have lead me to thinking about her and missing her. Instead, I thought about what I could be feeling and usually decided I'd rather not feel it right then: apprehension, urgency, lonely aching. I found myself hiding the emotions away again. And that only meant pain the next time I pulled them back in. What a fool. I knew better, but I hid them away and lived with the minor stabbing of pain as I shoved them back into their hiding place. And then the major stabbing pains.

When evening painted the sky, I formed out of the shadow, wincing. I had to drink sometime. Next to me, my horse buried his nose in a water bag.

"When is the last time you turned to God for help?" Farid asked

"It's my fault I hide my emotions away. I shouldn't ask for help out of my own mess." I bit off the words as the emotions scratched back into place.

"Does that make a difference, whose mess it is? You go to help repair another's mess. Will you ask God to help you then? If so, then why not now?"

"I need to do everything I can and then ask for His help," I said.

"Then you will fail."

"Are you saying I should just ask for His help and let Him do the work?"

Farid stared at me, waiting for me to answer my own question. This wasn't the first time.

I shook my head. *I'm sorry,* I signed, *I know I must do everything I can, as well as ask for God's help. It is still strange to me. When I prayed to Him out of habit, not expecting anything, I didn't mind asking for things. But now I know He answers, a part of me hates that He helps me in the little things, but He also lets one evil person hurt a kingdom of people. Shouldn't He stop that person, to preserve all the others? You said I should trust God because He is good and just. How is it good or just to let one person hurt others or even one other?*

Farid closed his eyes for several minutes, then he nodded

and disappeared. I rushed into the shadow after him and saw his outline fly toward me. I braced my feet and raised my arms to fend him off. A swipe to my leg, and I tumbled to the sand. A hand and then a knife-like point pressed against my neck. I froze. This was that sort of lesson.

"What is the most precious thing you could lose?" Farid's voice whispered through the air.

The point pressed firmly against my skin, not yet parting it. "My life?"

"Then to preserve your life, what are you willing to do? Lie, steal, kill?"

"No. My honor is more precious than my life."

"Could anyone take your honor from you?"

"I'm the only one who can," I replied. "Only when I stop being honorable, do I lose it."

"Do you mean, no one can force you to do what you don't choose to?" Farid pressed the point firmer, and my skin stung.

I tried to sink myself into the sand to reduce the pressure. How far would he go with this lesson? And what was I willing to do to get out of this? Could he force me? He could threaten me with all sorts of things, but it would still be my choice to do it. And I could always choose to die, instead. That choice would be harder if I had my emotions, but even then, it would still be my choice.

"My every action is always my choice. I can never claim someone else made me do something," I said, certain of the truth.

"Then there is one thing I can never take from you." He formed back into sight, a black-robed figure kneeling by me, still pressing sharpness to my neck.

I stayed in the shadow.

"And that," Farid continued, "is the same thing only you can give up: your choices. It is what makes you human and makes you God's child. You are more than an animal led by appetite, though many people descend to that level."

He pulled the point away from my skin. It was a rock, not a knife. He wasn't as rash as I'd thought. He laid the rock in his lap.

I took a deep breath and rubbed the beading blood.

God teaches us to do good, he signed, *and allows us to choose to follow His teachings. He allows the wicked to do evil because he honors our freedom to choose. If it were not so, we'd all be slaves to Him. He honors our power to choose more than we do ourselves.*

"Then God will never stop evil from happening, because he honors choice?" Even without emotion, this thought bothered me.

God honors our power to choose, but He does not remove the consequences of our choices. A man who plants fire rocks will not harvest figs.

It partly made sense. Every action had a consequence, for good or bad. "Can God only instruct but not enforce? Does He ever intervene against evil?"

Farid shook his head and signed, *He does stop much evil from happening, through those who choose good. His interventions and mercies are constantly in motion—in your life, in mine, in each of his children. We often do not recognize His mercy. It is in His time and way. Always has been and always will be.*

"I understand," I said.

"Hopefully, you are beginning to understand. Now, will you choose to keep hiding your emotions until you are in as bad a state as you were before, or will you choose to ask God for His help?"

I let go of my pride. Was pride a thought as well as an emotion? I experienced it even in the shadow. *Please God,* I prayed, *please help me carry these emotions, so I do not crush under their weight. And help me use my ability to choose wisely.*

27

THE WRONG END OF AN ARROW

HALAVANT

The King's Army grew each day. Men melted out of the trees and took step behind us until our forces swelled to three thousand. Galliard divided them into companies of a hundred men, each with a small flag showing the animal by which they were called: bear, porcupine, hare, garter snake, even sparrow. I stayed with the river hawk company, my personal calvary guard of a hundred. Though I should have been riding next to Galliard under the falcon banner, the royal symbol of my father and now me.

The Wilderland path ran half a day's march north of the road, wide enough for five men to march abreast, and must have taken years to cut, especially with the hills. I'd hate to try this path in the mud. The planning of these men was marvelous. How had they done it without the Queen's spies knowing?

We stopped to take a cold meal—parched corn again. The men made up for the monotony of food, and gambling was the preferred diversion.

A blond noble threw his cards on the ground. "Backstabbing Truvian!" He leaped to his feet and drew his sword. Two other card players grabbed the noble's arms, while the Truvian sailor scooted backward on his bottom. How were we to fight the Queen's armies if we couldn't stop it amongst ourselves?

We'd find out tomorrow.

I mounted and rode toward the edge of the wilderlands, shadowed by the Poet. We were close enough to the end of our path that I reached the edge of the Wilderlands within an hour. The King's Army would take much longer to march.

The Poet kept his horse slightly ahead of mine and constantly scanned the trees. What had happened to the distracted writer from sword training? Ever since Galliard assigned him to stay by my side, the Poet clung there as tenaciously as a leech and reported to Galliard with as much detail as my history tutor. All because Galliard said he trusted me to stay out of trouble about as much as he trusted a cow to stay out of spring clover. I hadn't done one impetuous thing since before the forest meeting.

I cast a baleful eye on the Poet as he settled down to write, then I studied the weed-strewn ground that stood between the wooded Wilderlands and the capital. Years ago, my father ordered a wide band of Wilderland to be leveled and the ground planted with choking weeds. It was an ugly scar at the edge of the rich farmlands but a protection against armies sneaking close to the capital. Tonight, we'd march exposed through leather-piercing thistles to the road, then over a wide river. A Queen's fort overlooked the only bridge, hopefully still as undermanned as our spies reported.

A cough brought me out of my thoughts, and a man stood

at attention. The buttons of the Queen's soldier's jacket strained across his chest as he squared his shoulders. The frayed hem of his pants sat an inch above his red leather shoes. Our tailors could only do so much with the stolen uniforms.

"Yes?" I said.

"Reporting for duty. Sir!"

"Quietly." I motioned to the open expanse and the stone fort in the distance.

The man relaxed his stance and smiled sheepishly. He was about my age. A ribbon held back his long, brown hair at the nape of his neck. He handed me a folded note.

I broke the seal. *Jerimah, son of Lord Karles, is our most likely man to convince the Queen's soldiers to get drunk, if you can persuade him to cut his hair. Please brief him for tonight. - Galliard.*

"So what do I do to get the King's Army past the fort?" He bounced on the balls of his feet.

He looked as impetuous as I often felt. Not the best combination for the task ahead. "You'll do exactly as instructed?"

He stiffened back to attention. "Yes, your Majesty!"

"Even cut your hair?"

I touched my own cropped hair. It still felt like a part of me was missing. He'd not do it, and we'd have to find another volunteer.

He fingered the brunette tresses that flowed down his back, as fine as any lady's. His face fell a moment, and then he looked me squarely. "Even that."

"Jerimah, once your hair is cut to soldier length, you will join the Queen's soldiers as a new recruit. You'll tell them 'The dice are weighted in our favor.' That phrase, plus your shorn head, should grant you trust, more than your ill-fitting uniform will. If they ask, you are the youngest son of a nobleman, forced into the army due to gambling debts. Make sure you get the fourth night-watch, and most important, make sure each of them drinks the drugged wine."

Jerimah chuckled. "But not drink it myself? That could cause a rat's nest of problems. Though, I suppose our army could get over the bridge even with me out cold, as long as the rest of the Queen's soldiers were, too."

I raised my eyebrows and tried to look stern.

He swallowed his chuckle. "I won't touch the wine. I'll be on the fourth watch. The Queen's soldiers will dream away."

The King's Army marched across the thistle-strewn land, filling the moonless sky with muttered curses. Thistles pierced soft shoes. Galliard rode out ahead, the falcon banner flapping above him. This was my army, under my standard, and yet I took my position near the middle, far from the standard bearer. Galliard didn't want anything to happen to me, but I'd have to face greater danger than a fort of drunken soldiers when we reached the capital.

I cringed as we reached the road and my horse's clopping hooves echoed along the hard-packed dirt. Ahead, a wooden bridge, wide enough for a regal parade, spanned deep and quiet waters. The stone fort stood on the far side. Jerimah stood atop the wall, lit by torchlight. He waved his hand to urge us onward.

The men who had boots took them off. We wrapped our horses' hooves in fleece. Even then, the muffled sounds of feet on the bridge echoed loudly. An hour passed, then two. At the edge of the horizon, the faintest tinge of light heralded the coming dawn.

Why did we pick the fourth watch? We'd taken too much time. The drugged alcohol would be effective for only so long, and we were making enough noise to wake even snoring Lord Kinash in a council meeting.

I watched from the shelter of a weeping willow ten yards east of the fort, far closer than Galliard liked, but he was too busy orchestrating the movement of men to force me away. My personal guard spread out about me, and the trailing willow bows acted like a curtain. I was safe enough. Jerimah made some hurrying motions with his hands, and the men continued to cross until only the tail end of our brigade remained.

As the last hundred or so neared the bridge, a gravelly voice rose from within the fort and carried to me on the breeze. "Oh, what a night."

Those on the bridge froze. I reached for my sword.

"Aye, it was," Jerimah said. "Surprised you're up already. My head is pounding like a door knocker."

"Mine's pounding like a parade on the Queen's birthday, enough to wake me," said the gravelly voice. "The captain's a hard man to stick you on this watch after you gave us the best drink we've had in years."

One horse pranced nervously. His hooves made muffled thuds against the wood.

"What is that?" the voice asked.

"It's just a farmer driving his cattle to better grass. You know how this land is, all barren and nothing growing," Jerimah said.

"I'll take a look. Wait, what are you doing?" the voice cried in surprise, as Jerimah disappeared behind the wall. "Foes! Stand..." The voice cut short in tumbled thuds.

The echo of the cry and the thuds died into the stirrings of the fort. Doors slammed and boots thumped over slurred shouts of command.

"Get out of there, Jerimah," I whispered. Between him and us stood an iron-shod gate or a twenty-foot drop from the wall.

The remainder of our army flooded across the bridge. A

horse screamed as an arrow pierced its leg. It thrashed about, knocking over men and cracking the bridge's side rail. The horse and two men fell into the deep waters. Another arrow flew into a knot of men. A man fell, tripping the rest. More men fell into the river.

"Archers, provide cover!" Galliard commanded, and the piper trilled the order.

Dark shadows of men scattered along the top of the wall. The torches now guttered in the early morning, and the sun didn't yet light the sky. More arrows rained over the bridge, poorly aimed, but our men were a dense mass even a toddler could have hit.

I drew my bow taut, touched the fletching to my cheek, and released. My target tumbled from the wall. The air thrummed with another hundred arrows being released. The Queen's soldiers ducked behind the parapet.

The rest of our army rushed over the bridge, and one crawled up on the river bank.

The wall stayed quiet, but we kept our arrows pointed toward it. Then one man leaped on top of the parapet and climbed over. Jerimah?

"Hold!" Galliard's voice cracked.

Two arrows sang through the air and the man fell backward, one leg dangling over the parapet.

The piper's trill came too late.

I dropped my bow and drew my sword, ready to strike down the archers. But which men shot? Then a grinding creak, and the fort's gates swung open. About twenty-five men tumbled out, their clothes misbuttoned and boots shoved on the wrong feet. Their blades stood bare.

"Halt, Carani scum!" growled a Queen's man. He wove unsteadily on his feet.

"Wolf company, surround them," Galliard ordered.

At the piper's trilling, a hundred of our men broke away from the formed ranks and enclosed the Queen's soldiers in a half circle. The sun lit a long leg and red shoe draped over the parapet.

I lunged forward.

The Poet wrapped his arms about my knees, and I planted my face in the dirt. I kicked and heard a solid oof, but he didn't let go.

I pushed myself up as far as I could with the Poet still clinging to my knees. "I'll not rush in."

The Poet loosened his hold. "It would be wise of your Majesty."

I cast him a dark look, then stood on my toes so my voice would carry over the heads of the King's Army. "I am Prince Halavant, son of King Luukas, and the rightful heir to the throne. To raise swords against me is high treason."

Some of the Queen's soldiers hesitated, lowering their swords, but others still held them defensively.

"We do not want to harm you. Drop your weapons or there shall be more bloodshed," I said.

A soldier, staggering near the gate, dropped his sword. "Not worth dying for," he muttered. A few more followed. Many soldiers wavered in confusion. A bull of a man charged from the ranks, sword extended. "For the Queen," he roared, before an arrow struck him in the chest.

Then mayhem broke loose. The remaining Queen's soldiers scattered. Some ran back into the fort, while our men chased after, preventing them from shutting the gates. Others threw their swords aside and sat upon the ground. But some charged our army. These fell by sword and arrow. In moments, it was over.

I lunged toward the fort again and stumbled as Galliard's voice bellowed next to me. "Badger company, secure the fort."

In a quieter voice, he said, "Then we will see to our young hero."

Four men carried Jerimah from the fort and laid him in the shade of the willow. Two arrows had pierced him, one in his shoulder and another below his navel. He looked up as I knelt beside him.

"I'm sorry," he rasped, "they didn't drink all the wine. When some men passed out with the second glassful, some stiff-brow broke the remaining bottles against the wall. Called me a young scoundrel and a bane on military order, but he never called me a spy. I couldn't leave to warn you. At least I got punished with the fourth watch." He grinned weakly, then fell into a half-faint.

It was our own arrows! Please don't let him die. Ye gods above, how do you stand to watch such things happen?

"Let me pass," a higher-pitched voice urged. "I must tend to his wounds." A tall boy in a loose tunic and a floppy hat pushed his way through the other men and knelt next to Jerimah. "You, with the scar across your eye, boil me water," the boy said briskly, with a bit of the Truvian lilt, "and you two, turn him on his side." The boy cut Jerimah's coat and shirt from around the arrows. There was something familiar about the healer. I tried to look under the floppy hat, but I had to drop my head to my knees as the fabric pulled away from the bloody skin with a sucking sound.

The boy hissed as he examined the back of Jerimah. "Only one arrow went through. The other lodged against his shoulder blade. Hold him fast." He broke off the arrow near Jerimah's navel and pulled the remaining part through his back.

I raised my head and wavered as I watched blood flow from the wounds.

"Hold this." He handed me two wads of fabric and placed my hands over the two wounds.

I breathed in through my nose and tried to clear the lightness from my head. I couldn't pass out here.

"I need help to pull out this other arrow." The healer grabbed the hands of another soldier and placed them on the arrow. "Easy, easy, pull smoothly."

The arrow ripped out, and my world hazed.

Sunlight hit my closed eyes. I put up my hand to block it.

"Good. You're awake." The voice sounded familiar. Like Lenora's. "Are you going to get up and help?"

I opened my eyes. I lay in the partial shade of the willow. It was still early dawn. I'd hopefully only been out a few minutes. Jerimah lay near me on a thin blanket, his torso bandaged and his face pallid, but his chest rose and fell with even breaths. An older man knelt next to him, his long, brown hair matching color with Jerimah's cropped locks, and his face creased with concern.

My army—no, *I* almost killed Jerimah.

"Are you going to get up?" The healer knelt, pounding herbs, with hat off and a long black braid flowing down her back. It was Aiden's oldest, Elise!

"What are you doing here?" I asked, angry she'd put herself in this danger.

"The same thing my mother did when your father fought the Carani," she replied evenly.

"Does your father know?"

"He does now."

He would. He was part of my company and would be about here somewhere.

Elise's voice pulled me from my thoughts again. "I could use help with these herbs. I sent the others away so it would be quiet here. I won't ask you to work with the blood again."

The Poet sat under a willow a stone's throw away. He nodded when my eyes passed over him. The tail end of the King's Army moved about in the near distance, cleaning swords and fletching arrows. A line of forty bound Queen's men sat along the fort wall, bandaged and glowering. Five men were stretched out next to small fires as others nursed their wounds. I glanced over and away from the row of ten bodies—legs straight, arms crossed their chests, a cloth over their face—some in Queen's red, some in peasant brown.

I could use Elise's distraction. I worked beside her, crushing herbs with a pestle. The woody and floral scents made me want to sneeze. I stifled my nose.

Elise hummed tunelessly as she lit several narrow sticks, doused them in boiling water, then dabbed a honey-looking mixture on the ends. She dipped them in the herbs I'd crushed. I focused my attention on Jerimah's face as she shifted bandages and thrust one stick into the shoulder arrow wound.

"Yie!" Jerimah yelped, his eyes flying open. "I've already been shot. You don't have to do it again!"

"My son," the older man said tenderly.

Jerimah turned his head. "Hallo, father. Sorry to be all trussed up like this. Met with the wrong end of some arrows."

The man shook his head, "Must you try my heart so? You are the only son I have left."

"Oh, you still have Anish. She is smart and brave enough to match me."

"But not replace you." The man brushed a hand across Jerimah's forehead.

Elise pulled me to the side. "He'll be fine. You better get back to your men. Keep safe." She reached up and kissed me on the cheek. "For luck." And she turned back to her work.

28

FALSE, FALSE, FALSE!

HALAVANT

The King's Army marched double-time through the day, along the royal road which ran through the weed-strewn land and back into the lush farms that surrounded the capital. There wasn't much use in secrecy now. Lines of men stretched behind and in front of me. Our company's blue flag with the red hawk flapped above the Poet. Fifty other flags flapped over the other companies—osprey, martin, boar. Three thousand against the Queen's Army of twenty thousand, but the Queen's Army was spread throughout the land, and many of them marched to fend off the *Carani attack*. If our spies were correct, only about three thousand remained in the capital.

Frightened faces peeked out windows as we passed. They might be some of the same people I'd questioned while seeking Katrin. I rubbed my chest where an empty ache throbbed, then fixed my gaze on the falcon banner. I was King Halavant, coming to free my people. What were these frightened faces thinking as they saw the king's symbol leading this army? Would I have believed it?

As the sun set, the capital city glowed before us. The cliffs rose behind, and the royal forest spread to the north. The city's three walls nested in each other in rosy gray—the lowest tier was the common city; next tier, the nobles' residents; and at the top, my home.

I closed my eyes for a moment and imagined I was coming back from hunting—two foxes hanging from my saddle, and a deer lying across my servant's horse.

"The general requests your presence."A bent-back man pointed toward an oat field where the falcon standard flew. Twenty men had already gathered in a loose circle, with a hundred more standing guard, arrows pointed outward. Not that there was any place for a surprise attack on us in this open farmland, and our spies reported the Queen pulled all her local forces into the city since we crossed the fort this morning.

My company rode with me and joined the guard as I entered the circle of leaders—Galliard, Devron, Aiden, the paunchy noble, the orange-haired tanner, and others—but not that trembling-lipped, thin-blooded noble from the first meeting. He'd been assigned to help the camp chef.

Galliard nodded welcome and then motioned to one of our spies. "Report."

"Lord Fredrick gained the Queen's permission to command the men guarding the north gate. He's assigned Queen's soldiers loyal to our cause to the gate and along the walls for fifty yards to either side of the gate. He'll try to broaden that reach."

"We'll keep our men to a ten-yard wide path," said Galliard. "Hopefully, it will get our men to the gate quickly but still keep them out of range of those not loyal to our cause."

The spy waited for another nod from Galliard. "To maintain the appearance of defending the city, the Queen's turncoats will shoot blunt, wooden-tipped arrows."

I spoke up. "Have the men wrap themselves in horse blankets. It won't be as good as armor, but it should turn blunted arrows. It helped against that hail storm last week. Has Fredrick taken care of the oil vats along the wall? Even with turncoat Queen's soldiers manning them, it wouldn't take much for one to change his loyalty again and set our men on fire at the base of the wall."

"I didn't ask." The spy turned green.

"Fredrick's a meticulous man," Galliard said. "He'll take care of that. Are the Raven, Bear, and Ferret companies ready?"

Three men nodded. "Aye."

"Then muster the troops."

I held up my hand to stop the leaders from dispersing. "Remember, we are only taking the outer wall today. Don't let your men spread through the city. We are still small enough we could be crushed if we don't keep together."

Galliard eyes creased in a silent smile while he kept his mouth stern.

I know we'd talked about this, but I wanted to make sure they remembered. I wasn't the only impetuous man here.

After we took the outer wall, then Fredrick's man in the palace would seek to parley with the Queen and her council. He'd announce I led this army and desired for a peaceful change of powers.

If the Queen refused, then we'd fight all the way to the palace. At what cost? *May the god of peace bless his efforts.*

"Lastly." I caught the eyes of each of the men. "I know some of the men mutter about taking their revenge on the Queen. If one does, he will be banished. We are seeking peace, not revenge."

Galliard raised an eyebrow.

I wasn't being a weak leader. I needed to talk to her, find out why she did what she did. A good leader didn't kill on second-hand knowledge. Then why was I part of this war? How many would die because of my second-hand knowledge? I swallowed. No! I'd heard and seen enough evidence to show the ruler must change, and this war was the only way.

Galliard continued to watch me, and the other men watched him.

I threw back my shoulders. "I declare this as your king."

Galliard nodded. "And I will obey our merciful king." He turned to the others. "If the Queen does not turn over the rule willingly, we will take her prisoner, uninjured if possible. Prepare to march."

We marched toward the city. The road before us split into three. One cobbled road led ahead to the central entrance of the city—a broad and ornate gate used by visiting officials and nobility. Another led south to the market entrance—an equally broad, but much plainer gate was crowded from morning until night. The third road, little more than a packed dirt path, led north to the commoners' gate—a narrow and paint-peeling entrance for those who didn't want the press of the market but didn't have noble blood. All three gates stood closed, and the outer wall bristled with the long spears of defenders.

A piper trilled the notes for *turn about left*, and the King's Army of three thousand turned in a ragged mass northward. We'd take the commoners' gate. We marched along, keeping more than an arrow's shot distance between us and the city wall. The city's defenders rained the arrows toward us, and all fell short. Still, some of our men faltered, cringing away from the city.

"They couldn't hit us if we stood at ten paces," a gruff voice called out in encouragement.

I smiled at his foolish boast. Hopefully, the commoners' gate would be quieter.

The piper trilled *Halt,* and the King's Army stopped twice an arrow's distance from the north gate. Soldiers in the Queen's red stood along the wall, as they had along all the rest of the city wall. Spears and helmets gleamed dully in the sunset behind us.

Please, ye gods of war, let Fredrick have truly taken the gate.

"Raven company. Forward march!" Galliard spoke and the piper trilled the signal. A hundred men wrapped in horse blankets rushed the gate. Arrows flew, and a few men stumbled. When they reached the wall, they spread along the base. The Bear company and Ferret company followed them. The hail of arrows increased, striking our men left and right, but they staggered on.

Then the trumpeting of a horn shattered the air. Our signal. The Queen's soldiers on the tops of the walls turned and aimed inward toward the city and toward the Queen's men further along the wall.

The rest of the King's Army marched double-pace, and the commoners' gate swung open. Our men at the walls poured in. I wanted to gallop ahead, to be with the first into the city, but the Poet caught my reins.

"I know," I said. "I'm too valuable."

"You wouldn't be a valuable pin cushion," he said.

I entered the gate anonymous in the midst of the river hawk company. I dismounted, stepping on one of the arrows, and saw the blunted wood tip. The arrows aimed at the Queen's men would be iron shod.

Galliard stood on a hastily constructed platform just inside the gate. He gave orders, the piper trilled notes, and companies of men split off in different directions. Some climbed the wall stairs to aid our allies in Queen's red as they fought the Queen's loyal soldiers. Others marched down streets, banging open doors and scanning rooftops, even as arrows rained onto them from the distant walls. Others started fires for food.

My stomach growled. It'd been a long day, and a long evening stretched ahead of us.

Lord Fredrick stood on a platform next to Galliard, scanning the men as they entered.

I saluted him. He'd done as he promised and made it so we could enter the outer city. Hopefully that was enough to get the Queen to agree to a parley. "Well done, Fredrick," I called out.

Fredrick leaped down from the platform. "My king." He waved me forward. "We must get you to cover." He opened the door at the base of the watchtower. Galliard gave one more command, then he and I followed Fredrick up the stairs into the circular stone room at the top. There was only one entrance, and Fredrick stationed men to protect it.

"The city is in turmoil." Fredrick plopped into a wooden chair. "All have heard of the Carani attack, and some think you are they. Others think you are rabble rising against the crown and ready to kill all in its path."

I suppressed a chuckle. I'd never seen Lord Fredrick so frazzled. Though I couldn't imagine what it must have been like, trying to figure out who he could trust to ask for help securing the gate and knowing he'd be hanged if he was found out.

"How many remain of the city's guards?" Galliard asked.

Fredrick bit his lip. "Almost a full three thousand. She only sent a thousand of the capital's guards against the Carani. I tried to convince her it was vital, that I'd fled my estate with barely my life. That they'd swarm the land if we didn't stop them, and we'd lose the harvest and face starvation this winter. But she said it was better to keep the crown safe, and the people would make do with what they had." He rubbed his neck, along where a noose could lie.

Three thousand trained soldiers against our three thousand

untrained men. This would still be difficult. But it was about what we'd expected. Poor Fredrick. He'd done all he could, and much more than his old heart should bear.

"Well done, Fredrick." I patted his shoulder. "We couldn't have gotten in without you."

The thumping of hundreds of feet marching echoed through the gate below. I moved to the window and looked into the city. This north section held a majority of the poor and homeless, prostitutes and released convicts, and some of the most colorful characters I'd ever spent time with. I'd snuck out of the palace to visit them three years ago and paid for the excursion with my first and only corporal punishment from my mother. If I were with her now, I'd get more than a slapped hand.

The fighting had moved into the distance as the King's Army swept through the streets and along the outer wall.

Not too far. Keep together.

Our breach of the city seemed to have rattled the Queen's men and sent them flying, especially since they didn't know who in the Queen's red might try to kill them. It had to be unnerving. Now the streets stood empty, except for the King's Army with a black cloth bound around their upper left arm, and our allies in the Queen's red, also binding black about their arms. Cooks stirred pots, and healers bent over the wounded.

A ragged blanket where a man once sat begging, was tossed to the side of the road. Its owner was probably hiding in some alley. Chairs and mattresses blocked windows. The thin wail of a baby and the whine of a dog carried over the deep thumping of boots. How long before the rest of the Queen's Army would turn again and attack us?

I turned to the window that faced the palace. "Fredrick. Do you think your messenger has sought parley yet?" If the Queen agreed, we should hear a trumpet inviting us to meet with her. I strained my ears for it.

Fredrick came beside me. "Soon, if he's not dead."

A gray, undulating cloud rose from the inner city. Part of it flew towards us.

"Messenger pigeons!" I grabbed my bow from the wall, then yelled out the window. "Shoot the birds!"

I released my arrow into the flock, and one bird fell to the ground. Cooks and healers grabbed bows and shot into the swarm of gray. Most of the birds escaped.

"Queen's wrath!" Galliard cursed.

Fredrick stared at the disappearing flock. "Queen's wrath is what we'll be facing if we can't take the city before the rest of her army comes."

The Poet entered the room, cradling a dead pigeon. I pulled the paper from its leg and stumbled as I read aloud, "Fairhaven is being attacked. The outer wall was taken by a traitor who claims to be the prince. Send troops, quickly. Kill—" I stuttered to a stop.

Galliard read over my shoulder. "Kill the traitor and all his followers."

I crumpled the paper in my hand. We had to act quickly. I didn't have time to weep over the woman who had been my mother. I clenched my fist over the paper and looked to Galliard. "I would like to join my company."

Galliard smiled sadly and placed his hand on my shoulder. "You are too valuable to be out in the open. Besides, some of our soldiers survived childhood in these neighborhoods and know these streets like a fox knows his den. Stay here and rest." Then his smile took a mischievous slant. "I don't want you to pass out again."

He'd seen me faint at the sight of Jerimah's wounds.

"Pass out?" Fredrick went to my side. "Are you injured?"

"No more than I was ten days ago. It's nothing."

"You there." Fredrick pointed to one of the soldiers in the room. "Make up a bed for his majesty. And you, get him food."

After eating, I sank onto a bed made of six thin mattresses stacked together and covered with coarse blankets. I didn't want to sleep. I needed to save my people. *My people. Will we take the throne before the other armies arrive? How many will die? I am a traitor to my mother, but I will not be a traitor to my people.* I soaked the mattresses with silent tears until exhaustion dulled even that pain.

Thump, thump, thump. The persistent banging echoed the pounding in my head. Why was my head pounding again?

It wasn't like the ache before Lenora drilled a hole in my head. More like too much wine. What time was it? No light came in the guard tower windows. I felt around my tunic. I needed water, something to dampen my parched throat and stop the thumping. My fingers closed around one of the small packages Elise gave me. It wasn't water, but the sticky fruitcakes would at least help.

I sucked on a small piece, and it eased the thirst. "What is going on?"

"Catapults. It's the Queen's Army attacking."

A flicker, and then a lamp glowed. Fredrick sat at the plank table, flanked by two soldiers. The rest of the room sat empty. Except this wasn't the tower room. This one was windowless and square.

"Where am I?"

"Somewhere safe," Fredrick said smoothly, all signs of frazzle gone.

"Where's Galliard? What's happening with my army?"

"They are currently safe, well out of the catapults' range. The Queen hasn't dared open the inner city gates and march out yet, though many buildings between the catapults and here will soon be gone."

"We have to stop it!" All those people. They had to get out of there.

"I can help you stop it. We can stop this whole war, and no one else will die."

I looked into his calm face and shivered. He couldn't make that promise. It wasn't in his power. Already people were dying. What was he doing?

"What did you put in my food?" I held one hand to my pounding head.

"Ah, so, you catch on faster than your mother. Although you are as predictable and as easy to sway as she."

"What have you done to my mother?" I lunged to my feet, ready to strangle him. The two soldiers caught my arms and thrust me into a chair. "You were the one! You ordered the death of Galliard's family and the enslavement of the foreign blooded and the, the—" I yelled, struggling against the men holding me.

"It's not in my power to make those orders. She did those things. I only fed her fears, suggested solutions, and let her carry it out. As I said, she's predictable and easy to sway, though she's gotten less so in recent years. She's become a bloodthirsty she-wolf. Even the best pawns can break."

My mother, corrupted by him! Turned into an animal, a she-wolf! "You'll hang for this."

"Not convincing words, considering you're my prisoner. You know I can get rid of you like I did the first Queen. She wouldn't be influenced by me, but pirates are easy to do business with. And your father—*Slow Wasting* is such a horrible thing to die by, as is *Heart's Weep* tea."

"Why don't you become king and be done with it?"

"I couldn't have gotten this far without your help and those armies the Yorel and Galliard gathered. I needed the people to be enraged with the monarchy and ready to overthrow it. They've been at a smoldering point for years. This last bit of insult—this threat to a third of the people—touched off a revolution. It all came together with your bit of brilliance, pulling away part of the Queen's Army with the threat of Carani attack."

"We are not your pawns, and we will not make you king."

"I don't want to be king." Fredrick's dry voice rustled like a snake. "The people are tired of the monarchy. Lansimetsa needs a stable ruler, one not led by passions and impulsiveness. The monarchy will dissolve, and I will offer my services as the father of a new oligarchy, ruled by men of wisdom and experience."

"I'll tell them."

"Oh, I wouldn't worry. Accidents happen."

I tried to think. I needed to know more so I could act. I strangled my anger. "And what do you want me to do?"

"You see being a pawn is better than death. You have a choice of willingly giving up your right to rule and supporting the rise of the oligarchy, in which I will let you live, or you can defy me and die."

He'd kill me either way. But if he let me speak to the people, I could at least warn them.

"Give me a night to think about it." I dropped my eyes so he couldn't see the anger gleam in them.

"You'll have until the Queen's trial in two weeks. I've already imprisoned the Queen, though her court thinks she's gone into seclusion since she learned you've openly rebelled against her. Even without the Queen to issue orders, her generals will continue the fight, and they will lose. I have men who will let your armies into the inner city and the palace. The King's Army will take the city, though I don't know how many will survive."

I hated him with every muscle. How many had already died

because of his duplicity? How many more would die before the army took the palace?

A thought and then a hope. He couldn't explain away my disappearance. They'd find me. And I'd tell them everything. I could—

"You won't be well enough to see any of this," Fredrick continued in his gratingly calm voice. "Your head wound, the one that healer woman so expertly treated, took infection while you marched along. You'll be unable to speak and burning with infection. The last words anyone will hear from you is your response to my question of *were you injured*. You said, *No more than I was ten days ago. It's nothing*."

I lunged forward. The two soldiers pushed me back again. I howled in frustration and fear.

Fredrick tsked. "The she-wolf's pup. Really now. You are more than an animal, though I'll muzzle you soon enough. This is what will happen. You will get a daily dose of *Lamb's Silence* and *Heart's Weep*. The one will make you unable to speak, the other will kill you unless you get another daily dose of the antidote. It's a secret not even your healer woman knows. You'll be free to travel about the city, though I fear you'll not feel up to it. But if you don't come back for the antidote, you'll die."

I'd be free to leave Fredrick's sight. I could escape in the time between the antidote and the poison. I could write and warn the people.

"You'll get the antidote," Fredrick continued, "at the same time as the next dose of *Heart's Weep*. Enough to keep you alive for another day. I'm not sure how many years you'll live this way. One man lived five. We'll take care of those hands, so you don't write anything. I know which crippling herb I'll use. This one has no antidote." Fredrick pulled a dull gray vial from his pocket. He waved it in front of me, taunting me with the crippling sap. "I'll concentrate on your hands for now. But if you don't do as I ask, I'll find other spots to cripple, and eventually, you'll be fully paralyzed. I hope you don't drive me to that point."

I howled again. I'd tear out his throat even with crippled hands.

"Howl all you want. Soon you'll be silent. In two weeks, you will appear in court. As your body adjusts to the poison, you'll slowly be able to do more things. Your testimony will be to simply nod or shake your head to my questions. If you cooperate, then I'll let you keep living with the daily doses of *Lamb's Silence* and *Heart's Weep*. If not, then you won't get the antidote the next day."

I'd not swallow whatever he gave me. I'd grit my teeth and clamp my lips. I'd pass out from lack of air first. I'd—I hollered as Fredrick thrust a thick needle into my arm. He twisted it around, sending fire up my shoulder and down to my fingers. He pulled the needle out and dipped a different needle in a red jar, then stabbed my arm again. This one numbed the spot, and the numbness spread slowly outward. I barely felt the last thrusts of a needle in the back of each hand. I slumped in the chair.

"You can take him back to the tower now," Fredrick said.

The two men carried me up steps, then out a trapdoor. Circular steps rose above us. We'd only been in the guard tower cellar. I tried to scream out for help as we passed the door to the outside, but nothing. I couldn't even make a sound.

I had to escape. I bent my fingers and found I could still move them. I'd warn them before I couldn't write. I'd find paper and tell them everything.

The men dropped me down on the bed, then spread out cards on the table. Chills ran up my neck and over my scalp. The mattress husking rustled under my shaking limbs. A fire burned behind my eyes, inside my throat, and through my chest, but my body wouldn't sweat.

Paper, pen, anything. Why was this the one time the Poet wasn't around? Galliard had turned over my protection to Fredrick and sent the Poet on some errand as if he had more use than being my shadow. Even if he were snoring beside me, I could find some of the paper and coal sticks he always carried. Wait. He'd given me that gift. I turned my back to the card-playing soldiers and reached into my jerkin. It was still there. My fingers seized as I tried to scrawl out words in the dim light on the minuscule paper.

Fredrick traitor. Poisoned—Heart's Weep. Need anti— My fingers dropped the pencil, and it rattled to the floor.

"What's that?" One of my guards stood. I stuffed the booklet inside the band of my stocking garter.

The lamp's circle of light took in my bed. The guard picked up the pencil, now broken in two.

"Trying to write a message, eh? Where is it?"

I didn't have to pretend to shake in fever as he searched the bed and me, rifling through my jerkin and breeches. But he didn't feel the bump beneath my garter. "Guess you didn't even have the strength to hold a pencil, let alone write with it. Get some sleep. Tomorrow will be worse than tonight."

29

LISTEN

YOSYPH

I'd never seen the city from the top of these cliffs. Farid knelt as he bound a rope through an iron ring secured to the stone. The sky above stood a clear blue in the early morning light. Behind us cut sharp mountains that had tried to kill me in shale slides and icy ravines. At my feet, the cliffs dropped away. A fall would last many seconds before ending on the rocks.

Below me, the capital city bulged from the base of the cliff in three tiers, each wall curving away from the cliff in the south and coming back to the cliff in the north. If I dropped a pebble, it would fall into the gardener's hut behind the palace. If I threw the rock, I could have hit the barracks. Katrin probably could have tossed a stone well enough to shatter the falcon stained-glass window in the palace's east tower. The cliffs bent eastward along the south of the city, which would allow late morning light to reach the palace. But for now, the whole royal grounds stood in the cliff's shadow. And I, a shadow, would enter, do my work, and be gone before the sun lit the rooms. That was the plan—except for the dark clouds rising from the outer city ring. The wind carried the faint sounds of the catapult's creak and the crash of buildings crumbling.

They'd attacked the city even before the end of the harvest. What had happened? Had Devron called our scattered groups together to attack? I scanned the city. It seemed most of the catapult attack fell on the northern part of the city. Masses of ant-like figures streamed from the central and south gates—people with carts and animals fleeing the city. Other figures moved steadily through the outer city toward the inner city wall, some disappearing as another building crumbled and dust blanketed the air. A horn call pierced the air.

Should I try to stop the advancing attack on the capital? Or should I capture the Queen first? Which would preserve more lives?

"I'll leave you here." Farid held the rope out to me. "May God bless and guide your path."

Thank you for guiding me and teaching me, I signed, then I flung the rope over the cliff edge. It tumbled down the face until it reached a rocky shelf partway down. Two more spans of rope and a pouch hung from the belt of my now unfamiliar breeches. Tucked safely in my tunic, I held my mother's letter along with a twisting strand of Katrin's hair—one I'd cut while she slept.

"Remember," Farid said, before turning back to the mountains and desert beyond, "what you want and what you should do are not necessarily the same thing. Pray often, listen intently, and be humble."

Had I learned yet how to listen? It seemed it took me almost dying before I recognized an impression. Would a kingdom almost crumbling be enough for me to hear God's guidance? Or would I wander the wrong way in foolish pride and let Lansimetsa disappear into the horrors of anarchy? If I took out the Queen and the generals, then the battle would be over. But if I could get the attacking army to pull back into a siege, fewer men would die, and I could take out the corrupt leaders.

I *quawlaar'd* and stepped over the side of the cliff. My leather shoes, wrapped with gummed rope, gripped the face as I walked down the cliff, hand under hand. "Please, God," I prayed as I descended, "should I stop this battle or find the Queen first?"

An image of the prince jumped to mind. He stood as I'd last seen him, glowing with sweat from our spar. What did he have to do with this?

Find him, a thought whispered.

Find him? He'd be at the palace, yelling insults from the walls.

I reached the shelf. I bound my next rope through another ring set into rock and descended again.

I'd find the Queen and secure her, then find him. That must be the answer.

Thank you for helping me, I signed after I dropped to the ground behind the gardener's hut. No one seemed to be around. They must all be hiding away from the approaching battle. Not that I needed to worry. No one could see me, and if they discovered the rope, it would distract them from the battle and perhaps save a few lives.

I ran through the kitchen gardens, passed the emptied barracks, and dashed through the steward's door. Marble walls stretched down arched hallways, and high windows let in the light. Pages and servants skittered nervously from place to place. Where would the Queen be? I'd never entered the palace before.

I followed one well-dressed servant and found myself in a room that could have held our whole market square. An empty throne sat at one end. A table sat a little to the side, and two men bent their heads over maps. I slipped over to listen.

"There is a breach in the nobles' wall. The south gate is taken," one man wheezed, his face blotchy with fear and anger. "Some she-wolf's pup is letting them in!"

"When I find him, I'll string his entrails over every gate in the city."

I looked sharply at the speaker. He had General Jonstone's voice—the confident, paunchy, drinking chief of the Queen's spies—but he'd shrunken to a hollow-cheeked man.

"Do you believe that snake who tried to parley with us? Do you think the prince leads the rebels?" the first man wheezed.

The prince? They thought the prince was leading this? What crazy brilliance led to spread that rumor?

"If it's him or an imposter, I'll gut him the same," Jonstone bellowed. "He about killed our Queen when he snuck off a month ago, and now this. She won't even let me in to consult with her. And the rebels keep breaching our walls."

So he wasn't in the palace. He could even be leading this attack. I'd have to find him. But first, I would capture the Queen.

Jonstone shifted a map and pointed where to move the troops. Before anything else, I needed to remove him and this other man. I fingered the four vials in my pouch. Four poisons prepared by Farid. One ridge on the vial meant debilitating stomach cramps. Two ridges—muteness for a day. Three ridges—death-like sleep for a couple days that could lead to never waking. Four ridges—swift death.

I touched the four-ridged vial. It would be easy to end them now, stop them from ever plotting another death. But which vial would aid Lansimetsa and its people best?

The wheezing man reached for his goblet after I slipped the single-ridged vial back into its pouch. I re-tightened the cap on the three-ridged vial. Jonstone would sleep through the rest of this war, which would be more pleasant for him than his companion. Hopefully, he would wake for questioning.

Now to find the Queen. She must be in her rooms, but where would those be? I could wander for hours without finding her. I slipped back into the marbled hall.

A drudge, carrying a dirty bucket of water, plodded down the hall. Years of mundane exhaustion erased all emotion from her features. I caught the handle of her bucket and walked beside her. She shook her head as if confused and then plodded on.

"Where is the Queen?" I whispered.

She didn't even scream. She slumped to the floor in a faint, the water forming a gray puddle around her.

I tried asking a young man who was rushing by with a platter of roast ducks. The ducks took flight in one direction and he in the other.

I'd feel frustrated if I could feel. I found a servant who wore finer clothes and was about my size. I could have sent him into paralytic shock by whispering to him, too, but thought it quicker and kinder to strike the side of his head. I dragged him into a broom closet and gathered my emotions. Along with the expected emotions, a new one grated at me—something was horribly wrong, even more so than the battle outside, and I needed to hurry. I slipped into the servant's clothes and strode out to find non-fainting information on the Queen.

"What are you doing here?" A shrewish voice snapped at me. A woman in a gray high-necked dress glared at me.

"I have a message for the Queen."

"Guards!" the woman shouted.

I *quawlaar'd,* and her shouts turned to screams. Soon the whole palace would be filled with stories of ghosts.

I ran down halls until her screams faded, then slipped back out of the shadow. Again I felt urgency, and I wasn't in the right place.

I'm trying, I signed. *Can't you help me more than this pestering feeling?*

A pale kitchen maid came around the corner, her apron filled with sprigs of herbs. She stopped and looked at me. A shy smile played across her lips. Maybe she could help.

"Please, fair maiden," I said. "Could you help me? I have a message for the Queen but I don't know where her quarters are."

She blushed and motioned for me to follow her. We strode down one narrow hall after another through the servants' back ways. Finally, we reached an ornate door.

"She's through there," the maid whispered, "but it's locked. She's not well. Susanne said she barely eats and won't let anyone other than old Ana tend to her. But if you could help end her, then maybe this war could, too."

I jerked. How did she know?

She laughed and tweaked my ear. "The Queen never allows servants from the desert. She hates them more than any other blood. Besides, you speak too kindly. I'd wondered when one from the King's Army would make his way into the palace."

"Thank you. You'd better go."

She slipped a sprig of lavender into my buttonhole. "For safety."

I waited until she turned the corner, and I *quawlaar'd* again. It took me about a minute to set all the tumblers in the lock and slip into the room. Dark curtains cast everything in shadows. My eyes slowly adjusted as I searched the room for the Queen or anyone. Empty chairs, smoothed bed, tables. I opened every closet, rifling through the heavy silk and brocade gowns. I looked beneath the bed and opened every curtain. No Queen. No old Ana. No one.

Late morning sun poured through the now open windows. I knew when I left the shadow again, urgency would yell at me. I hadn't listened.

30

SILENCE

HALAVANT

Every word, every scrape of the chair across the floor, made me want to scream. But no sound came from my burning throat. I tossed and turned in as fine a bed as I had in the palace, every muscle shrieking as if I lay on nails.

That morning, the King's Army took the next ring of the city, and I was now sequestered in Fredrick's doubly guarded mansion. I was protected from those who would kill me, by those who would kill me.

I opened my eyes as the door creaked. Galliard entered and took a seat beside me. "So you've decided to greet the day." His eyes were deep with sadness. How much death had he seen? But he didn't talk of that. "I have good news. Lord Fredrick's men will open a breach in the fortress wall in half an hour. We may win the throne for you before the day is out." He bathed my head with a cloth.

His face swam in and out of focus. I tried to make my eyes alarmed and my face full of warning.

"Elise, how is he?" Galliard asked.

Elise was here? I turned my head. She stood at the other edge of the room, mixing herbs silently.

"I wish I'd been here this morning when the infection first set in," she replied, pouring hot water over herbs. "It's now spread through his body."

I had to warn them. But when Galliard had visited before, he didn't get the message, despite all my mouthing words and alarmed looks. Every part of my body responded sluggishly, and maybe my attempts to mouth words looked like nothing more than mumbles. Galliard had looked at me in concerned alarm. Maybe Elise would understand me better.

She came to my side and I mouthed the word 'help.'

"I'm trying to." She held up a cup to my lips, and I sipped. Bitter Monk's Sleep. I pushed it away, pleading with my eyes for her to listen. She didn't force it back but watched my face.

I mouthed, 'Fredrick traitor.'

She tilted her head and watched my lips carefully.

I mouthed again, 'Fredrick traitor.'

Her hands stiffened as she bathed my brow. She nodded.

'Poisoned.'

"I feared so," she said.

Galliard looked from me to her. "Can you understand him? He's been delirious all morning, but he seems calmer with you."

One guard stopped eating and came to hover over Elise.

"He's still delirious." She gave my shoulder a squeeze. "He mouthed the words *frothy toads* and *pudding*."

The guard stifled a snicker and went back to his lunch.

Galliard glared at the guard, then turned to Elise. "I wish

your mother was here. I've sent our fastest rider to fetch her, but it will be several days."

Even with her mother here, it wouldn't do any good. But Elise understood me. She could help.

The door opened. Fredrick walked in, his face creased with false concern. Behind him came a man in a physician's robes.

"I've found a physician to care for him," Fredrick said. "He's one of the finest in the city, and he was brave enough to stay around when others fled. He felt it was his duty to tend to the wounded, and there are all too many of those—pierced, crushed, thrust through. It is a hell out there."

I pushed myself up to half-sitting. I'd create worse for him in here.

"Careful," Galliard said, as Elise gently urged me back to lying. "The war is almost over."

Then Galliard pulled Fredrick to the side. I could hear every whispered word. "Be more careful what you say."

"I'm sorry," Fredrick said. "That was thoughtless."

Hah! Every word was a planned barb, a reminder of his power over me.

"Elise should stay," Galliard said. "The king seems less agitated since she arrived. And I'm sending some of my own men to stand guard over him."

"By all means. A loving hand always helps in healing. Select whatever men you can spare from battle, but we must return now. My men removed the drainage grating under the wall. I doubt it will remain a secret for long. We can't lose this chance."

Galliard and Fredrick left to their war, and the physician approached. "My dear," he said to Elise, "I will examine his majesty. You will want to leave the room."

Elise looked at him with her serious brown eyes. "I have helped my mother examine many patients. I will stay and help."

If he found the message! I rolled so my back was to them. My arms were already beneath the covers. If only I could get the booklet to Elise without him knowing. I fumbled about with rigid fingers. My stockings were gone, my legs bare! One of the guards must have found it after I slipped into sleep. And now Fredrick would poison me in some new way. I glanced at the physician and shuddered. I'd not let him win.

Elise came over to one side of the bed, while the physician worked to undress me from the other side. I looked into her face and mouthed a word. She shook her head, took my hand in hers and I felt a small flexible square. I sucked in my breath.

"Shh," she said, "it will be all right. We'll figure this out."

31

BROKEN

YOSYPH

Clouds of dust blocked the noon sun. The Queen's soldiers packed the palace's walls like seabirds on a nesting cliff. Men tumbled backward, pierced with arrows. Ladders rose against the walls and fell away again as Queen's soldiers thrust them with pronged poles. Diagonal beams braced every gate. Four creaking catapults flung stones. Beyond the walls clashed the cacophony of metal, the boom of battering rams, shouts, splintering wood, and the fife piping out the signals I'd created last year. *Buzzard, flank left. Otter, attack center right.* Its shrill notes trilled without hesitation. My men remembered their training.

I would feel proud for them later. For now, I would make a way for them to enter and then go find the prince.

I wove through the crush of soldiers running about the courtyard. Thrice I knocked into a man, but in all the jostling, no one noticed. Three men strained against the lever to set one catapult, the ropes taut enough to start untwisting. I pulled my ridged knife against the strands six times, enough to fray the rope. The catapult creaked as the men lifted a stone into the wooden basin. Then *whoomp,* the lever released, and the arm rotated forward. The stone flung over the wall, and the rope snapped. I jumped back as the rope whipped around and caught two men across the chest. Shouts of dismay rose around me as men scurried to pull out the ruined rope and find a new one.

I slipped toward the porter's gate. It stood only a cart wide, narrow compared to the main gate, but still wide enough to allow a press of men through if it were opened. Two cross beams and two diagonal beams braced it shut. One cross beam was smaller, used every day. The other was a solid oak beam that would be difficult for one man to shift. Dozens of men guarded the porter's gate. I pushed against one of the two diagonal bracing beams. It lodged fast. What would have enough force to pull it free?

Along one wall stood a black charger, saddled and slick with sweat, its hooves big enough to crush a man's head. That would do.

I pulled a length of the discarded catapult rope inside my cloak. I bound the rope about one bracing beam, then snaked the rope along the ground to the horse. Two men in the Queen's red stumbled over the rope, but continued their dash to the top of the wall to fill in gaps where other soldiers had fallen. I worked quickly, but without a feeling of hurry, knotting the rope around saddle pommel, careful to not brush against the horse. Then I slapped the charger on his right flank and howled the wolf call.

The horse spooked, flying away and to the left. The rope pulled taut and rose to shoulder level, sending several men into the air. The air filled with yells of surprise and the groan of the diagonal bracing as it scraped over the cobble and fell away from the gate. The Queen's soldiers jumped away from the spooked horse. One rushed in to sever the rope, while the rest of the gate guards pressed in to force the beam back into place.

"Even the dead are fighting against us," cried one man, cutting away the taut rope from the bracing.

I slipped between the press of men and hefted the thick oak beam that sat cradled across the two doors of the gate. A battering ram boomed, and the gate shuddered, pinching the beam. Then the pressure eased. I heaved upward, and the oak beam slipped free and thudded to the ground.

The Queen's soldiers about me startled back with cries of "Ghosts!" and "Shadow demons!"

I leaped back from the gate as the ram boomed again. The gate burst open in a shower of splinters as the smaller cross beam shattered and hinges screamed. Men tumbled as the iron tip of a ram swung into the open space. Men with a black band about their arms rushed through the open gate, slashing through the scattered Queen's soldiers. The call of the fife outside trilled orders. I'd opened a way for the battle to end sooner. The black-banded men—my men—would take care of the rest.

I pushed my way through the surge of soldiers, around the edge of the gate, and along the outside wall. The tide of men, some in the Queen's red and others with black-banded arms, swirled and clashed about me, funneling through the gate. Company flags fluttered above the swarms of soldiers, and a large falcon banner hung from a third-story balcony of a mansion across the square—the old king's symbol. Six rectangular shields, each about the height of a man, formed a barrier along the inside edge of the balcony, preventing me from seeing who stood behind, though the piper's trill came from that direction and arrows continued to rain upon it from the palace curtain wall.

I ran along the outside of the square, hugging the wall and staying mostly out of the fray. After an arrow scored my cheek, I yanked a shield from a Queen's soldier and sprinted on. The men who saw the floating shield ran, but their cries of shock melded with the other cries of war, and soon they were pulled again into the torrent of fighting.

A wooden gate stood closed in the mansion's stone wall. I climbed over and landed in a grassy yard filled with wounded soldiers, both in the Queen's red and the black armbands. Women, girls, and young boys rushed between them, giving them water and tending to wounds.

One tow-headed boy dashed into the carriage house carrying a heavy jug. Timothy? I dashed after him and caught his arm. He hollered and jerked away. I came out of the shadow. I swayed at the push of urgency coupled with the horror of the dead and wounded and my kid brother standing in the middle of it.

Timothy pulled away from me, but I held firm. "Yosyph?" he asked. "Are you a ghost?"

"No. But I'll make you one if you don't get away from this battle. What are you doing here?"

"Helping King Halavant take the throne away from the Queen. Are you sure you're not a ghost? You just appeared out of nothing." Timothy looked at me with curiosity.

"I'm not a ghost. I learned to shadow walk. I need to get into that mansion and talk to Prince Halavant."

Timothy looked up at the balcony with the falcon banner, then pulled me toward the back garden of the mansion. "He's not in there, and I can't tell you where he is, because someone might hear, and then they might go assassinate him. But I can lead you to him."

That would do. *Thank you, God, for sending me a guide.*

Timothy clambered over the stone wall and dashed through the wide noble's streets, past ornamental gardens trampled and stained red, and led me beyond broken-windowed mansions. The sounds of looting pouring through open doors. The anarchy was already beginning. The image of Farid's broken water jug played before my eyes.

"Prince Halavant is ill." Timothy cut across the muddied lawn of a red brick mansion. "His head wound took infection again."

"Head wound?"

Timothy turned and ran backward. "Don't you know? He left the palace because he couldn't stand the corruption of the Queen. Men tried to assassinate him, and he couldn't even speak until the healer woman cut a hole in his head. And—"

I put my hand on his shoulder to stop him from running into the wall as we came to the edge of the lawn. What had happened these last months? It didn't sound like the prince. Left the palace? Almost assassinated? A hole in his head?

Timothy turned around and jogged through the streets.

"He found out about the planned enslavement of the people and gathered the King's Army. He planned a surprise attack from the Carani—but it was our men—to pull away the Queen's armies. But he is ill again, and we have to win this war for him, so he can get better and be our king. He'll be so much better than the Queen."

How much could I believe of the gossip of a twelve-year-old? But Halavant must have done some good things to have these stories and for the leaders of my army to respect him enough to give him leadership, even if it was in name only.

"Why do you need to find King Halavant?" Timothy turned down another wide avenue.

"I need to help him."

Timothy stopped running and turned to me. "We have our best healers and physicians taking care of him. There's not much you can do for him there. But you can help us win this war. Can you disappear like you appeared? I thought you could only be unnoticed—but invisible? You could go kill the Queen and all her generals. You could scare the rest of them into surrender."

"I've already taken out the generals. I have to talk to Halavant."

"But he can't talk. His head wound—remember?"

What was this feeling of urgency? I couldn't help him as a healer. I only knew rudimentary herb-lore. He couldn't speak, so he couldn't tell me anything vital to this war. He was being cared for and protected by a whole army.

"Just take me to him." I turned Timothy around and gave him a little shove forward.

Timothy looked back at me as I glared, then he shrugged. "You got a whole lot more stubborn since you left. But the Yorel knows better than me. This way."

The wide streets were littered with injured, both soldiers and civilians. We ran through a thick archway of the noble's wall, its massive gates unlatched from the stone wall and lying on the ground, then through rubble-filled streets of the northern part of the city. An hour later, Timothy knocked on the door to the guard tower over the commoners' gate. The neighborhood sat silent, the door unguarded, though locked.

"He's in there." Timothy pointed to the top of the guard tower. "Keeps him away from the battle, and it's where no one would think to look."

It didn't make sense for him to be there. No guards, in an

unprotected part of the city. I set the tumblers in the lock, pulled open the door, and sprinted up the stairs to an empty room with a pile of thin mattresses and a table, and down to the cellar—a table and a few chairs in the middle of boxes and barrels. Then under the winding stairs—empty hooks for shields and swords.

Timothy followed me. "He should have been here. That's where they said he was."

Why hadn't I just found who was commanding in the mansion with the falcon banner? He'd have known. "I don't believe they'd let the whole army know."

"Oh." Timothy's face fell, then rose. "Father will know. He's part of the meetings."

"Is he closer than where I found you?"

"Yes."

I followed Timothy through a maze of narrow streets until we came upon Father's tavern, the White Goose, except now the sign above it held the ornately penned name of the Royal Hazel. The Queen must have taken ownership after Father went into hiding. And now in the battle, Father had reclaimed it.

Father stood in the wagon in front of the tavern, directing the line of women carrying wine casks and barrels of mead. "Careful," he reprimanded one woman as she stumbled forward with a small cask. "If you break the seal, it will bubble out before you can get it to the wounded."

I dashed to my father.

"Yosyph!" He clambered out of the wagon. "Did you bring an army?"

His first words and I had to disappoint. "No."

"Ah, well, you are back, and that is a needed mercy."

"I have to find Prince Halavant."

He looked at me sharply. "He's fighting on our side now. Don't you go trying to kill him. I have so much to tell you."

"I'm not. I don't have time to listen. I have to find him —now."

He raised his eyebrows. I was never one to rush into things. If the prince had changed, so had I. He studied me for a long minute. "I've heard he's in Lord Fredrick's mansion, But I can't be sure. Galliard will know."

Fredrick's mansion was in the south noble's section. Another far jog, but closer than returning to the mansion outside the palace to seek Galliard. I sprinted away.

Hours lost. Hours wasted. I ran across the city only to find Lord Fredrick's mansion deserted, even the servant quarters abandoned. I searched the outbuildings and then the mansions close by. If only I could find a horse. The sun had set, and moonlight filtered through the dusty air. Galliard would know. I should have gone back to the battle when it was still early afternoon.

Please, God. I've looked. I asked. If I'm to find him, I'll need your help. My prayer felt repetitive, as I sent it heavenward again. I stopped glancing at the mansions, wondering if the prince was in one of them, and turned my focus to the trek toward the palace.

Laughter echoed down a side street to my left. Probably more looting.

"Attention!" The command rang from the same direction. I turned and jogged that way, my sprinting wind long left behind.

Soldiers in the Queen's red, but with a black band about their arm, stood in front of a moldering mansion, set far from the road in unkept grounds. Lanterns on the wall behind them cast their faces in shadow. A man in an embroidered jacket faced them. "You are a disgrace to your duty. Get back to your stations, and don't let anyone enter this building, or I'll send you to the front lines."

I *quawlaar'd*, feeling cold relief from my self-recrimination, and slipped past the guards into the building with the man in the embroidered jacket. He strode up several flights of stairs and knocked on a door. A young lady with black hair opened it. "His Majesty is asleep," she said in a low voice.

The room's lamp lit the man's face. It was the Poet. He was one of our best intelligence officers, gathering and remembering information from a conversation the rest of us missed, and an effective assassin. "Galliard sends his regrets he can't spare a man from the battle to change out the guards. Can you put up with these oafs for a night? The war should be over by morning, one way or another."

"What has happened?" she asked.

"It seems the Queen's generals were poisoned, but some young officer has rallied the Queen's men and forced us from the palace grounds. The fighting is back to the nobles' section. I must return." The Poet turned and leaped down the stairs two at a time.

I could do something about that. Before, the battle was in our favor. But now they needed my help. I could do as Timothy had urged. It made the most sense. All this wild goose chase for the prince. All this time wasted. I'd misunderstood the impression. I would return to the battle.

I almost turned when I glanced past the young woman. A man lay on a bed. Prince Halavant? He looked a man, his boyish round face now lean and with the start of a beard. His blond hair was cropped short and marred by a line of stitches. Gnarled fingers lay on the coverlet. What had happened to him since we sparred a month ago?

A thought passed through my head. *Stay by him. This is your place now.* This thought was followed by a memory of Farid's words. *You'll likely have impressions to do things that go counter to what you've planned. Do you hold to your pride and keep going your way? Or do you listen?*

I slipped into the room under the weight of those thoughts, turning my back on all logic said I should do. I would hate myself for the deaths. Why was this the impression?

32

BLINKS IN THE NIGHT

HALAVANT

I woke to a dimly lit room. The lamp showed the physician sleeping on a padded chair and my two nighttime guards playing cards at the table. I could finally try to communicate with Elise. I turned my face toward her and winced in pain. My muscles seized with the movement.

Elise looked up from packing herbs into little cloth sacks. "Where does it hurt?"

Everywhere. How I wish I could speak.

She pulled a jar from her satchel and rubbed a salve down my legs. It soothed the muscle spasms. Soon the physician would poison me, but it hadn't happened yet. The fever burned hotter. How soon would the *Heart's Weep* kill me if I didn't get the antidote?

"I can't read what you wrote," Elise murmured as she leaned

over me. Her voice blended with the hum of the crickets and the distant sounds of battle. "Did you earlier mouth *Fredrick traitor*? Blink once for no, twice for yes."

I blinked twice.

Her hands tightened as she massaged my arms.

"What poison?"

'Heart's Weep' I mouthed.

"Hearth sweep?"

I blinked once and mouthed 'Heart's Weep' again.

She bit her cheek. "If I spell out the letters of the alphabet, can you blink when I get to the right one?" She softly sang a lullaby as she massaged my arms. After one verse I realized each word started with the next letter of Lansimetsian. She rotated through the fourteen letters each verse, and though each verse the words changed, the letters kept repeating.

My head ached as I tried to follow the song and blink on the correct letters. The fever made the words blur together. It seemed like hours later when she murmured back to me. "*Heart's Weep*."

I blinked twice, and my head rolled to the side.

"There is no such herb as *Heart's Weep*," she whispered, frustration seeping through her calm. "He's playing with your head, as he is with the rest of us. Is it in your food?"

I blinked once. If *Heart's Weep* didn't exist, what was he poisoning me with?

"The punctures on your arms then."

Two blinks.

"When? Last night?"

Blink, blink, and shuddering. Elise scooped more salve and massaged my stiffened hands.

"When you are done with him," called one of the guards from the table, "I could use a shoulder rub."

"Quiet, fool," said the other guard. "We're on duty, and we leave the girl alone."

"All we do is sit and play cards," the first shot back. "No one will get past the guards outside. Do you plan to ignore a pretty girl like her for two weeks?"

"Quiet," the other hissed, backhanding his table-mate.

Elise bent close to me. "Two weeks? He'll keep you alive for two more weeks?"

Blink, blink.

"Then we have time." She turned me on my side.

"My dear, are you still awake?" The physician's gentle voice sent me into a new fit of shivers. How could a man about to poison me have such a voice? He stood from his chair.

The physician came to Elise's side. "My dear, you must rest. It is near midnight."

"Is it time?" Elise kept her eyes on me.

I blinked twice.

"Yes, there is a lovely room right across the hall all made up for you. No need to sleep in a chair like an old man like me."

"But I always stay next to my patient."

"If you won't leave, I'll ask the guards to escort you out. It's for your health. Who knows if you'll catch this infection if you wear yourself out, and what good would that do the young king?"

"Should I go?"

I blinked twice again. They'd hurt her if she stayed. But she could warn Galliard and others now.

"My dear child. You are exhausted. Go. You can tend to him again in the morning. Do not come back before then."

"Halavant." Elise took my hands in hers. "I'll be back with the dawn." Then she kissed me on the cheek and walked solemnly from the room, taking the last bit of light with her.

33

THE BROTHER BOND

YOSYPH

I stepped to the side as the young woman exited the room, and the prince's show of confidence crumbled. He took a couple of shuddering breaths and warily glanced from the physician next to him to the two guards at the table. He was a wolf, trapped and wounded.

I moved toward the man in the physician robes. He pulled three jars from a satchel and set them on a little table by the bed. None of them were labeled. One was red, another gray, and the third white. Then he pulled out a needle.

I grasped his wrists.

His eyes pulled wide. He jerked away from me and tumbled to the floor.

"What's going on?" One of the guards laid down his cards.

"Something grabbed me," the physician stuttered.

I strode to the two guards and lifted a card from the table. It floated in the air, and then I flicked it sideways so it cut the cheek of one of the guards. Both guards scrambled away from the table.

"Ghosts!" One guard ran for the door.

The physician tried to follow, but I hooked his foot, and he tumbled to the floor again. His nose flattened against the wood.

In a crash, a stumble, a yank, and a slam, the two guards were gone.

"Please," the physician whimpered. "Please go away."

"Tell me the antidote to the poison," I whispered behind his ear, placing my hand on the back of his shoulders so he couldn't rise.

"I don't know," he stuttered. "I'm only doing what Lord Fredrick commanded. He promised me an earldom. I don't know what the bottles do. Please let me go."

He was a cowardly murderer, but he seemed to be telling the truth. I struck the back of his head, and he slumped.

A groan sounded from the bed. I looked up from binding and blindfolding the physician. Halavant stared at the unconscious physician, his face white and his lips parted. Another groan. Whatever had kept him from speaking was wearing off.

"I'm here to help." I came out of the shadow. Halavant's face blanched, and his eyes rolled back. I stumbled under the rush of emotions. One unexpected feeling was compassion for the man lying on the bed. I touched his forehead. Fever burned. His breath came shallow. I had to find the antidote. Would one of those bottles be it? But the others were surely poison. I couldn't start dosing him with them.

Why, I signed, *Did you lead me here, to see my brother die?*

I felt a coldness, similar to being in the shadow, as if a warm presence withdrew.

"Please," I stuttered out loud. "Help him. Don't make him suffer because of my pride."

I took the cream the healer girl had been rubbing on him. I could at least do that. Surely Fredrick would come to check on him, after the stories those guards would tell. I could force the knowledge of the antidote from him. But I had to keep my brother alive until then. I rubbed his spasming muscles, bathed his fevered brow, and moistened his cracked lips. The physician sagged, bound, gagged and blindfolded in the corner.

Halavant moaned again, and his eyes fluttered open. He stared and shuddered, either with fear or fever.

"I'm not a ghost," I tried to reassure him. "I'm—" I paused. Do I tell him I'm his brother, or the Yorel, or just the commoner, Yosyph?

"You speak?" he rasped. "You were mute before."

I chuckled. I did not expect him to recognize me, much less think about my muteness. "Less so than you were today."

"Are you a shadow demon?"

"No. Well yes, but I'm an honorable one."

"Good." He pushed himself to sit. "Kill Fredrick." The fury of his words exceeded his strength, and he fell back to the pillows.

"What has he done?"

"Killed my father, corrupted my mother, provoked a war." Halavant panted.

The latch of the locked door rattled.

"Guards!" an annoyed voice called. "If you've also left your post on some ghost story, I'll have you strung up. Open the door."

I *quawlaar'd* and opened the door. A pasty-faced noble entered, casting his eyes about the room. Lord Fredrick. He'd sent help in many ways to our cause over the years. Though we'd never met officially, I, as mute servant, had watched him in many of our illegal meetings.

He jerked as he saw the physician trussed in the corner. He almost backed out again, but I grabbed his left wrist, drawing him farther into the room.

"Fredrick," I said. "Your day of reckoning is here."

"Luukas?" Fredrick froze in his struggles against my grip, "Luukas, you don't understand. I was helping your son. I've done all I could to keep him alive."

He thought I was my father? I could work with that.

"False and foolish man." I intoned, my emotionless voice fit the ghost well enough. "Do you think you can lie to the dead?"

Fredrick's knees gave out, and he slumped quaking to the floor. He clasped his hands in front of him. "Please, Luukas. You know I've always sought the best for our beloved nation. It is a hard road, and I've hurt with each dark step."

"Your torment is assured." I squeezed his wrist tighter. "It may be lessened if—"

"If what?" Fredrick's voice took on a tone of hope.

"If you tell me the antidote to the Heart's Weep."

"Antidote? There is no antidote."

"You lied." Halavant cried from the bed.

"Yes, I lied. You are poisoned, but not to death." Fredrick turned his head toward me. "Luukas, please believe me, your son is already pulling out of the depths of the poison. The one only made him mute for a day. The other was not *Heart's Weep* but rather *Love's Broom*. A miserable, but not deadly, herb that brings on a fever. There is no antidote but time."

"You'd have me believe you when you killed me," I said.

Fredrick's face morphed. Suspicion replaced fear. "You're not Luukas. He died of the *Slow Wasting*. You must be that shadow demon the people call the Yorel."

"Yes."

"You stole the voice of my best friend," Fredrick said.

"Friend? How could you be my father's friend when you

tried to kill my brother and destroy the country my father fought to preserve?"

"Your father?" Fredrick shuddered. "Your mother is that cursed desert woman?"

"Yes."

"Can't be. She was barren, and the pirates assured me she died."

He was the one. He was why my mother slaved and died. Thousands of thoughts and memories and what-ifs rolled through my mind, all cold and bereft of emotion. Fredrick still knelt before me alive because I was in the shadow. I didn't know if I would choose to let him live if the emotions buffeted me along with the thoughts, in spite of my honor.

"Brother?" Halavant yelled, a bit belated.

"Later," I said.

I placed my knife against Fredrick's neck. "Tell me the antidote, and no lies."

"I told the truth," Fredrick whined. "Time is the antidote. I didn't want the prince to die, only to be my prisoner and speak for the formation of the oligarchy. Luukas felt the monarchy held too much power and wanted to change it to more of a balanced rule, but he died before he could do more than dream about it."

"I think," I said, "you don't know what's the truth or a lie anymore. I'll let you live. But if my brother grows worse in any way, I will peel your skin slowly until I can uncover the truth."

"Brother?" Halavant said in wonder. "I'm brother to a shadow demon. And it's raining inside."

I struck Fredrick across the head, much harder than I had the physician, and ran to Halavant's bedside. His skin poured with sweat, his pillow and coverlet soaked. The fever had broken. He slipped into a deep-breathing sleep.

Dawn poured through tall windows, turning the oak and rose-papered walls gold. Halavant lay sleeping and free of fever. Fredrick was trussed next to the physician in one corner. The healer girl would arrive soon, and with help, if I didn't misunderstand her last words to Halavant. I dared not leave him alone in the room, even with those two poisoners bound. But others would come. I stayed out of the shadow. I needed to feel the impressions, to know how to help Halavant.

Thank you, God, I signed for the hundredth time. *Thank you for preserving my brother.*

I looked at Fredrick and acid emotions rose again. I pushed them down, burying them under what needed to happen next. They pushed upward again. I shoved them down with a growl. Then without intending to, I flickered into the shadow and out —once, twice, three times. Each time, as the emotions rushed back, they burned me until I thought I'd pass out. "Please help me with this burden," I gasped. "It is more than I can bear."

Quiet words whispered through my head. *The shadow will always pull you when you try to bury strong emotion. It is my blessing to you. You can not hide your emotions again, and you will be reminded to turn to me. Well done, my child.*

I collapsed to the ground. I didn't think I'd ever get used to hearing the voice of God. I sat in a dazed heap until laughter pulled me from my thoughts.

Halavant lay with his eyes closed and chuckles rippling from his throat.

"Halavant?" I moved to his side.

"I don't know what parts were a dream or not." His eyes stayed shut. "But I hope the part where Fredrick babbled and pleaded like a scared little girl was true. The ghost of King

Luukas, come back to haunt him." Tears squeezed beneath his lids. Laughter blended with sobs.

"Or the part," I rejoined, trying to find the humor in the dark of last night, "where the guards about strangled each other in their dash for the door."

"I'd have run, too. Are you really my brother?"

"Yes."

"And the fabled Yorel, and a shadow demon, and," Halavant opened his eyes and studied me, "mute but expert swordsman?"

"I'm Yosyph."

"Well, Yosyph Yorel Shadow-Demon Mute-Swordsman—my brother, I don't feel like I'll be up and about for many days. You sound like you have four lifetimes of stories to tell. They have to be better than the ones rampaging through my head."

"Is that an order from my baby brother?"

"A kingly request."

A gentle rap sounded on the door.

"A request that will have to wait." I slipped into the shadow and opened the door.

Elise stood there, her serious eyes red-rimmed. She didn't even notice the men in the corner, but ran to the bed where Halavant lay grinning.

"You're doing better." A smile touched her face. "What happened? Where are the guards?" She saw Fredrick and the physician bound in the corner and brought her hand to her mouth.

"It's a long story," Halavant said. "Did you bring help?"

"They are in the hall. I didn't want the guards to hurt you if we all rushed in. But all Fredrick's guards are gone. What happened?"

"I think," I came out of the shadow, "we'd better call them in and stop this war."

Elise did what no other person had yet had the sense to do.

Instead of screaming, fainting, or running away—she stared at me, studied me, and then nodded. "That explains much. The Yorel has returned."

The news of Lord Fredrick poisoning the prince and imprisoning the Queen had a greater effect on the war than anything else. The Queen's army, both the part within the city and the part that arrived in a forced march, accepted Galliard's white flag of parley and held the first meetings for peace.

We found the Queen locked in the cellar of the moldering mansion, her nails long gone from scratching at the wooden door. Her voice had been silenced by the same poison as Halavant's. I pitied the men now guarding her. She tore the air with curses to turn even a pirate scarlet. She was our prisoner until we came to a full peace.

Pulling information from Fredrick was like making a picture from a shattered mirror. His view of reality was fractured distortions. Yet he sometimes answered my questions when I stayed in the shadow state. And occasionally, he even slipped back into thinking I was my father's ghost.

So this was why I had to learn to shadow walk. It wasn't to win a battle by taking out the leaders, but rather to act as my father's ghost and pull the needed information from Fredrick. Only God could have known this was needed. If I'd ignored Him and followed my own wisdom, we'd still be mounting deaths in battle.

I shuddered and stole into Halavant's room.

This was in a new hiding place. Assassination was more likely than ever by those who abhorred the battle under the falcon banner and the changes were sure to happen. I'd always thought I'd be instigating those changes but Halavant, even in his weakened state, proved to be an astute and compassionate leader. This land needed him. Where was my place in all this? A shadow in his service? It would be better than a throne.

Galliard looked up as I entered. He sat holding Halavant's hand on one side of the bed and Elise on the other. Halavant had just woken from sleeping most of the morning, and color tinged his pale face. I stood aside and listened. I was not his friend and confidant.

"*Love's Broom,*" Elise murmured. "Yes, that would cause the fever and spasming muscles, and in repeated doses, it is deadly. You were so weak yesterday, I don't think you could have handled a second dose, no matter what *master poisoner* Fredrick thought. He thinks he's so witty, playing with words—heart's weep, heart sweep, love's broom. But your hands? Did he tell what he used on them?"

Halavant's fingers continued to curl like claws in the hands of his friends.

"I'll pull it from him." Fredrick still refused to answer that question. I flickered in and out of the shadow, then hissed through gritted teeth. This *blessing* could grow annoying.

"If I didn't hate him so much," Halavant said, "I'd feel sorry for him."

"Leave a piece of him for me," Galliard said. "He has yet to pay the debt for my family's deaths."

And my mother's, and my father's, and thousands of others.

34

THE KINGS' TRIAL

HALAVANT

Yosyph and I are much alike. I scratched the pen over the parchment, my words large and wobbly. *Same green eyes, same stubborn jaw. Same propensity to get into trouble. And we love the same woman. He denies it, but he also flickers in and out of sight each time he talks about her. I'm not sure how I'll handle it when we see her today. It's only been two weeks from the battle, and she showed up demanding to see Yosyph—not me, but Yosyph. But we, the Light and Shadow Brothers as the people have started to call us, are protected by more guards than a caravan in robber country, and tied up in more meetings than there are hours in the day.*

So she's waiting until this afternoon, and Yosyph's been blinking in and out every few minutes. I'd suspect him of sneaking off to see her, except he's too honorable for that. Or too scared. He doesn't say. That is where we differ most. Where I speak without thinking, he thinks without speaking. Trying to pull stories from him is like pulling cold taffy—too fast or hard, and it breaks. If I ask too much, he turns mute, and if I persist, he disappears. But if I ask a little at a time, then glowing tales of adventure fill the room, one tiny segment at a time. He refuses to tell me how he feels about her. If I knew, then I could—

"Blast these crippled hands," I cursed, fumbling to push the full parchment to the side. "And blast Fredrick for killing himself." I'd never know what he used on them, or if there was any way to restore their movement. A brace wrapped around each forearm and ran down to my fingers. A pen was strapped to my right hand. I could hook my fingers through the two handles of a mug to drink, have a spoon strapped to my forefinger brace to eat, and I was back to the kingly indulgence of a page dressing and grooming me. What a bother.

A knock interrupted my thoughts.

"Come in," I grumbled.

Yosyph entered, his dark features and green eyes serious, and his unadorned black clothes in dull harmony. I'd tried to get him to wear color, or something finer than cotton, but he seemed to think the black dullness befitting a shadow demon—no, a shadow walker.

It was time to go. I stood as Yosyph dropped to the chair across from me. I sat back down. Yosyph glowered. Why? Was he afraid of seeing Katrin?

Yosyph leaned forward. "You have to order the Poet to stop."

That was what he was worried about? I chuckled. Yosyph refused the crown and refused the praise. He'd be happy to stay a shadow. But the Poet wouldn't stop his songs. "The Poet is doing his part to heal the rift betwixt our peoples."

"It's exaggerated beyond belief. He should write songs about himself instead, assassin and survivor of arrow and sword."

"You are a hero and of the desert blood. You can put up with shameless praise to help heal the feelings toward your kin in this land."

Yosyph stared at the table, dropping a mask over his emotions.

"It's not only you. There are songs about Lenora—the Truvian miracle worker—and the giant-blooded blacksmith who lifted a city gate to rescue a trapped child. If songs and plays can build up walls of prejudice, they can help tear those walls down again."

Yosyph sat silent, his face hiding a thousand thoughts. He finally looked up. "Have you seen your mother today?"

I shook my head. I'd visited her a week ago in her comfortable and well-guarded room. Her vehemence overwhelmed me till I wished I could disappear into emotionless shadow like my brother.

"She's asking for you. Maybe she'll tell you something that will help us repair this country. She turns as silent as a sleeping volcano when I enter the room. For our people, you should try."

I shuddered at the thought of mother's vitriol. "I'll go, if you'll tell me how you feel about Katrin."

Yosyph grew silent, flickered out of sight a few times, then looked me in the eyes. "I love her. I love her enough I won't ask her to marry me. I can never show my love to her the way you can. I'm too silent, too dark, too much of the shadow. I can't even feel strong emotion without disappearing. What woman would want a husband like that?"

"You only disappear if you are trying to hide your emotions. You'll find someone when you stop hiding." And I would be happily married to Katrin by the time he'd figured out how to stop hiding. My hope for the coming meeting rose.

Yosyph nodded. Thinking and not speaking.

Katrin leaped up from the divan as we entered. She looked from Yosyph to me to Yosyph to my hands and back to Yosyph. I drank in her eyes, her sun-darkened face, her slim form dressed in white desert robes. It seemed a lifetime ago, and she stood before me—a song and a flame.

"I'll never trust you again." She stepped toward Yosyph with each word. "You left me in the middle of the desert. If Naven hadn't been there, I'd be married to Qadir's grandson." She now stood half an arm's length from him and glared into his face.

The guards at the door stepped forward, lowering their spears.

I waved them off. "He'll be fine." Half of me wanted to take her in my arms and kiss her soundly. The other half of me shook with laughter. I'd been on the receiving end of her anger, but nothing as burning as what Yosyph faced.

He flickered from sight and back again.

"Don't you dare disappear." Katrin grabbed the front of his cotton tunic.

"I'm sorry, Katrin," Yosyph stuttered. "I couldn't take you with me, and I didn't know how to say goodbye."

"Like this." She stepped forward until their toes touched. "I don't care for you even though we survived brigands and wolves, desert and shadow together. So goodbye."

"Katrin." Yosyph caught her arm as she turned away from him. "I do care for you. We survived brigands, wolves, desert, and shadow together. I never want to say goodbye again. I love you."

"Oh." Katrin went wobbly.

My heart held its breath. When the Yorel decided to speak, he didn't hold back.

She shook off Yosyph's touch. "You say you love me—you

care for me." Her voice started at a cold calm and rose with each word. "Yet you didn't trust me enough to tell me!"

Yosyph glanced at me and gulped, then turned his eyes back to Katrin. "I'm trying to tell you now." He dimmed almost to transparency and poured out his words. "I want to always be with you. Will you be my wife?"

I'd have punched him if I could have balled my fingers into a fist.

"Wait!" Katrin stepped back a pace from Yosyph.

I lowered my partly raised arm. If I struck Yosyph now, in the middle of his proposal, Katrin would turn colder to me than a doused fire.

Yosyph flickered again. His face contorted in pain each time he came back into view.

"Yosyph, stop it." Katrin demanded. "I didn't say no. I don't know yet. Why didn't you say something before?"

Yosyph pulled himself into solidness and gripped the arm of the divan.

Katrin closed her eyes and took shaky breaths through her nose.

Now was my time. I touched her hand. "I still love you." I poured all my emotion into my words. "I love you enough to leave the palace, live as a beggar, almost die, and lose the use of my hands."

Katrin plopped onto the divan, her head in a hand, her shoulders shaking. I sat down beside her and placed my arm around her, pulling her closer. Her warm form fit against me more perfectly than my many memories.

Minutes slipped by too quickly. She pulled away from me. "You two are awful!" She laughed, tears streaming down her cheeks. "Halavant, you are part of my earliest memories and many of my best. Yosyph, you've brought me safely through the depths of hell. I love you both for different reasons. And you expect me to decide?

"No." She shook her head. "I won't decide today, or this week. Give me a year, and then I'll choose. Give me time to truly get to know each of you. Because, Halavant, you've changed. And Yosyph, you rarely opened up to me."

She stood, still shaking with laughter and tears, and walked toward the door and the stunned guards. As she reached the door she turned. "No foul play, or I'll hate you forever and marry Qadir's grandson." And she was gone.

It felt like a flame had whooshed over me, leaving me stunned and a bit singed. Life with my brother got a lot more complicated. Wasn't rebuilding a nation enough?

I reached my braced and stiffened hand to Yosyph. "Looks like we are both on trial. May the one who loves her most win."

Yosyph nodded, taking my hand in his. "A pity. I was beginning to like you."

35

THE KING AND HIS SHADOW

YOSYPH

I strode across the courtyard, my body slick with the sweat of sword practice and my fingers muttering thoughts I wouldn't speak out loud. *I admit my love to Katrin, and she tells me to wait a year for an answer. Why did I listen to Halavant's advice to stop hiding my emotions? I should have stayed silent and just let her marry Halavant, then I'd not carry out this hope and fear for a year. Do I pursue her? Wouldn't Halavant be better for her? But I love her, and I can't bury my feelings anymore. What then?*

I took a deep breath, trying to untangle the emotions rising within me and not push them down.

Whomever she chooses, I must put my people first. And to do so, I must work beside my brother. He's a good man, one I will not hate.

I flickered.

"Please, God." I whispered my prayer. "I don't want to hate him."

I stood still, waiting for the peace to come. It came, in part, but the ache still sat heavily in my chest. I could not stand there all evening.

I entered the long halls, visible. Servants bowed as I passed. I wanted to *quawlaar*. I'd never get used to this. I felt too open, too noticed. Finally, I entered Halavant's rooms. Would he even want to see me after our meeting with Katrin?

He glanced up from his writing desk. It was covered with books and parchments. He looked weary. I'd heard how he'd practiced the sword to deal with sorrow and stress, and now even that was taken from him. I'd turned to the sword practice to relieve my emotions because I could no longer bury them. How much had we changed to become like each other?

I took a seat across from him. "I'm sorry about Katrin."

He shook his head and glanced down. He wasn't ready to talk about it either. He picked up a paper I'd sent to him that morning, detailing my ideas for a test that would ensure we had good leaders for our people. He'd marked several parts of the page with wobbly ink. How many times had he read through it?

I broke the silence. "Have you thought about it?"

"Yes," he snapped. "And creating a ruling body based on those who can pass a challenge is insane. Many good statesmen would die if they had to sleep on their back porch, and you want them to survive a week through the Wilderlands."

I leveled my voice. "My mother's people have a long history of peace because their council is created from those who passed such a challenge. Only those with honor, wisdom, and courage can rule."

He shoved the papers to the side and leaned towards me. "That same council about killed our father, and they banished your mother."

Yes, they'd done that, but they'd kept their people at peace for generations. Couldn't he see? "It is better than the oligarchy Fredrick wanted. Corruption will abound under a group of old-blooded nobles grown fat on the labors of serfs and servants."

"I don't want an oligarchy," he said. "I want to let each town choose a man to represent them in a council and rule the land by the voice of the people."

"And how would you ensure these men were good and wise men? What would keep men like Fredrick from talking their way into power? We have to have a trial to test their honor."

"We'd have all the others in the council to help balance out the few dishonest ones. Can't we trust the people to make good choices?" Halavant rubbed his temples, his hand braces making the motion stiff. He'd been rubbing them this morning, too, after he'd proposed to the royal court we give a portion of the power to the people. The court went from open-mouthed silence to ear-aching yelling.

Halavant dropped his hands and smiled slightly, like he'd just had an idea. "We'll go back to the old monarchy. And you can be the king."

I grayed. I would never be the king. He knew that. Why did he bring it up again?

He continued. "You can rule this people with honor and wisdom, because you've passed the King's Trial. And you can send your children to that trial, and the one that survives can rule after you."

I felt myself fade with each of his words until I could see the empty table through where my arms had been. I flickered back into sight as pain etched my body.

Halavant winced. "I'm sorry. That was cruel. But you know the people can do great things, noble things. Can't we trust them? Can't we teach them? If they learn to govern themselves, to choose their own leaders—good leaders—to help us make decisions, then our land shouldn't fall again."

"It will take at least a generation to teach them. And many still want you, or I, or both of us, dead. We're destroying the way things were, and it is not a comfortable thing."

"Ah, but that is the lot of kings. It shouldn't be new to you. You've been a hunted criminal for years."

"I wasn't sitting on a throne then."

Halavant smiled sadly. "You still aren't. Though I'd gladly hand you that burden."

I would never sit there. We'd create a better government, one ruled by wisdom and law. But while we made those changes, the people needed a strong leader. They needed King Halavant. I stood and bowed in deference to my younger brother. "I'm sorry, but they need you. A shadow could never be king."

Halavant let out a weary breath. "I hope Katrin will need only me. But the people need both of us."

He didn't need to fear I'd leave him with the burden. The people would get my every waking moment and each of my sleepless nights. I would slip in where Halavant needed ears, watch unseen where he needed eyes. I would be the king's shadow.

THE JOURNEY CONTINUES IN

THE KING'S SHADOW - **coming autumn 2019**

Two brothers rule a war-torn country after overthrowing the tyrant, only to discover one of them is dying.

If you liked *The King's Trial,* please leave a favorable review on your favorite rating site. And please, share with a friend. I created the book, but the story lives through readers like you.

UPDATES AND FREE SHORT STORY

To get updates on my next book, *The King's Shadow*, and a free short story, *East of Apollo's Palace,* sign up for my newsletter at: https://storyoriginapp.com/giveaways/74715c6a-70c5-11e9-8307-03a7e997bade

ACKNOWLEDGMENTS

Thanks to my husband, Jesse, for listening to my story ideas, brainstorming with me, and cheering me on. God truly blessed me when I married you!

Thanks to my six children for giving me years of experience even when I wasn't writing, and time to write in recent years.

Thanks to my alpha and beta readers, especially James Farb, Tori Gullihugh, Shelly Ruble, Rebecca Lamoreaux, and Hayley Chow.

Thanks to my editor, Martha Rasmussen, for finding all the little things that make the difference between a good story and a well-told one.

Thanks to my cover artist, Rachael Wilkinson. You create beauty wherever you go.

Special thanks to my sister, Erin, for asking for bedtime tales and then encouraging me to write them down. And to my cousin, Rachael, for being my first writing buddy. You both were there from the first “once upon a time.”

ABOUT THE AUTHOR

As a youth, I made up stories to help my little sisters go to sleep. It backfired. We stayed up for hours continuing the tale. The King's Trial was born in those late, whispered nights.

Ever since I climbed up to the rafters of our barn at age four, I've lived high adventure: scuba diving, mud football with my brothers, rappelling, and even riding a retired racehorse at full gallop—bareback. I love the thrill and joy.

Stories give me a similar thrill and joy. I love living through the eyes and heart of a hero who faces his internal demons and the heroine who fights her way free instead of waiting to be saved. I read fiction and true-story adventure. I write both, though I'm starting with publishing the fiction—fact will come later.

I create high fantasy, fairy tale retellings, and poetry. I live a joyful adventure with my husband and six children. I am a Christian and I love my Savior.

You can contact me at:
mlfarb.author@gmail.com
www.facebook.com/MLFarbAuthor/
https://mlfarbauthor.wordpress.com/

Made in the USA
Columbia, SC
29 August 2019